LIVE ECHOES

Also by Henry V. O'Neil

The Sim War Series

Glory Main
Orphan Brigade
Dire Steps
CHOP Line

LIVE ECHOES

The Sim War: Book Five

HENRY V. O'NEIL

HARPER

VOYAGER
IMPULSE

An Imprint of HarperCollins Publishers

This is a work of fiction. Names, characters, places, and incidents are products of the author's imagination or are used fictitiously and are not to be construed as real. Any resemblance to actual events, locales, organizations, or persons, living or dead, is entirely coincidental.

Digital Edition FEBRUARY 2017 ISBN: 978-0-06-247174-1
Print Edition ISBN: 978-0-06-247176-5

Harper Voyager, the Harper Voyager logo, and Harper Voyager Impulse are trademarks of HarperCollins Publishers.

HarperCollins is a registered trademark of HarperCollins Publishers in the United States of America and other countries.

FIRST EDITION

17 18 19 20 21   HDC   10 9 8 7 6 5 4 3 2 1

For my beloved mother
Patricia Chard O'Neil
1927-2016

"What a chimera then is man!
What a novelty! What a monster,
what a chaos, what a contradiction,
what a prodigy! Judge of all things,
imbecile worm of the earth; depositary of
truth, a sink of uncertainty and error;
the pride and refuse of the universe!"

—BLAISE PASCAL

CHAPTER 1

"I've been here before, Mirror." Olech Mortas spoke to a man who appeared to be his exact duplicate. Tall and blond but going gray, bearing the same facial features down to the wrinkles of middle age. They walked side by side down a carpeted hallway, and Mortas wondered again if Mirror was marked by the same abdominal and leg scars that he'd received in the war. He'd been fifteen at the time, and the wounds had whitened and faded, but they were still there.

"Of course you have. You lived in this place for five years. Both of your children were born here."

"That's not what I meant. You and I have been here before."

"There is no such thing as time in this realm, Olech. No before, no after."

"So you keep telling me."

Mirror suppressed a laugh. "That was very funny."

"We've had discussions, you and I. Many of them, since I arrived . . . wherever I am. How can that not have happened in the past?"

"We have talked. But as there is no time here, it couldn't be in the past." They reached a paneled door, on which hung a set of pink baby shoes. Olech touched an old crack in the wood, painted over so many times that it was almost invisible. He'd forgotten that defect many years before, and marveled at the completeness of Mirror's memories. "How else could we be revisiting the events of your life?"

"I was hoping you'd explain that to me, at some point."

"That would defeat the purpose." Mirror flicked his blue eyes at the door, indicating Olech should open it. Knowing what would happen, he reached down for a pocket that hadn't been there when they'd started down the hall, for keys that hadn't been in the pocket. When he looked up, Mirror was gone.

That made sense, in a way, because now Olech Mortas was no longer gray or wrinkled. He was thirty years old again, the keys were something he handled every day, and he couldn't wait to get inside to share the big news with Lydia.

Opening the door carefully, knowing that one of the bureaus was just a little too close. Passing the bassinet in the center of the living room, seeing it was empty just as he heard his wife's voice from the office.

"Yes, Senator Mortas thought the speech went quite well. He's very involved in matters important to veterans, as you'd expect from one of the Unwavering." Mortas chuckled as he walked through the bedroom, still amazed at Lydia's ability to work his war record into every conversation. Her words continued, warm, friendly. "I certainly will pass your congratulations on to him. And now that we have your contact information, you'll be hearing from the senator more frequently."

Despite the limited space, the apartment was spotless as always. The bed had even been made. Olech stopped in the office doorway, watching Lydia type at the keyboard with one hand while holding the baby with the other. Ayliss was strapped to her mother's chest, reaching in vain for the dark hair that was firmly tied up out of reach.

"Well you certainly had a good day." Lydia spoke before turning around. "I watched the whole thing. You were brilliant."

He went to them, kissing his wife deeply before planting a gentle peck on Ayliss's head. "I thought I rushed the middle."

"I thought you sped up because your audience has a short attention span."

"Apparently not." The prideful smile spread across his face. "When I got done, I swear the whole Senate shook my hand."

"Even . . . ?"

"Yes. Horace Corlipso himself. He was leaving the chamber, but he patted me on the shoulder and said, 'Very good job, young man,' as he went by."

"Told you."

He kissed her again. "You were right, as always. Did you see the reaction to the paragraph about increasing disability payments?"

"You mean the part I re-wrote over your objections?"

"That's why I mention it." Ayliss was tugging at the blood-red ribbon on his lapel, the medal awarded to the few survivors of the child army known as the Unwavering. He held it in place between thumb and forefinger, but leaned in so she could see it more clearly.

"So was that all Senator Corlipso said?"

"He really was leaving, so there was no chance to speak with him."

"You should have tried."

"Better not to look too eager." The smile returned, and he pulled the two women in close. "But he did notice me. Horace Corlipso. How about that?"

He was back out in the hallway now, but that was no surprise. The memories were always sandwiched between solitary discussions with Mirror. Olech felt the years gradually return, and saw himself again in the graying man before him.

"You adjusted that speech so it conformed with the

platform of a faction dominated by Senator Corlipso."
Mirror began. "Why was that?"

"Just a second." Olech looked back at the apartment
door, savoring the last sensations of having actually
been there, wherever *there* was. He waited until it had
all dissipated, and whispered to Mirror. "Those were
the happiest years of my life."

"I know. How could I not?"

"So is that what this is? You're experiencing my
memories?"

"Did that feel like a memory?"

"No. It was much more realistic than mental recall.
I was actually *there*, back there, back then. I had all the
thoughts that were in my mind that day. Things I'd
completely forgotten."

"Exactly. Human memory is imperfect, even when
it's intact. The intriguing element here is that all of that
data is available to you. You just don't know how to
access it."

"Did you learn that from studying humans in the
Step?"

"Yes. That's why your experiences here are so
vivid and complete."

"If you've already accessed this information, why
are you running me through this? What do you hope
to learn?"

"Humans demonstrate a worrisome inconsistency
between their aspirations and their actions. From

studying you in the Step, I know you made numerous decisions in the human realm that ran counter to your values. I seek to understand this, and cannot do that merely by observation."

"You couldn't have asked me about it?"

"Faulty memory is not the only obstacle here, Olech. Your fellow humans display a strong capacity for self-deception and rationalization, sometimes in the face of obvious factual contradiction."

"That's true." Olech felt a lightness in his body, or whatever was representing his body. It was a sensation he remembered from other conversations with Mirror, despite the being's insistence that there was no time in this place. It almost always meant that Olech had accepted an uncomplimentary observation as accurate. "I doubt I'm going to be able to explain the inconsistencies in our natures."

"Explanation is not the goal. You and I will achieve comprehension."

"Why is this so important to you? You said you found our inconsistencies worrisome."

"Not all of them. There is another human inconsistency, where your natural instinct to survive is overridden by other impulses. In some cases these impulses are of a very low order, such as greed or lust. In other cases, the impulse is highly noble, such as seeing an ideal, a person, or large numbers of persons as more important than yourself. You displayed that inconsistency when you went to war as a teenager.

And when you embarked on the voyage that brought us together."

"What happened to me, in that voyage? I keep coming into awareness here, with you, but I have no recollection of what happened." Olech experienced a tremor of fear, which was surprising. Despite his confusion about Mirror and this realm, his conscious time in this place had always been accompanied by an abiding calm. "Am I dead?"

"You are physically alive, and your body is perfectly safe." Mirror's image began to blur, a signal that this period of awareness was about to end. "It is still inside your spacecraft, suspended between the realms, and it has not aged. Time is a thing of the human realm."

"So time is passing, where I came from?"

"That is of no importance." Mirror had turned transparent, and the corridor walls were following suit. Olech raised a hand, seeing right through it. Mirror's words seemed to vibrate the vanishing atoms of his being. "Nothing there is of any concern to you at all."

"**C**aptain Varick. Lieutenant Mortas. Please stand to hear the panel's findings."

Jander Mortas pushed his chair back in stages, struggling with the brace that ran the length of his left leg. The brace itself wasn't the issue; the pant leg of his dress uniform barely fit over the contraption and made every movement difficult. Erica Varick leaned down to help him, muttering under her breath.

"Come on. Stalling's not gonna change the verdict."

Mortas came to attention next to the tall Banshee, looking at the men on the raised platform. The room made him think of auditoriums at university, and he'd had to remind himself more than once that they were on board a spacecraft in the war zone. The *Silenus* was a bloated, luxurious transport for high-level politicians, and he'd deeply enjoyed its accommodations for the past days and nights.

"I should have known you were gonna get me in big trouble." Varick whispered without moving her lips, staring straight at the panel. They were so far from the rostrum ahead and the half-moon tiers of seats behind that they probably could have conversed at normal volume, but that would have been unwise.

"Nobody made you flush that thing out to space. And I did offer to take the rap, if you recall."

"I should have let you. They won't do anything serious to Reena Mortas's stepson. Me, they'll probably draw and quarter."

"Or worse—send you back to that staff job."

"Not funny, Jan."

The panel's president, a corpulent senator named Bascom, cleared his throat. The audience behind Varick and Mortas came largely from Bascom's oversized retinue, and they made noises indicating they were on the edges of their seats.

"Having reviewed your reports, and heard your answers to our questions, this panel declares its duties completed." Senator Bascom's ruddy cheeks glowed with self-importance. "Captain Varick, Lieutenant Mortas, we thank you for your cooperation, and we commend you for your bravery."

Loud applause broke out in the tiers, and somehow Mortas knew the audience had come to their feet.

"Color me impressed." Varick hummed. "Your stepmother's man wasn't lying. The fix *was* in."

"When a Mortas family agent tells you everything's been arranged, you can bet everything's been arranged." Jander concentrated on standing at attention. "Besides, their questions made no sense. I bet they didn't even see the real report."

The applause died down, but Senator Bascom wasn't ready to surrender the limelight. "I believe I speak for the entire panel when I offer my regrets that your mission to Roanum turned out to be a hoax."

The word brought a searing memory into Jander's mind. A pretty, blue-eyed woman with reddish-brown hair, raising him over her head and throwing his body thirty yards through the air.

"Don't say a word," Erica hissed, sensing his sudden tension. "For once, just let things work out for you."

"That 'hoax' threw me into a river full of snakes."

"And I fished you out."

"Those things almost killed us both. And my leg *is* killing me."

Jander's eyes shifted minutely, studying the other panel members. An aged admiral named Futterman glowered at him from Bascom's right, despite having said nothing during the brief proceedings. To the senator's left, Timothy Kumar nodded in solemn agreement. Tall and good-looking, Kumar was now a close adviser to Jander's stepmother Reena, the woman at the head of the human alliance in the war against the Sims. Kumar had spent the previous day lobbing a series of easy questions at Mortas and Varick.

"Well maybe you shouldn't have sneaked into my quarters last night." Varick stifled a laugh. "Give your poor leg—and the rest of you—a break."

"You came to my cabin last night."

"Oh, you're right. They're all blending together."

The comment distracted Mortas with the memory of an unexpectedly long chain of golden evenings spent with Erica. Coming together during the Roanum mission, they'd been harshly ordered to Earth following its chaotic end. Those orders had then been countermanded, leaving them waiting in space on a cruiser called the *Ajax* that had been their guardian angel while on Roanum.

The ship's captain, a Mortas family loyalist, had left them to their own devices until being ordered to rendezvous with the *Silenus* inside a protective ring of Human Defense Force warships. Once transferred to the *Silenus*, they'd been surprised to find themselves assigned luxurious cabins right next to each other. The panel hadn't convened for another week after that, and the two HDF officers had made pleasurable use of the time.

Bascom interrupted Jander's reverie.

"I would like to extend my personal thanks to both of you for having undertaken this dangerous mission, and for your composure when Gorman Station was attacked. I wish you a swift and complete recovery from your injuries, Lieutenant Mortas. I know you're working hard at your therapy. "

Jander nodded at the senator, catching the flutter in the corner of Varick's lips. He'd made her laugh the night before, and could see she was on the verge of starting up again.

"Thank you, sir. I'm giving it all I've got."

Varick's entire body twitched just once, and she gave off a tortured peep.

"You're as dedicated as your father was, Lieutenant. I worked with him closely over the years." Senator Bascom seemed ready to launch into a long anecdote, but Admiral Futterman cleared his throat with force. Bascom blanched, and then continued. "Your stepmother is waiting to see you on the *Aurora*, and we won't delay your reunion. This panel is concluded, and you are both dismissed with our thanks."

Seats clattered closed behind them, but Varick and Mortas stood frozen.

"The Chairwoman of the Emergency Senate came all the way out here?" Erica offered in a stunned monotone. "I *knew* you were going to get me in trouble."

"Come on. Let me introduce you to my stepmom."

What do you think she's going to do to us?" Varick asked as they waited outside the hatch of Reena Mortas's office on the flagship *Aurora*.

"After that phony inquiry, I'd guess she's going to conduct an in-depth debriefing."

"That makes sense."

"But she could also be very angry that we killed the alien. I can't be sure. We were never close."

"Damn you, Jan!"

Nathaniel Ulbridge appeared in front of them as the hatch opened.

"Jan." Short and blond, Ulbridge was well muscled and attired in the gray uniform of Mortas family security. "I'm sorry about Hugh."

Jander shook the offered hand, and gave a brief nod. Hugh Leeger, Ulbridge's boss until recently, had defected to the slave rebellion on Celestia under mysterious circumstances.

"Hugh made a choice, and even I have to respect that." Leeger had been Jan's bodyguard for most of his childhood. "He was always his own man."

"No he wasn't. Personally, I think that's what broke him."

Ulbridge ushered them into the office. Standing ramrod straight, the two officers marched up to the desk of a middle-aged woman with short red hair wearing a severe black tunic. Reena Mortas regarded them without emotion, and Jander saw that she'd aged considerably since he'd shipped out to the war zone over a year before.

"Captain Erica Varick and Lieutenant Jander Mortas reporting as ordered, Madame Chairwoman," the Banshee said.

"So there you are. The two junior officers who decided to incinerate humanity's only proven means of communicating with the Sims. Forty-plus years of fighting an opponent that looks just like us but chirps like a bird, and you threw away the only chance we ever had of conversing with them." The blue eyes cut into them. "And then you were stupid enough to confess to that, in a report that would have leaked all over the alliance if the skipper of the *Ajax* hadn't sat on it."

Mortas stared at the unadorned wall behind his stepmother, trying not to shake his head. This was just the kind of political nonsense he'd hoped to escape in volunteering for the war.

"Did you read the report, ma'am?" Varick asked politely. "We gave a clear explanation for our actions."

"You think so? The document I read told me that you conducted a highly successful meeting with the Sim delegates, using the alien shapeshifter as a translator. First time anything like that has been achieved in the entire war."

"We did," Jander responded. "Ma'am."

"Then you said that a mercenary force kidnapped the shapeshifter, and you recovered her alive when the *Ajax* captured the mercenaries' ship."

"*It*, ma'am," Erica answered. "The shapeshifter only took the form of a human female. It remained an it."

"You think that's important?" Reena let the words hang in the air. "You recovered it alive, helpless inside a Transit Tube, and then you jettisoned that tube to burn up in Roanum's atmosphere."

"The report also mentions that the shapeshifter tried to kill me when the mercenaries showed up." Jander spoke without looking at Reena. "It confessed that its true purpose in contacting us wasn't to arrange a cease-fire, but to gain information about the Step."

"I see. And you didn't think we could have kept that information from it, forewarned by you, if you'd passed the shapeshifter up your chain of command?"

"May I speak freely, ma'am?"

"I thought you were. Go ahead, Jander."

"I'm certain it would have gotten what it was after—even if we'd warned you. The alien had a firm grasp of human nature, and told me it was going to manipulate our top leadership to learn how the Step works. It was playing us the whole way, and it only revealed its true mission because it thought it was about to kill me."

Reena rolled her chair back, and stood. "I believe it referred to the top leadership as the 'half-bright ego-maniacs you let run your lives'—am I remembering that correctly?"

"Yes, ma'am. It understood us quite well."

"Do you agree with that, Captain? That it was going to fool us? Fool me?"

"I couldn't take that chance, ma'am. The thing said a Sim armada would descend on the settled planets to wipe out humanity as soon as they gained an understanding of the Step. And that there was no way to stop them."

"It communicated that last sentiment telepathically, from inside the tube?" Both officers nodded. "So tell me this. In that final communication, did that thing sound like an ally of the Sims—or one of their creators?"

"One of their creators." Varick and Mortas answered in unison.

"According to your report, it never said that explicitly."

"It wouldn't do that. It wouldn't solve the biggest puzzle of the entire war." Varick spoke in earnest. "Jan's right. That thing was toying with us from the start. And it was laughing when we flushed it."

Reena walked around the desk and stood in front

of them. "You do understand that there was no way we could share the truth about your mission with the rest of the alliance, in its current state of flux? Your actions forced us to spread the story that this was all a hoax."

Jander frowned. "But the word was already out, that another shapeshifter had appeared and that we were communicating with it. That's why the mercs tried to kidnap it. And even though they're all locked up, the Holy Whisper colonists on Roanum know about the meeting with the Sims. Their leader, Elder Paul, was with us."

"As a group, the Whisper is commendably tight-lipped. That comes from having their beliefs ridiculed at every turn." Reena shook her head. "You had no clearance to bring their Elder to that negotiation. What were you thinking?"

"As pacifists, they were overjoyed about the possibility of a cease-fire. They were the first ones the shapeshifter contacted, and we didn't feel it was right to exclude them." Varick's voice softened. "Given what happened later, perhaps we should have."

"They don't blame us for the mercenary attack on the colony. I was personally contacted by the Whisper leadership, thanking the *Ajax* for its intervention. And since this Elder Paul died in the assault, any stories the colonists tell about the meeting with the Sims can be dismissed as rumor."

"It's wrong to be covering this up, ma'am," Jander whispered. "The alien said there were thousands more just like it, and that we couldn't possibly keep them from getting another impostor through and learning about the Step. We need a plan to stop that, and instead we're denying this ever happened."

Reena's eyes flashed. "Just a moment. Through most of that report you insisted that the shapeshifter was lying to us. So what are you telling me? That it started telling the truth right at the end, when it knew it was doomed?"

"It doesn't respect us at all. It wanted us to know we're the ones who are doomed."

"I'm going to have to take your word for that." His stepmother walked around the desk and sat back down. "Because that's all I have. I'm left with only your notion of what that being was really trying to do. When I actually might have gotten to the truth if you'd let it live. And maybe even could have used it to arrange a cease-fire with the Sims.

"But I'm one of those half-bright egomaniacs, aren't I? Too stupid to be allowed to even speak with that thing."

Standing like statues, neither officer responded.

"Nathaniel is going to debrief you now. We need to analyze everything that happened on Roanum, this time without your high-blown judgments. I don't care how long it takes. After that, you're both going back to your units—where, if you've got any sense at all, you won't breathe a word of this."

"Because someone might punish us?" Jander couldn't stop himself. "Ma'am?"

"No, Lieutenant. Because no one will believe you. I'm making sure of that."

Ulbridge sealed the hatch behind the two officers, and walked over to Reena's desk. The Chairwoman had sagged into her chair, as if exhausted.

"How did I do, Nathaniel? Did I give away the secret?"

"Asking if the alien acted like it was one of the Sims' creators was a bit too close for comfort, but I think they missed it. I'll confirm that during the debriefing."

"Thank you. Dig deep with the questions, but don't let them figure out what we're really after."

"Yes, ma'am. I'll report back as soon as we're done."

Reena didn't notice when he left. Her mind had already called up an image, impossibly far from that spot, in a desolate region of space. A gray planet, one of several in a star system that she'd learned about through someone else's dreams. Camouflaged probe spacecraft had come close enough to surveil the unremarkable orb, but so far had detected no activity at all.

She'd code-named the planet herself, believing her missing husband had shown it to the dreamer as the possible source of the Sim enemy. Reena breathed out the word with her eyes shut.

"Omega."

"**Y**our stepmother is up to something." Erica whispered the words many hours later in her cabin, intertwined with Jander.

"She sits at the top of the biggest bunch of backstabbers in human history. I'd be surprised if she wasn't."

"No, it's more than that. Did you notice she didn't mention your father even once? I don't care how mad she is at us; you're his *son*, and this is the first time she's seen you since he went missing. And yet she didn't bring it up. She was concentrating on playing a role."

"That's my family. They've always got some game going on."

"Not your sister. From what I'm hearing through the Banshee grapevine, she's doing her damnedest to be a good troop."

"She sure took the long way to get there. Last time I saw Ayliss, she was scheming against my father. Apparently they patched things up before he disappeared."

"Why does the Chairwoman believe he's still alive?"

"Nathaniel explained that to me, after the debriefing ended. One of the Step Worshipers—their leader,

I guess—had a series of dreams where she thought my father was communicating with her. Just crazy talk. His capsule's been missing for months."

"The Chairwoman's under a lot of strain. She's hiding that, too."

"Be careful drawing conclusions with this crowd. They wear a lot of masks. Sometimes for years."

"I think she doesn't want you to go to Celestia."

"That's where the brigade is. And since you're hell-bent on getting back to the Banshees, what else would I do?"

"You should stay here. At least until your leg's healed."

"I belong with the Orphans. Colonel Watt will put me to work somewhere." Their looming separation took a step closer, and he kissed her hard, as if to ward it off.

"Colonel Watt." She laughed. "You believe he actually *threatened* me over your safety? When you see him, tell your colonel what I did to bring you back. Tell him about the snakes. Then tell him I said he can kiss my ass."

"Look who's getting ornery. You haven't even shipped out yet." The silence enfolded them for an instant. "You know, I could ask my—"

"No. I'm headed back to the war. Been gone way too long. I need this."

"I had to try. You know I had to try."

"Just one thing. Don't tell your Colonel Watt to kiss my ass." Varick's tone softened. "Tell him I'm not giving you back. You're just on loan."

In her office on the *Aurora*, Reena Mortas finished reviewing the transcripts of the debriefing Ulbridge had conducted with Jan and Varick.

"So what do you think?" she asked the security man.

"We can't assume that the shapeshifters are the entities creating the Sims, but I think it's highly likely. Its story about the origins of the Sims has holes just where you'd expect them to be, if it was trying to hide that connection. And the Sim delegates refused to offer their version, despite their obvious affinity for Jan and Captain Varick."

"That's not surprising, now that we know why they're fighting us. They believe humanity is persecuting them. No matter how friendly the conversation got, they think we're trying to eradicate them."

The decades-long war with the Sims had begun the instant human space explorers had encountered the humanoid race. According to the shapeshifter, the Sims believed they were the mutated descendants of ancient human long-range space missions, unfairly attacked by an enemy they referred to as the "cousins."

"I found it interesting, that the alien said it doesn't believe the Sims' creation story."

"How so?"

"Jan is convinced that the shapeshifters don't fear us at all. That sense of superiority might have caused the alien to include hints of the real truth in what it told them. Kind of a sick joke."

"Are you saying it was giving us clues?"

"Rejecting the Sims' story allowed the alien to propose how that tale got into the Sims' heads in the first place. It said it believed what we've always suspected—that the Sims are a designer enemy, meant to oppose our expansion. Its suggestion that the Sims' creators telepathically implanted that creation story—along with individual Sims' different skill sets—is just a little too close to what the alien already demonstrated it can do to humans."

"Telepathic communication. Jan and Varick heard it laughing when they jettisoned it."

"It also spoke to them, briefly, without opening its mouth. On Glory Main, the original alien essentially downloaded data into Jan's head. Awfully similar to what the shapeshifter said the Sims' creators do."

"Do you think that might also apply to what it said about their numbers? That there are thousands more?"

"I do. Why would it say thousands? Why not millions, or even billions, if its intent was to convince us that keeping them from learning the secret of the Step is futile?"

"Another clue?"

"I believe so. Stating their true numbers, or exaggerating them by only a little, might be just part of the fun."

"Or it might just be a fact. They don't need big numbers, with their abilities. All it's going to take is for one of them to slip by."

"That is true."

"So we've got to beat them to the punch." Reena rolled her chair back, and stood. "Is everything proceeding?"

"Yes, ma'am. Half the convoy will return to Earth, while we go with the other half to the Construction Zone. General Merkit is waiting for us."

"My husband put him in charge out there to put a stop to the profiteering. Who would have guessed he'd put the perfect man in the perfect place for us?"

CHAPTER 2

Sealed inside a Banshee fighting suit, Ayliss Mortas was having the time of her life. The feed from dozens of microcameras gave the false impression that her helmet had vanished, and she half-expected the falling snowflakes to land on her face. Coursing down through the pale atmosphere, driven by a wind she could hear but not feel, the ice crystals either slid past at the last second or stopped inches from her eyes before melting against the face shield.

Her arms and legs moved easily inside the now-familiar armor, but the freedom of actually traveling on a planet's surface was astounding. All of her previous suit experiences had been aboard ship, in stationary simulators or large compartments, and there had been no room to simply run.

Now she was doing that, uphill, through an open

forest covered in white. The briefing had told her the temperature on this part of Secured Planet 3157 was lethally cold, and her suit's readouts confirmed that, which made it all the more marvelous. Heat exchangers kept her environment at a constant, comfortable temperature regardless of how much she exerted herself. A foot higher from the ground than normal, encased in an armored body loaded with high technology and powerful weapons, Ayliss thrilled to see the terrain passing by much faster than she could run.

"Slow *down*, Mortas!" Cusabrina snarled in her ear.

Still bouncing forward, Ayliss turned her head to the right. Her helmet was fused to the shoulders of the suit, so a forehead-and-neck assembly rotated with her and changed the camera views. Reaching the limit of her neck's mobility, Ayliss laughed as the view continued to shift until she was essentially looking backward. Twenty yards behind and twenty yards away, Cusabrina's suit blended in with the snowy landscape. Bulging mechanical legs spread into an armored torso before sloping up into the bell-shaped helmet. Cusabrina carried her rifle in one swollen glove, reminding Ayliss that the veteran had insisted she leave her own weapon clipped against her back. The weapon was called a Fasces because of its multiple barrels, and could fire everything from large caliber rounds to grenades.

"How many times do I have to tell you, Corporal? My name's Rig!" she called brightly, bringing the view back to her front before reluctantly slowing down.

"And how many times am I going to have to tell you I'm not an NCO?"

"Sergeant Tin said it would be easier to just call you Corporal. She said you go back and forth, promoted one day and busted the next."

"This one's permanent. Not that I care." The older woman coursed into her peripheral vision, weaving among the trees. She admired Cusabrina's ability to move while bent forward, reducing her overall silhouette. Ayliss and the other new Banshees had been assured they would eventually pick it up, but her earlier attempts had always ended with a tumble. "See that boulder to the west? Get down behind it."

Ayliss punched her tongue into the suit's tube control, calling up the basic patrolling menu. The helmet materialized somewhat as the electronic display showed her a compass, her heading, the distance to the next course change, and a small schematic of the rest of the squad. Sliding her tongue, she shifted the schematic over and enlarged it to see where the others were.

Her Banshee Basic squadmates had been assigned as a group to Sergeant Tin's squad, and so each of the five newbies had been given a veteran minder. They moved all over the snowy mountain in pairs, sweeping the ground for an enemy that was not expected to be there. More seasoned Banshee squads were slowly converging on the summit of a high mountain to the east, where the suspicious electronic emanations had originated.

Reaching the snow-covered rock Cusabrina had pointed out, Ayliss dropped to a knee and peered through a scraggly bush. She now looked down the other side of the slope, seeing more untouched whiteness and denuded trees. Cusabrina moved up, coming to a stop just short of the crest twenty yards to her right. They were scouting a broad ridgeline that split from the eastern side of the target mountain, and the squad's other teams were spread out to the west at half-mile intervals.

"This is Cusabrina. We're at Checkpoint Four." A red circle glowed in the corner of Ayliss's display for a few seconds, before dropping onto the schematic where they were located. "No sign of Sam. Or anything else."

"Hold in place," Tin responded, paired off with the Banshee that the training cadre had nicknamed Plodder. Biggest of the five newbies and a former military police officer, Plodder's quick temper called for extra supervision. "Tabor, what's the holdup?"

Ayliss studied the schematic, seeing that the team on their extreme left had fallen behind just a bit. Tonguing a map onto the schematic, she studied the incline and decided it wasn't steep enough to be holding them up. Tabor was an easygoing veteran, and so she'd been paired off with the equally low-key Legacy.

"Just pickin' a few flowers." The drawling voice almost made her laugh. "Something to brighten things up when we go back aboard."

Two short beeps sounded inside the helmet, and Ayliss immediately looked over at Cusabrina. She didn't hear Tin's answer, because her partner had hit the override.

"You awake over there, Rig?"

"Yes, Corporal."

"Then why aren't you seeing this?"

Embarrassed to have been paying too much attention to the electronic display, she quickly scanned the trees to their front. Heavy with snow, they blocked the view as the ground fell away. Ayliss was about to switch to infrared when a distortion seemed to flash across the snow.

Zooming in on the undulating blanket of white, she finally saw it. Saw them. Sliding, slithering, pulling themselves along, a pod of pale, tentacled creatures crawled away two hundred yards down. Perfectly camouflaged, they zigzagged along with a fluid grace that was both beautiful and disgusting. Ayliss decided they looked like jellyfish back on Earth, except these ones weren't anywhere near the sea.

"Got 'em. What are they?"

"Some of the monitoring stations reported seeing these things from time to time. Harmless. They call them Snow Squids. You need to read the briefing materials better, newb."

The pod slid out of sight, and even though they were obviously abandoning the area to the armored intruders, Ayliss shivered when she realized their patrol route went in the same direction. "That was revolting."

"All teams, move out." Tin came back up on the net. "Keep your eyes open."

"Not if I have to look at those squirmy things," Cusabrina muttered, and it took Ayliss a moment to realize her partner had only spoken to her. "Hey, Rig. Let's stay put for a few. Give the octopus tribe plenty of time to clear out."

"**M**aking final approach. Everybody in position?"

Ayliss listened to Sergeant Pelletier, the leader of the squad tasked with the actual reconnaissance of the summit. On a high peak to her east, intermittent electronic signals had been detected by passing Force ships. The Sims were well known for emplacing stealth navigational beacons throughout the war zone, and that was what the Banshees expected to find here. Most of the space lighthouses were unmanned, but there was always a possibility of enemy contact.

Tin's squad, having found no sign of the Sims on their assigned ridge, had then spread out in pairs to form part of a ring of Banshee teams surrounding the target area. Cusabrina had selected a good hide position for them, halfway up the slope where they could observe the distant mountain and the low ground between them.

Stretched out in the snow, Ayliss felt a rush of accomplishment when Cusabrina told her to unclip her Fasces from the back of the suit. She now alternated between looking through the weapon's scope at the white valley below and checking the overhead imagery provided by orbiting ships and stratospheric drones. The trees stood out on top of the target mountain as they presumably had for millennia, and no readings of any kind—heat, electronic, or otherwise—indicated there was anything there.

Pelletier's squad had separated into two elements, carefully working their way up the final hundred yards of the summit using the forest for cover. Although the suits dissipated their heat signatures, Ayliss could easily make out the reddish glow of each Banshee against the frozen ground.

The footage of the mountaintop changed abruptly, with a dashed line of red spurting down the slope toward the approaching teams. The heat dots indicating the Banshees immediately jumped left or right, seeking cover from whatever was firing at them. Looking across at the peak, Ayliss heard the subdued rumbling of a heavy weapon even though she couldn't see any of the action. The recon squad quickly filled her in.

"Contact on the crest! Sim machine-gun emplacement! Marking target!"

Going back to the imagery, Ayliss saw a digital cross appear where the stuttering red line began. As for the line itself, it was sweeping back and forth while the Banshees down the slope pulled back in a pre-rehearsed response. Pelletier spoke, and Ayliss thrilled at her composure.

"Fire control, fire control. Requesting bunker busters on pre-set target Purple One. Camouflaged emplacements, obviously been here a long time. Double the volley."

"Banshee, this is fire control. Rockets on the way. Get your heads down."

"Everybody open your eyes," Tin coached her dispersed squad. "Sam's no fool. That gunner knows we're about to drop the boom-boom on him. He's attracting attention while his buddies scoot. They could pop up anywhere."

Ayliss felt her heart thudding against the armor. Tonguing the imagery aside, she searched the ground with her rifle. Nothing moved, but in her mind she imagined a host of Sim soldiers, clad in snow-camouflaged combat smocks, fleeing right toward her.

"This is fire control. Twenty seconds to impact. Twenty seconds to impact."

Snow fell in clumps from the trees on the far side of the valley, and Ayliss gasped in anticipation. Movement.

"Stay cool, Mortas," Cusabrina purred. "Let's see what it is before we light it up."

The veteran started reporting the unidentified motion to Tin, but Ayliss's entire world shrunk down to the gunsight reticle before her eyes. The Fasces was tied into her suit's systems, and the reticle told her the range as she shifted her view.

The first figure broke from the tree line, and adrenaline shot through her just before Ayliss saw that it wasn't a Sim. Ice-blue and majestic, it looked like some kind of stag. Curved antlers rose up from its head, and long aqua fringes hung down from its neck. The beast stopped as soon as it came out in the open, and Ayliss saw more behind it. Smaller versions of the stag, some with antlers and some without, skidding to a halt inside the trees.

"They don't like the gunfire. They're clearing out," Cusabrina explained.

The leader sniffed the air while the fringes fluttered as if caught in a breeze. Ayliss watched in wonder as the feelers stretched away from the creature, obviously testing for some indication of a waiting enemy. The test didn't last long.

The far peak exploded in flashes of fire, the first throwing snow everywhere and the others coming in behind it at one-second intervals. The startling concussions stampeded the animals below, and they surged across the valley in a wild-eyed mob. Perhaps thirty in total, all sizes, they kicked powder all around before hitting the dead center of the low ground. For an instant Ayliss thought they'd broken the ice of a snow-hidden stream, as the ground under their powerful hooves cracked and flew up around them.

It was only after the herd had disappeared into the far trees that she detected the wounded motion in the snow, the damaged tentacles reaching for the sky and then dropping, while the whiteness changed to a soupy gray that darkened into blackness. She watched as the surviving squids slowly dragged themselves away, many of them lurching on obviously shattered tentacles. The sight nauseated her enough that she looked away.

And wished she hadn't. Many yards up the valley, a light blue figure surged and struggled as if caught in a tangle of white underbrush. Panicked by the explosions just like the others, it had separated from the herd and run across the squid creatures all by itself. No antlers, no fringes, it looked like a doe. Kicking madly, it leapt into the air only to be yanked back down. More and more of the tentacles wrapped around it, and Ayliss saw its wide-eyed terror as it craned its head back to bellow a call for help that she didn't hear.

The others didn't hear it, either. The doe fought on for just a little longer before slowly freezing in place, quivering as if its muscles had turned to stone. Ayliss dumbly wondered if the Snow Squids had some kind of poison in them that had paralyzed the beast, just before the knot of twitching muscle pulled it down.

"Contact to the south!" Pelletier called out from the summit. "Blast doors opening. Looks like a hangar. Marking target."

Ayliss gratefully switched back to the imagery, seeing the new designator on the southern slope. The snow was crumbling away, showing heat that registered as a narrow slit probably fifty yards wide.

"Shuttle inside. That's gotta be their escape craft. Can we have a gun drone?"

"Already inbound."

More heat slid out from the wintry hill, and then it detached into a tiny rectangle. Ayliss's suit systems automatically targeted it, surrounding the emerging craft with a blinking circle that identified it as a Wren shuttle.

The pilot was smart, diving instead of climbing, banking down the mountainside. Pelletier's squad didn't bother shooting at it, because the drone gunship had appeared. A jet of exhaust shot from its belly when it fired the missile. The Wren swept around the western side of the mountain, appearing five hundred yards in front of Ayliss and Cusabrina just before the rocket caught up. It exploded in an immense fireball, flaming chunks falling into the trees while a starburst of smoke blossomed in the pale sky.

"Target destroyed," Pelletier reported. "The hangar doors are still open. Wanna toss one in there?"

"Negative. Intelligence wants to examine the site. Security cordon, remain in place. Reconnaissance squad, continue your mission. Evaluate bomb damage on the peak and enter the site if possible."

Acknowledgments flowed over the radio, but the feed stopped in mid-sentence. Ayliss turned troubled eyes toward Cusabrina, knowing the veteran had muted the link.

"Can you imagine being assigned here? Hilltop in the middle of a frozen nowhere?"

Ayliss tried to come up with a snappy response, but the dead doc filled her mind. So frightened, so helpless, doomed by forces beyond its understanding.

"Yeah, I guess this was a really lousy assignment, even for Sam." she offered.

"Naw, that's not what I meant." An armored hand lightly swatted her. "I was asking, what do ya think the odds are that Command might make us stay here?"

This complex is something we haven't seen before." An unseen speaker narrated the video as it played on a large screen back aboard ship. "The Sims don't usually leave troops with their covert navigation beacons, but this installation was meant to be permanent."

Ayliss had already seen the footage, shot from the cameras of the Banshees who had entered the wrecked position. The antennae and tracking equipment had been destroyed by the rockets, which had blown the top off of the hollowed-out peak. Looking up from the counter where she was cleaning her dis-assembled Fasces, she saw the beams from the suits' shoulder-lights playing over the darkened interior.

"Living quarters, a mess area, and even a room for physical training were dug into the rock. Most inter-estingly, four different hangar doors were created and camouflaged so that the escape shuttle could launch in the safest direction."

"Didn't do 'em any good," Dellmore commented. The counter where the squad members were work-ing on their weapons was L-shaped, and the veterans were seated together. A seasoned Banshee, Dellmore used her size to intimidate the new arrivals. She'd been paired with Lightfoot because the dark-skinned rookie had demonstrated a talent for deflecting her barbs. "All that hard work, just so they could get smoked while running away."

"Sam knows we're stretched thin out here. They didn't used to put that kind of effort into one of those sites." That came from Zuteck, seated next to Dell-more. Medium-sized but well muscled, she'd been paired with Bullhead, the natural leader of Ayliss's Basic Training squad.

"While this particular site was far more extensive than the normal setup for a navigational outpost, Command stresses that this does not represent an es-calation of Sim presence in this sector." The briefer finished the presentation, and the screen went dark.

"Sounds like the very definition of an escalated

presence." Legacy offered, from the leg of the counter where the rookies were working.

"You catch on fast," Dellmore replied. "You figured out that Command lies to us."

"Hush now, Dell," Tabor cooed, attaching electrical leads to her rifle's control system and viewing the readout on her handheld. "My newbie did just fine today."

"How about yours, Bree?" Dellmore called to Cusabrina. "Was Minister Mortas worth anything without a team of reporters?"

Ayliss felt her face flush, but didn't respond. Dellmore had a particular dislike for her, made all the worse by the battle fought on a planet known as Quad Seven. As the newly appointed governor of a colony of discharged veterans, Ayliss had fought alongside them when they'd been attacked by smugglers. A brief clip of a blood-and-dirt-covered Ayliss had received a great deal of circulation on the Bounce network, aided by Reena Mortas's propagandists. Ayliss sensed that Dellmore's real problem with Quad Seven was that their squad leader had been there. Ayliss had carried the wounded Tin off the battlefield herself.

"How about it, Bree?" Dellmore repeated.

"I'm sorry, Dell. As usual, I wasn't listening to you. What did you say?"

"I was saying—"

"Don't bother. I'm not listening anymore."

"Okay. So how'd you like it, Mortas? Just a dull

operation where we all did our jobs and nobody got featured on the Bounce."

"I learn something important with everything we do." Ayliss responded, well aware that as a newcomer she had almost no status among the Banshee company's veterans.

"Glad to hear it. Can't tell you how much we like being saddled with five pups who didn't even complete Basic."

"Speak for yourself, Dell," Zuteck growled. "Stop saying 'we' like that."

"We were doing fine in Basic." Bullhead spoke flatly. Though much smaller than Dellmore, she stared across the compartment in obvious challenge. "You know they sent us to the fleet because Zone Quest tried to murder us all on that jogging trail."

"Relax, Bontenough. I'm not worried about the three of you who were already in. I'm just wondering why they put all five of you in one squad."

"You ever happy, Dell?" Cusabrina asked. "You bitched when we were understrength, and now you're bitching because they gave us replacements."

"Replacements? Trading seasoned fighters for these babies?"

"Weren't no trades at all," Tabor murmured. "Harter's new pancreas never did fit right. We were kidding ourselves, thinking we were going to keep her."

"Borlov and Crater were bound to get transferred

sometime." Cusabrina picked up the litany. "Put themselves in the sick bay with their stupid dares—"

"Lay on enough salve, you can wear a suit over burns like those," Dellmore responded. "They shouldn't have been reassigned—"

"—for the *third time*," Cusabrina finished. "They had to separate those two. So you saying you wanted a squad with only five live bodies?"

"I'm saying I want a squad with bodies I can depend on. Not some showboat rich kid who comes out here with her own babysitter."

Lightfoot chuckled loudly. "I would *love* to hear you say that to First Sergeant Blocker's face. You know he's back in the bay with the support crew, cleaning up our suits even as we speak."

Dellmore ignored her. "How'd you swing that one, Mortas? Get your old bodyguard sent to the war with you? After he already did two tours."

Ayliss lowered her weapon to the counter. "It's Rig."

"What now?"

"Rig. That's my name." Ayliss pointed down the table. "That's Plodder, Legacy, Lightfoot, and Bullhead. Just like we told you."

"You are such a bunch of hopeless rookies. You're not supposed to keep your Basic nicknames. You're not supposed to like those names. They're *insults*."

"Not Bullhead," Plodder corrected her. "See that

scar above her eyebrow? That's where one of those landscaping 'bots caught her with a leaf line. We fought them off with no weapons at all, flying at us with everything from saws to clippers."

"Don't forget the insecticide," Legacy offered. "I'm still coughing that up."

"You amaze me." Dellmore stood, her size arresting the attempted banter. "Those things attacked you because of a beef between Zone Quest and the Mortas family. You almost got killed for a rich kid who only enlisted to beat a murder rap."

"I didn't kill anybody that day. First Sergeant Blocker and Sergeant Tin had to do that, and Ewing was forced to kill Rittle." Ayliss stood as well, feeling a deep weariness instead of the expected fear. "The whole thing was my fault, though. They're back out in the war zone because I made a mistake."

"I'd say you just made another one." Dellmore started walking toward the far end of the counter.

"Ladies." The voice, calm and confident, came from the open hatch. All heads turned to see Sergeant Tin, dressed in fatigues. "Good to see you're all so far along with cleaning your weapons."

Dellmore gave Ayliss a meaningful stare before returning to her seat, and Tin walked into the center of the L. The entire squad wore their hair cut close to the scalp, but for a moment Ayliss saw Tin's dark hair flying as she delivered fatal punches and kicks to the Zone Quest security man who'd been guarding Vroma Rittle. Rittle had hired the smugglers who had tried to murder the veterans on Quad Seven, and Ayliss had sworn to kill him at the time. Tin spoke, driving away the shameful memory of how Rittle had actually died.

"We'll have a detailed after-action review once all the equipment is stowed away. I was very pleased with your performance out there. For a first time in the suits, I'd say our newest members did just fine."

An electric field of tension filled the room when no one responded, but Tin continued as if she hadn't noticed. "From here on out, I don't want to see you segregated this way. Old hands will sit with the newcomers, and vice versa. We're one squad, and we have to depend on each other."

"Even if half the squad has zero combat experience as Banshees, and two of them were civilians two months ago?" Dellmore presented Tin with an unpleasant smile.

"Breena." Tin spoke while facing Dellmore.

"Yes, Sergeant." Cusabrina answered.

"I'm reinstating you as a corporal."

"I don't think the skipper will like that, Sergeant."

"Captain Breverton isn't the skipper who demoted you."

"Yes, but she knows I got busted for yelling at the old skipper."

"Were you wrong?"

"No."

"Well then Captain Breverton would have been on your side. I'm going to go clear it with her now." Tin took a step forward, directly in front of Dellmore. Though dwarfed by the seated Banshee, she seemed not to notice. "Pardon me, Dell. Did you say something just now?"

"No, Sergeant."

"I think we should all try a little harder at working together as a team. What do you think?"

"That's a good idea, Sergeant."

"Thank you, Dell." Tin left the compartment, and no one spoke for almost a minute. Cusabrina broke the silence by sliding her stool back and taking Tin's place in the center of the room.

"I'm your new assistant squad leader. From time to time, the squad will break up into two elements, one led by Sergeant Tin and the other by me. In the meantime, when Sergeant Tin isn't with us, I'm in charge. Understood?"

"Yes, Corporal." The chorus came from every Banshee present, and Ayliss guessed Cusabrina had given this speech before.

"You're all equal in my eyes, as long as you pull your weight. Anybody slacking off will get my special attention. Anybody giving one hundred percent will get my full support. Any questions?"

The silence continued for only a few seconds.

"Good. Now let's drop the chitchat and get done

with these rifles. We've got a debriefing after this, and I don't intend to miss chow for that."

"Slow. Slow. There. That's it." Ayliss only heard the words, because her entire field of vision was deep inside the armored leg of her fighting suit. "Now tighten it down."

She twisted the locking mechanism using a set of long forceps, and felt the click when it seated home. Ayliss stepped back from the lower half of her suit, looking at a tall armorer named Jerticker. The support soldier was stooped over an internal monitor that magnified the channel where she'd just replaced a tiny heating coil.

All around them, mechanics and other specialists worked on the squad's equipment in a large maintenance bay. Following the debriefing and a hot meal, they'd all joined the support personnel who kept their suits up and running.

"Jerticker, how do you know so much about our gear? First Sergeant Blocker said you were running a repair bay on Larkin when we were there." Following the killing of Vroma Rittle, several veterans who had served with Blocker had decided it was wise to leave Larkin, re-enlist, and join him with the Banshees.

"Oh, I've always been good with machines. Cleaning them, fixing them, taking them apart."

"Don't forget stealing them." A deep voice spoke from behind them, and Ayliss happily turned to see Dominic Blocker. The senior-most NCO in the support company, he wore the camouflaged fatigues from his earlier service as a combat soldier.

"If I hadn't been a little light-fingered as a civilian, the Force never would have gotten the benefit of my talents." Jerticker grinned at Blocker while disconnecting the feeds on the monitor. "You gotta admit, First Sergeant, you've taken full advantage of my skills."

"That I have. Now let me borrow Private Mortas."

"Not a problem. We've done as much as she's allowed to do, anyway. Now I gotta watch a video on how to re-route her elbow camera's wiring."

"I won't ask if you're allowed to do that."

"Allowed. Not allowed. Those are just words."

"I didn't hear that." Blocker took Ayliss by the arm and steered her away from the work line.

"How did it go out there?" Blocker asked, once they'd stepped into the shadows.

"Have you ever been in one of these things?" She pointed back to the line. The bay was purpose-built for Banshee suit repair, and segments of armor passed overhead while others stood up on racks where robot arms worked on them.

"Yes, I have. They're not just for the ladies, you know."

"I really enjoyed running around out there. So

much *power*. The air was freezing, but I didn't feel it at all."

"How about your squad? They teaching you and the other newbies?"

"Sergeant Tin's making sure of that. I'm paired off with this old hand named Cusabrina. She's a little sarcastic, but I think we worked well out there." The image of the struggling doe returned, its unheard calls for help rising from its straining throat. "I . . . saw something happen, and I can't stop thinking about it."

"Tell me." The big man studied her with fatherly concern.

"There were these ice jellyfish things, sliding over the snow. The rockets spooked this family of stag-looking creatures, and they trampled them."

"What else?"

"One of the does bolted away from the pack, and the jellyfish things . . . they got her. The rest of them ran off, and it was left behind, trapped in these horrible tentacles, fighting to get away. It died right there, because of something that shouldn't have happened."

"It bothers you. The randomness of it."

"Yes. Yes, that's it. It was meaningless. That doe just took a wrong turn, and it died for it." Ayliss realized that the bay had dissolved around her, and that for a minute she'd been down on the snow planet again. Coming back, she remembered she was talking to someone who'd survived two complete tours in the war zone. "Well listen to me, going on about a life form I never saw before, like what happened to it was important."

"It was. To that creature, it was the most important thing that ever happened."

"It just looked so helpless, so scared, so . . . forlorn."

"I know that feeling. I got cut off once, when I was a private. Big fight, I got turned around in the smoke and spent the next two days trying to find friendlies."

"You telling me you messed up in combat, Dom?"

"I'm telling you I almost got killed, while doing everything I was supposed to. In the middle of all that chaos out there, nothing you do is guaranteed to be safe. Jumping left has just as much chance of getting you hurt as jumping right."

"That can't be it. You're saying it's all luck?"

"I'm saying you have to put this out of your mind entirely, or come to terms with it. Anything else, and you'll be too scared to move. Which makes you a hazard to your squad."

A flash of anger. "I will *not* put my sisters at risk. No matter what."

"There's the answer. Keep thinking of the Banshees right next to you, and you'll do fine." He patted her on the shoulder, and walked away.

CHAPTER 3

Jander studied the terrain beneath him as the medical shuttle flew him back to the war. The transport ship that had brought him to Celestia had offloaded dozens of replacements in standard shuttles from orbit, but a fussy technician had insisted that all returning medical cases rode on the medical bird.

As the only passenger, he'd found a comfortable seat that allowed him to prop up his leg brace while looking out the porthole. His handheld kept updating his location, and the medics on the shuttle had assured him that the capital city of Fortuna Aeternum was his correct destination. Apparently the Orphan Brigade was operating not far from the city, and he would have little difficulty catching a ride back to his unit.

A medic passed, and he waved the man over. Pointing out the porthole, he observed: "We seem to be following a chain of Force units and refugee camps."

"We'd better, sir," the man answered. "There are so many ex-Forcemembers with the rebels that nothing flying this low is safe. It ain't like fighting old Sammy the Sim. We got too comfortable with Sam not understanding a single word we say. So when this thing started, everybody was still broadcasting in the clear. Locations, arrival times, entire mission orders, and the Rogers were listening the whole time."

"The Rogers?"

"Roger the Rebel, sir. What we call them. It's creepy, knowing our opponents speak our language, know exactly how we operate, all our vulnerabilities . . . sometimes you can't be sure if the uniform next to you is one of them or one of us."

He headed up the aisle, and Jan went back to viewing the ground. Like so many of the settled worlds, much of Celestia was uninhabited. Great expanses of untouched territory passed beneath them, in between the sprawling bases with their towering defenses and the temporary encampments of the troops hunting the rebels. Despite the large numbers of Force units redirected to Celestia, the refugee camps dwarfed the military sites. Most of them seemed to have been thrown together, with acres of ramshackle roofs made from all kinds of discarded material ringed by watchtowers and miles of anti-personnel wire. From this height, it was hard to tell if the wire was meant to keep the enemy out or the occupants in.

His handheld announced the approach of Fortuna Aeternum, and he pressed his temple against the porthole. He'd once visited the capital city as a boy, as part of his father's entourage, but already knew that place was long gone. Once the most opulent metropolis in the galaxy, the rebellion had turned Fortuna Aeternum into something out of Earth's Dark Ages. The ground outside the city looked like a mud flat, denuded of trees by people desperate for fuel and churned up by thousands of patrol vehicles. The blue waters of the River Bellona were now a murky brown, filled with the refuse from the stricken city's inhabitants. The wide river passed right through the metropolis, feeding numerous canals that were likewise polluted.

The city's size had actually increased during the war, and its outskirts looked like just another refugee camp. First he saw acres of tatterdemalion shelters, connected in a quilt of necessity so tight that it was hard to see if there were any streets or even alleys. Next came the burned-out shells of the outermost neighborhoods, destroyed in the initial bloodletting, likewise covered with anything that could serve as a roof.

Following the river, they passed through a ring of checkpoints that appeared to be the first lines of defense for the city's core. Armored vehicles, stone pillars jutting out of the ground, and rolls of anti-personnel wire surrounded each of the strongpoints. The buildings inside this ring had seen a lot of repair work, and Jander decided the checkpoints were a demarcation between the haves and the have-nots.

"Some things never change." he muttered.

The shuttle descended until he could make out the high wall that encircled the Seat of Authority, also known as the SOA. Though fighting on planets in distant solar systems, Jander had heard of the infamous compound where the planet's former rulers now held court. The wall itself was completely new, surrounding several square miles in the city center where Horace Corlipso and the other oligarchs had once lived. Towers stood out from the gray battlements, loaded with heavy weapons and festooned with surveillance gear. A two-hundred-yard killing ground had been cleared all the way around, and the River Bellona had been diverted to form a stinking moat on one side.

The shuttle passed over the wall, surprising him. Mortas looked down at his handheld, and felt sudden apprehension at seeing it had gone blank. He saw the same medic approaching.

"We're being diverted, sir. Right to the roof of the Security Ministry." The man's earlier openness had been replaced by cold distance. "Apparently Governor Asterlit wants to meet you."

"Lieutenant Mortas. Welcome to Celestia." The man was taller than Jan's six feet, with the physique of a stevedore. His tunic was jet black, with a high collar that pressed against a bull neck supporting a shaved head. "I'm Damon Asterlit."

Mortas extended his hand, wary of the individual who had been Horace Corlipso's chief assassin. Asterlit had regained control of Fortuna Aeternum by ruthlessly crushing the slave rebellion in its streets, earning the unquestioning gratitude of the surviving oligarchs. It was Jander's understanding that Asterlit had effectively replaced Horace as the ruler of Celestia.

"Do you greet every replacement lieutenant who comes through?" he asked, trying not to look away. They stood in an empty corridor one level down from the Ministry's long roof, where the shuttle had landed. The uniformed attendants who had escorted Jan had been terse in their greetings, and they'd disappeared as soon as Asterlit approached.

"You're hardly a replacement." The words were bloodless, the eyes probing. "Your record with the Orphan Brigade is quite commendable. But no, I don't greet every Force officer on arrival. Just the ones who knew the traitor Hugh Leeger."

Jander fought the flutter of panic that had started when the medical shuttle flew away. The Orphan Brigade knew he was due to arrive that day, but not that he'd been diverted to Asterlit's headquarters. In the months since the rebellion's start, Jander had heard the rumors flying around the war zone about Asterlit's cruelty and his iron rule on Celestia. A man in such a position could cook up any story he liked about why Jander Mortas never reached the Orphans.

In the back of his mind, Mortas remembered the voice of a Force interrogator, telling him he could be made to disappear if he didn't cooperate. Asterlit had clearly done his homework, so Jander decided there was little chance of successfully lying to him about Hugh.

"He practically raised me until I went to boarding school. But in my family that happened when you turned twelve."

"He was your father's chief of security after that, and then your stepmother's. Also an impressive record, until he conspired with the servant girl Emma to murder my friend and mentor, Horace Corlipso."

"I was in the war zone when that happened. I have no idea what occurred."

"I'm surprised by your lack of interest in one of the key leaders of the rebellion." The tone never changed, carrying neither emotion nor urgency. "You do know that Leeger has risen to command a large band within the Orange?"

"Excuse me, the Orange?"

"That's the name we gave to a particularly difficult faction among the rebels. They're hiding in the mines west of here, and once you stay underground long enough your skin turns orange."

"I didn't know that."

"Your Captain Pappas will no doubt fill you in when you rejoin your unit."

"I expect he'll brief me along with the other officers. It's part of his job, as the battalion's intelligence officer."

"He'll have a lot to tell you." Asterlit raised a large hand, indicating that they should walk down the passageway. "The Orphan Brigade is being redeployed from their current duties, and their new area of operations is a well-trafficked rebel corridor near Orange territory. Any information you could provide about Leeger would improve their chances of success."

Although his left leg was encased in a brace that allowed the knee joint to bend and his recovery was progressing, Mortas emphasized his limp as they walked. The dead stillness of the corridor seemed wrong to him, and he realized he was comparing it to the busy hubbub of Unity Plaza, his father's headquarters on Earth. Unlike Unity, there seemed to be no one else around.

"The brigade's been here for over a month, so I expect they'll be telling me more than I'll be telling them. About Leeger or otherwise."

They turned a corner, and he was actually relieved to see two armed guards standing on either side of an ornate double door. He didn't recognize the uniform—forest-green fatigues and black boots—so he assumed they were some kind of special security detachment for Asterlit. The governor hadn't slowed down to match his labored gait, and so the man stopped just short of the tall entrance.

"I might be able to help you there." Asterlit said, before waving a hand at the sentinels. They both wore helmets with darkened visors hiding their eyes, and one of them tapped the side of his headgear before giving the order to open the hatch. The two doors swung silently, and Jander followed the governor through them.

He stopped just inside, baffled by the layout. The chamber was a large, long rectangle with tiered seating to either side facing inward. At the far end, roughly fifty yards away, a set of stairs led up to a broad platform and a chair that could only be described as a throne. Low and broad, it looked like it had been carved out of a single piece of black stone. Although the seats on either side of the approach were accoutered with all of the electronic equipment the governor's staff would need during a conference meeting, the throne itself was bare.

"What's this room used for?" Jander asked, studying Asterlit's reaction. He was only mildly disappointed, as the big man finally responded with something akin to emotion. His bald head canted a millimeter, and his brow furrowed.

"I would think that was obvious. I hold staff meetings here." Reaching across one of the nearest desks, he produced a remote control device. "You may want to sit down."

"I'm fine, thank you."

Asterlit clicked the remote, and the lights in the cavern dimmed. A familiar sight coalesced in the center of the room, a swirling ball of light that gradually expanded until the seats and walls were replaced by the ghostly image of a three-dimensional recording. This one was gold in color, from a bright sun that had been shining overhead and the yellow of the open ground. A moment later he stood in the middle of a crude road, with military trucks spread out on either side. Freeze-framed images showed drivers bailing out with weapons while their infantry security force raced up the road. Somewhere in the distance, the cannon on an armored car blossomed into what looked like the flaring of a match.

"This video was recovered from an ammunition convoy ambushed by the Orange not long ago. It's a composite of multiple camera views."

Sounds erupted all around them, and Mortas flinched. He recognized the blast of the shoulder-fired HDF rocket launcher known as a boomer, and then the armored car was tossed bouncing out of view. All around him soldiers took up firing positions around the trucks, shooting madly until the air was filled with the roar.

Another boomer round hit something behind him, and Mortas turned to see another armored car belching flames at the back of the column.

"Notice anything?" He heard Asterlit, but couldn't see him.

"No incoming small arms fire. They don't want to blow up the trucks."

"Or kill their own people."

As if materializing right out of the ground, a bare-chested figure leapt up next to Jander and then raced for the nearest soldier. Wearing light-colored trousers wrapped tightly to his legs by strips of cloth, the wraith appeared to be covered head-to-toe in the soil of the ambush site. Sprinting forward, he swung his arm at the back of the trooper's neck. Jander managed to see the fighting knife just before it punched straight into the muscle.

More concealed positions burst open near the trucks, and moments later dozens of camouflaged men and women were swarming over the defenders. It was over soon after that.

"The Orange study the responses of our security people better than any other rebel band. No matter how we change procedure, they adjust within days."

With the action ended, Mortas saw that the knife-wielding ambushers weren't camouflaged at all. Their skin was bronze, and the few of them with unshorn heads showed the same tone in their hair. They were soon joined by many others, bearers who ran up with empty pack boards hanging from their backs. The rebels quickly broke the bulk ammunition down into cases, which were strapped into place and carried off by multiple relays.

"You'll recognize this one. His skin hasn't changed yet."

Walking down the center of the road, accompanied by a bushy-haired child who was completely orange, Hugh Leeger spoke into a small radio.

"No. Stay up there and keep your eyes open. If they've got a react force waiting, you're our warning."

Jan studied the face of the man he knew so well. Unlike the others, Leeger wore a complete set of fatigues and boots. He'd lost some weight, but seemed otherwise unchanged from when they'd last met in Roanum's orbit.

"Got it all?" the Leeger image asked a rebel who had run up as if to make a report, and the woman nodded before jogging after the departing pack train. "Okay, burn 'em."

Flames sprouted all over the stripped convoy, shrinking the picture as the heat consumed the cameras generating the video. The footage flickered as the different devices died, and Leeger and his young bodyguard appeared to melt in the inferno before the throne room returned.

"As you can see, Hugh Leeger is one of their leaders."

"I'm not surprised."

"So there's nothing you can tell me that might help us catch him?"

"The man I knew wasn't a traitor, so I doubt anything I've learned still applies to him." The words burned in his mouth, but Jander wanted this interview to end.

"All right." Asterlit brought the lights back up. Stepping closer, he loomed over Mortas. "Keep this in mind. We caught his protégé, the operative known as the Misty Man, and hanged him in the courtyard outside. We're going to catch Leeger too, and I promise you his passing will not be nearly as quick."

The governor stopped talking, waiting for a response with the face of a statue. The whole performance rekindled the resentment of overbearing authority that Jan had developed early in life, but he managed to keep silent. Finally accepting this response, Asterlit made a motion as if to lay the remote control on the nearest table.

The room dissolved again, instantaneously this time, into strobing light and throbbing shadows. It was another video, shot right there in the throne room, and so he was in the dead center of the replay. Loud music boomed out a disturbing, discordant beat, which he felt in his teeth.

All around him, men and women in different stages of undress were writhing and wrestling. Facial masks abounded, as did strange loincloths and mesh clothing.

The darkness made it difficult to determine exactly what was taking place, but it was obviously a violent orgy. In one flash of illumination he saw several men ganging up on one female, a single bare arm reaching into the air for help. Several yards away a large woman in a mask was lashing someone with a cat-o'-nine-tails, her laughter rising above his cries of pain.

Seated in the throne wearing a robe open to his midsection, Asterlit looked on without any emotion at all.

The projection disappeared a second later, leaving him back in the room with Asterlit.

"I'm sorry." The governor spoke without remorse. "I hit the wrong button."

Knowing Asterlit wanted a reaction, Jander gave him a bemused smile.

"Something struck your fancy there, Lieutenant?"

"Struck my funny bone, is more like it."

"Excuse me?"

Mortas feigned sudden contrition. "Oh, I'm sorry, Governor. That was rude of me. I'm sure you felt that was quite a party."

"And you don't?"

"I'm in the infantry. What you just showed me, for us that's not even good pornography."

Asterlit appeared flummoxed, but spoke anyway. "I imagine you've seen your share of true pornography. Out there. Outright obscenity."

"Yes." Jander considered stopping there, but the

ham-handed attempt at rattling him had struck a nerve. "On Fractus, I killed a Sim infiltrator by beating his head against a boulder. That was after he and his buddy had killed two of my men and then emasculated them. They also killed my medic right in front of me."

"Certainly sounds obscene."

"You may get to see it yourself, one of these days. There's a whole Sim armada out there somewhere, trying to find a way to get to the settled planets without being detected. When they figure that out, you may wish you spent more time supporting the war than torturing slaves."

"So it's true. You did speak with them."

"No." Jander decided he'd already gone too far. "I just believe the rumor about that armada. It's been going around the war zone a long time."

"What were they like? Did they seem malleable? Suggestible?"

"The only Sims I ever encountered were actually quite obstinate."

Asterlit studied him a moment longer. "You're more like your father than you think, Lieutenant Mortas."

"I'll take that as a compliment."

"My attendants will show you back to the roof. Another shuttle is on the way."

"Thank you, Governor." The notion of the sun and the breeze on the empty rooftop was suddenly quite appealing, and Mortas tried not to show his relief. "It's been an honor meeting you."

An armored shuttle carried him from the SOA to the sprawling base where the Orphans got their logistical support. As a separate brigade, the Orphans had no permanent parent organization or dedicated sources of supply and maintenance.

That didn't appear to be a problem once Jander limped down the ramp from the shuttle. Ten miles south of Fortuna Aeternum, the base could have been a city in its own right except that none of its temporary structures was higher than two stories and most were only one. The spacedrome where he stood roared with activity, with transport planes, shuttles, fighters, and drones lifting off or landing. Movers, trucks, and armored cars were parked in seemingly endless fenced-in lots, and in the distance he was just able to make out the cannon on a row of tanks.

The shuttle had been diverted from another mission to pick him up, and so the crew had no idea where Jander was supposed to go once he landed. Normally his handheld would have synced up with the Force systems running the base, but the device was still useless. The sun was high overhead, warming him as he scanned the row of tan huts where he'd been dropped off. Various signs displayed acronyms that probably made sense to base personnel, but were total gibberish to him. He'd decided to enter the nearest hut to ask directions when a voice called out.

"Is that the famous Lieutenant Jander Mortas?"

He turned to see a tall, slim captain coming toward him in desert camouflage. He wore no insignia, but Jander knew him well as First Battalion's intelligence officer.

"I'm not famous when I'm in the same spot as Captain Erlon Pappas. Legendary explainer of military graphics, sometime weather forecaster, and tolerator of the infantry." They embraced after exchanging salutes.

"Who says I tolerate you assholes? You guys kidnapped me from a cushy headquarters job."

"*Long* before I got to the brigade." Jander leaned in to study the other man's short hair. "Longer than I thought. You going gray on us?"

"Blonds don't go gray. We go silver. Come on. I've got a mover waiting."

They walked between two huts, with Pappas studying Mortas's gait. "How's the leg?"

"It's coming along, but I re-injured it on Roanum. You hear what happened there?"

"That part of the story didn't make it onto the Splat."

"The Splat?"

"Sorry. That's a new one. We don't call it the Bounce here. News might rebound all over the galaxy, but everything that happens here gets censored really hard. It doesn't bounce so much as go splat."

"I think I hate this place already."

"No reason to wait. Everybody else hates it." A

broad parking lot spread out in front of them, but Pappas stopped just on the other side of the huts. "You'll get the full briefing, but this whole scene absolutely sucks. That asshole Asterlit somehow got appointed as the governor, and Command decided that means he runs the show. You hear about him yet?"

"I just met him. That's why I'm late."

"Uh-oh. What did you tell him?"

"What could I? I only just got here."

"Not what I mean. He's got a strong propaganda arm, so just assume he taped everything. Get ready for him to twist that on the Splat so you sound like his biggest fan."

"Son of a bitch."

"Don't worry about it—nobody believes any of that nonsense anyway." Pappas made no move toward the vehicle park. "What did he want to talk about?"

"Hugh Leeger. He wanted to know if I had any tips for fighting him."

"Do you?"

"Yes. *Don't.*"

The mover took them to the other side of the airfield, passing enormous hangars and maintenance bays. Jander was staring at a sea of cargo containers when Pappas leaned over the back of his seat. He handed Mortas a new handheld, and took the old one.

"It's a completely different war here. Sammy Sim

might not understand our speech—" Jander thought he felt the intelligence officer's eyes drilling into his memory of meeting the Sim delegates on Roanum "—but the Rogers sure do. Worse, half the Celestian units mutinied when they were sent back here. So our opponents have got lots of trainers telling them how the Force operates."

"I heard it was bad."

"It is. We've fielded encryption that should have secured our comms, but that's only been partially successful. Some of the defectors must have been commo experts, because they're still getting into our systems. A week ago, they juked a target identifier on this one Tratian outfit. It shifted the rockets right on top of the guys calling for them."

"Shit."

"It gets worse, but that's gonna have to wait. Right now you need to meet your new assistant, Sergeant Strickland." The mover stopped outside a long segment of fencing, and through the mesh Jander could see it was a motor pool.

"Supply? I'm working supply?" Mortas was already well acquainted with Sergeant Strickland, who was widely respected as First Battalion's supply NCO.

"We would have put you on the battalion track team, but we don't have one, and you can't walk."

"I have no training in this at all."

"Don't worry—that's the new job description. We haven't had a real supply officer in this battalion since

Drew Follett." The name brought back a memory from Jander's first days with the Orphans, when he'd met Captain Follett. The man had been vomiting outside the battalion HQ late one night, and he'd died a short time later. Obsessed with finding new sources of food for Orphan units locked in combat, Follett had been ingesting small portions of captured Sim rations even though they were deadly to humans. "It's a temporary position, until you can walk again. Strickland's been running this show on his own, whether he's had an officer to babysit or not. He'll bring you up to speed."

Mortas took this as his cue to dismount, which he did with reluctance. His mind pushed back against the very idea of the new role in such an unfamiliar environment. Varick's face appeared unbidden in his mind, compounding the sensation of letdown. In an effort to push that thought away, he made himself focus on the job. "What are we doing right now? The battalion, I mean."

"We're moving."

Pappas's words were borne out by the scene in front of him. Laden movers were marshalling in files, engines running, while soldiers ran around them securing last-minute additions. A hundred yards away, he could see even more activity inside a row of open-air maintenance bays. Deciding that the trucks were someone else's concern, he started limping across the ground.

As he drew closer, Mortas felt consternation at not recognizing anyone. Half the troops were bundled up in body armor, helmets, and tactical goggles, but the remainder had stripped down to fatigue pants and T-shirts and Jander felt he should have seen a few familiar faces. He'd almost reached the bays when an armored man crossed in front of him. Medium height and carrying a Scorpion rifle, he resembled many of the other soldiers in the area. Even so, recognition clicked somewhere in Jander's mind.

"Dak? Sergeant Dak!"

The man turned and looked around as if not seeing him.

"Sergeant Dak. Don't recognize your old platoon leader?"

A smile spread across the man's dark skin while he slid his goggle lenses up under his helmet. "Lieutenant Mortas! When did you get back?"

Elation flooded Jander as he stumped up to Dak and swatted him on his armor. "Just now. How's the platoon?"

"As good as can be expected. They've had us pulling every job the Orphans were never meant to do. Guarding the perimeter, riding shotgun on supply convoys, heck there was even a rumor they were gonna make us take over security for the SOA. Can you imagine that? Palace guard for Asterlit."

"So what are we doing now?"

"Finally a real mission. We're bustin' loose from this rear-echelon grab-bag and heading for the boon-docks, where we always shoulda been. We're gonna be hunting Roger in a big patch of nothing, right between two sectors controlled by the Orange and the Flock."

"Heard of the Orange—who's the Flock?"

"Nutty bunch. Mostly ex-slaves, high on freedom. They tattoo bird symbols on their faces. Free as a bird. Get it?"

"This place is crazy."

"You always did catch on fast."

"How are the men?" Having been gone for the entire time the brigade had been on Celestia, Mortas couldn't make himself ask if there had been any casual-ties.

"Not too happy, but nobody is. I didn't join to put down a slave rebellion, or to keep fat cats safe behind a wall. Never thought I'd say this, but I miss Sam."

"But they're hanging together? The platoon, I mean."

"Of course. Lieutenant Wolf's made some good moves, volunteering for the lousy jobs before we could get assigned to the really shitty ones."

"Lieutenant *Wolf*? That's his name?"

"No, but everybody calls him that. His real name's hard to pronounce, and it's a thank-you for him and his scouts saving our hides from the wolves the night you got nailed."

"Are you kidding me? He got there for the last five minutes of that fight, riding in an armored car." Mortas was barely able to keep himself from saying the nickname should have been his by all rights. His wounded leg throbbed, as if in confirmation.

"That's true, but most of us would be dead if he'd been a minute later." Dak pointed at the leg brace. "Admit it, sir. We put up a good fight, but those brutes had us by the balls at the end."

"I guess so." Jander's mind whirled with the overload of information and his platoon sergeant's obvious affection for his replacement. "So, any idea where you'll be tonight? I'd like to drop by."

"We're going straight out on patrol, three days at least, but I'm sure we'll catch up." Dak started walking away. "What are they gonna have you do while your leg heals?"

"I'm the new battalion supply officer."

Dak laughed. "God help us, then."

"Yeah, don't eat your last ration." Mortas called, but the man had already disappeared.

"Lieutenant Mortas? Over here, sir." The voice belonged to Sergeant Strickland, standing next to a flatbed truck under the maintenance awning. The short man went back to supervising a team of soldiers who were tightening straps around a trio of large metal tubes that looked like rockets.

"Hey, Sergeant Strickland. Good to see you again."

"You too, sir. Sorry your leg is still messed up, but you'll have plenty of time for rehab, where we're going." Strickland squatted down, inspecting the underside of the flatbed.

"Where are we going?"

"A smaller version of here, but out in the boonies. A supply base we'll be sharing with the support out-fits from a couple different units."

"Who's running security there?"

"Not Orphans. The brigade's shuttling out to dif-ferent patrol areas in that vicinity. It's a real hot spot for the rebels." Strickland stood up, wiping sweat from his dark skin. "You'll be riding in one of the only shuttles going right to the base. I'll see you there in a few hours."

"I'd rather go with the convoy."

"No armor, goggles, or weapon, and you can't run. You're flying on this one, sir." The NCO gave him a sympathetic look. "Once we're unloaded at our new home, I'll get you outfitted and briefed."

"Makes sense." Mortas gestured at the rocket-like tubes on the truck. "What are these things?"

"A holdover from Captain Follett's time. He was always trying to find different ways to deliver rations to the troops." Strickland paused. "I'm sorry, sir, I forgot you met him."

"Briefly. He cared a lot."

"Yeah, he did. And it killed him. Anyway, these things here are a kind of space dart. One-man capsule, launched from orbit, with automatically deploying parachutes to slow them down before impact."

"I've heard of these. From the Spartacan Scout I was marooned with on Roanum." Mortas put his fingertips on the bed and inspected the darts. Twenty feet long, with a single porthole and engines near the fins. "He said they were deathtraps."

"He was right. They got phased out a couple years ago. So Captain Follett found a whole yard full of 'em gathering dust and thought they'd work fine for emergency food deliveries."

"Have you used them?"

"Not the way Captain Follett thought. The original configuration had almost no guidance to it. But Sergeant Leoni got some missile training somewhere along the line, and he attached those engines that you see near the fins."

"That's impressive. Is Sergeant Leoni somebody new?"

"*New?*" a jovial voice barked from the other side of the truck. Mortas watched a set of worn combat boots cross behind the vehicle, and then a man with a full head of gray hair appeared. Stripped to a sweat-dotted T-shirt, he had a barrel chest and a bit of a gut. A merry smile showed gaps between his teeth, and then he was shaking Mortas's hand. "I been in this war for thirty years, young lieutenant. Done everything from grunt infantry to general's driver. I even did a turn in the stockade."

"From the gig as the general's driver?" Jander gave the man a wild grin, recognizing the archetype.

"What can I say? He objected to my off-duty use of his vehicle. I owe him one; I met a better class of people in the lockup."

"I been there. Except I was in solitary."

"Really?" Leoni studied his face, reappraising him. "You're gonna have to tell me about that sometime."

Strickland tried to redirect the conversation. "I was just showing our new battalion supply officer how you improved the darts."

"Aw, it wasn't just me. The boys and girls in my company are pretty handy with tools. They cooked up a simple launcher so we can load these beasts up with food, shoot 'em into the sky, and then the guidance takes 'em right to troops in the field. We lost a few of 'em, getting it right." A secret grin. "Crashed one of 'em into the personal shuttle of a Tratian general who was asking too many questions. Not while he was in it, of course. Anyway, we finally worked out all the bugs and can put rations down just about anywhere you like."

Strickland grinned. "Best part is, this being our own concoction, Roger can't hack in and redirect them. No HDF system even picks them up."

"Excuse me, Sergeant Leoni, but you mentioned your *company*? What company is that?"

"The First Independent Transportation Company, sir." Both NCOs laughed. "We're the truck-driving equivalent of the Orphans. You see, with all the desertions when Force units first came here, there were a lot of outfits getting broken up. Left a lot of truck drivers without a home. Since the Orphans have no organic transport, I just started picking up a vehicle here and a driver there, and asked Colonel Watt if we could be of use."

"You're not an Orphan?"

"Oh, I'm an Orphan, sir. Back before your brigade was ever called that."

"You're gonna have to tell me about that sometime."

"I will, sir. But right now we have to get this show on the road and you need to get to your shuttle."

"All right." Mortas looked toward the airfield. "Can you point me in the right direction?"

"We can do better than that, sir. You're with FITCO now. We can always find you a ride."

CHAPTER 4

"**S**enator Mortas. What is your vote?"

Olech came to with a start, just as he had on the day when this memory had occurred. He looked left and right in confusion, noting the tense muscles of the senators seated closest to him. The semicircular desks rose behind him and fell away to his front, where the chamber's speaker was calling for his decision.

All the sensations of that day returned—the nausea from the uncharacteristic binge the night before, the grinding doubt at what Lydia said was the smart move, the gnawing belief that this was just plain wrong. The wounds inside his abdomen, which had quieted during his years in the Senate, had come alive that morning. They clawed at him as he stood.

"I vote . . . nay."

His decision seemed to echo across the chamber, but

it elicited surprisingly little response. Olech thought he heard someone blurt out, "What the hell?" in the rows behind him, but his eyes were firmly planted on the desk when he sat.

"Senator Mortas has voted against the measure." The speaker called for the next ballot, but Olech heard none of it. Slowly raising his eyes, he saw two faces turned around in their seats, stamped with disapproval and anger. Not a week earlier he'd assured both of those senators that they could count on his support.

Finally finding the nerve to seek out the only face that mattered, Olech blanched to see that Interplanetary President Larkin, specially invited for this important vote, was staring directly at him. He'd given his word to the white-haired man, and then gone back on it. Instead of resentment or hostility, Larkin's lined features bore a long-suffering stillness, as if this latest affront was nothing when compared to all of the other betrayals in that hall.

Acid burned in his stomach, making him wish that the old wounds had reopened, anything to take him out of there. The vote went on and on, but Olech now began to see it as something that had already happened, that Larkin's reform had been narrowly defeated. Control of officer promotions in the Human Defense Force would remain with the Senate, and so the command structure of the Force would become even more political in its behavior.

Olech's fingertips tingled, and he saw with relief

that the long table was fading away. His next view was the raised gallery walkway outside the Senate chamber, normally packed with staffers and reporters, but now empty except for him and a graying man walking beside him who was his duplicate.

"What just happened, Mirror?" The shame of the event rode the words. "Why didn't you speak to me before this memory?"

"Of all the votes you cast as a senator, this one baffles me most. I did not want to prejudice your reaction."

"That wouldn't have made any difference. I feel now the way I did then. Sick, ashamed, and stupid. I knew it was wrong, but I did it anyway."

"Not an unusual event in the history of your race."

"My wife always had excellent instincts for the smart play, but somehow on this one she called it wrong."

"It cemented you in place with Horace Corlipso's faction, which was one of the goals you and your wife chose early in your career."

"Just because it got us what we wanted didn't make it right. The Force was already riven with its own factions—hard not to, with an interplanetary alliance—but commanders in the war zone were starting to make strategic decisions based on political factors because the Senate controlled who got promoted. Larkin recognized that danger, and almost managed to wrest that power away from them."

"You promised to help him."

"Of course I did. I'd been out there, I'd fought in the war, I knew the threat this represented. How could it not be bad for the troops, or for just winning the conflict, if decisions in the field were being made to please politicians on different planets?"

"You could blame this on your wife, you know. She pushed you to do it."

"She was listening to the wrong people."

"She was a political operator, in the same environment as everyone else. And she was your closest adviser and confidante. She had an obligation to provide better counsel."

"It was a joint decision."

"You and I both know it was not."

"Oh, but it was, Mirror. We both wanted status. We both wanted power. And we both fooled ourselves that we were only going to do it the one time."

"You look fifty pounds lighter than the last time I saw you, General." Reena Mortas spoke while walking down a long, cylindrical passageway.

"That was quite some time ago, Madame Chairwoman," General Merkit, the commander of the disjointed space city known as the Construction Zone, answered comfortably. "I never got the chance to thank you for making me go rebuild the Orphan Brigade. It changed my life."

"And I thought I was just making it difficult." Reena laughed once. "You've done a splendid job out here."

"It wasn't half as hard as it at first seemed. So much activity, so many convoys coming and going, factory stations as far as the eye can see, all infiltrated by the worst kinds of profiteers and schemers you ever met."

"I'm not sure about that last part. I am from Celestia, you know."

"This gang would have given them a run for their money, ma'am. But as with most overblown bureaucracies, there's usually one big rule or a single powerful agency that can bring it to its knees."

"And that was?"

"The security authorization to work here. As military commander, that one's all mine. Doesn't matter if you're the richest ore hauler in the galaxy or a board member with Zone Quest; if I yank your credentials you have to leave. I did it a few times, just to prove I would, and even now I have to toss a hard case every once in a while. But you threaten their ticket to making money, and you get their attention."

A large security detail walked behind the pair, the Chairwoman's bodyguards mixing with Merkit's protectors. When Olech had installed the general in the Construction Zone with the unpopular mandate of ending the rampant corruption, he'd surrounded Merkit with a hand-picked team from his own force. Although the two guard teams had barely spoken to each other, the gathering had been a bit of a reunion.

"Ulbridge tells me you've made some key personnel changes out here."

"That part was easy." The corridor ended at a circular hatch guarded by armed men wearing the gray tunic of Mortas security. The door stood open on enormous hinges, and it glistened with counter-surveillance gear. "When I pull the credentials from some crook in the hierarchy, I get to pick the replacement. You'd be surprised at how many of the discharged veterans working out here have a deep hatred of Zone Quest, Victory Provisions, and their cronies."

"No, I wouldn't." Reena stepped over the hatch's raised opening, followed by Ulbridge and Merkit. The room was two stories high and cylindrical, and its walls were covered with large viewing screens.

"So I had a ready talent pool of people who'd been blackballed by the corporations. They're grateful for their new jobs, and enjoy rooting out corruption. They're also hooked into an extensive, informal intelligence operation among the vets and the low-level workers; very little goes on that I don't hear about."

The hatch closed behind them, and the lights came up. A single command console stood in the center of the room, encircled by two half-moon tables with several chairs.

"This is the most secure compartment in the whole Construction Zone, Madame Chairwoman. We can speak freely here."

"My people already swept the place, ma'am."

Ulbridge slid between the tables and activated the console. Different screens flickered into life while Ulbridge slotted a highly encrypted disc. Reena and Merkit took their seats.

"So what can I do for you, Chairwoman Mortas?" Merkit asked.

"A small favor." Reena breathed the words out like a prayer. All around them, the walls took on the darkness of space. Stars twinkled into existence a few moments later, and then one of them slowly brightened as the focus intensified. Planets orbiting the star began to take shape, as well as numerous dead asteroids, but then the resolution stabilized on a single gray planet.

"Name it, ma'am."

"General Merkit, you're going to win the war."

"—**W**hich brings us to the star system that we've been covertly studying for almost a month." Reena had been walking back and forth for much of the last thirty minutes, describing the unlikely chain of events that had brought this group of unexplored planets to her attention.

"I have a question before you proceed, ma'am."

"You think it's crazy that I'm accepting a vision from a Step Worshiper's dream as an indication that these planets are the origin of the Sims."

"I am skeptical of that part, but it's not my question." Merkit shifted in his seat. "You said that the alien encountered by your stepson detailed the creation story which the Sims believe—that they're the mutated descendants of long-duration human space voyages that got lost out here."

"Yes, but the alien also maintained that the Sims' belief was a lie, implanted in their brains by their actual creators."

"I understand that. But I believe your stepson is probably correct in suspecting that much of what the alien told him is somewhat based in fact."

"Why is that, General?"

"I've spent a lot of time around accomplished liars. Many of them try to stay close to the truth because it's harder to disprove what they're saying. And some of the good ones think they're so darned slick that they can hand you a giant clue and you won't catch it."

"I remember a general who was like that."

"My time with the Orphans showed me I'm not slick at all. But back to my question. The Sims believe they're the mutated descendants of humans who came out here with the equipment to artificially create succeeding generations. If that's true, the Sims would be a self-sustaining race. However, we've never detected anything at any time during the war that suggested the Sims have this capability. Its absence seems to blow a giant hole in the alien's description of this Sim creation story."

"Very good, General." Reena nodded at Ulbridge,

who began tapping keys on the console. "The Sims who met with my stepson shied away from discussing their origins, so there was no opportunity to compare their beliefs with the shapeshifter's description. However, one part of the alien's explanation suggests an answer. The Sims are supposed to have been receiving convoys over the decades of the war, each one being the next serial in a staggered arrival of more and more important elements of Sim civilization. The ability to generate life artificially is so crucial to their survival that they may believe that equipment won't arrive until the very last convoys."

"So the Sims' actual creators could be manufacturing the newest generation, keeping them in a form of stasis while feeding them memories of a nonexistent past and the skills they would need upon awakening," Merkit mused. "That way they'd retain control of how many Sims are produced. And when the Sims won the war, their creators would just shut off the machines."

"That is exactly the assumption we followed." Reena shifted her gaze to the screens, which now retreated from the solar system under observation. The bright star became just one among many, and then digital indicators began to appear at a great remove. "Although we couldn't risk going near the system, we did ring it with covert monitoring systems."

"What did they show?"

"Nothing, at first. Three entire weeks passed with

no activity in that system at all. I was on the verge of ordering closer reconnaissance when this happened." The view intensified, rushing in toward the suspect planets again. The largest of them appeared lifeless until a tiny spark popped into life on its gray mass. Like an ember rising from a fire, it left the dark planet and then swung away into space.

"That was a launch." Merkit stated, coming to his feet.

"Yes." Reena's lip curled, still relishing the discovery. "It's a sizeable craft, and it moved out of the system at a speed consistent with Sim vessels."

Ulbridge entered more commands, and the screens switched to a blurred image hurtling through space. Still observed from a distance, it was a wedge-nosed craft with the boxy fuselage of a personnel transport. Merkit walked toward the picture as if in a trance.

"Tell me you were able to track where it went."

"It was a risk, but we had to know. A robot probe followed it, all the way to a region of space well outside the war zone. This spot right here."

The screens resolved into another black view, but Merkit didn't notice. The dark void was nothing more than the background to a tableau of astounding significance. Arranged like ships at anchor, hundreds of spacecraft similar to the one launched from the gray planet hung in the gloom as if frozen.

"We believe this is the next convoy of new Sims. The ship we tracked slid right into place with no additional adjustments, the way it would if the entire complement were asleep. Or, more accurately, not yet born."

"Our ships do the same thing, before and after a Step."

"Yes, but at the end of a voyage our people wake up. The energy readings on our vessels climb substantially during and after that process. The new vessel appears to have gone into an energy-saving mode, and hasn't moved. They're all just sitting there, powered down, with no emissions indicative of signals or scans."

"What have we learned about the planet of origin?"

"Long-range surveillance says it has gravity and a weak atmosphere, but that it's not habitable by humans." Reena waved a hand, and the view focused on the forbidding gray orb. "So far we've detected nothing unnatural about its surface. No structures, no antennae, no monitoring stations. The launch originated inside the planet itself."

"So whatever's happening there is hidden."

"Right now, yes. But we've developed a plan to find out what's going on inside."

"And that's what you want me to handle."

"Yes. There are too many eyes on me, and too many ways for this to be discovered. You've got total control of the stations out here, and so much activity that you could take this over and get us the answers we need."

"It would be my pleasure, ma'am."

Reena stood next to him, staring at the screens. "We cannot let them know we're onto them. Proceed cautiously. I've assembled a team of experts in a wide range of disciplines, all of them loyal, who will be arriving here in small, disjointed batches that I'm sure you can disguise as something else. They've been studying this planet visually, and have drawn some conclusions about its makeup.

"Other teams are augmenting robotic reconnaissance to get us closer and, ultimately, to enter the planet itself. You will do that only on my say-so, and only after completing all other studies on this planet, and on every other planet, moon, satellite, and asteroid in this system."

"Yes, ma'am. You can count on me."

"It is imperative that we determine if the shapeshifters are here. You'll be provided with the data gleaned from the scan of the original alien at Glory Main, as well as the scan of the moth-like particles it burst into just before being incinerated. We also have scans of the most recent shapeshifter, provided by the commander of the *Ajax* while orbiting Roanum. The creature gave us the slip most of the times it walked back into the desert, but on two occasions it burst into the same particles as were observed on Glory Main. It's possible that those moth-like things are its natural state."

"That's highly intriguing."

"If this planet is what we think it is, I would love to vaporize it from a distance." Reena stepped up to the glowing wall, and touched it with her finger-tips. "Unfortunately, that would still leave us with a vast region of space controlled by Sims who believe they're fighting us for their very survival.

"To convince them that they won't be receiv-ing any more convoys of new Sims, and that their creation story was a lie, I'll need detailed evidence. Hopefully we'll be able to get microbots inside this planet and gain the footage of what's going on in there, but we have to be prepared for any eventuality. That includes an all-out ground assault that may even go subterranean."

"But it's not a Hab, Madame Chairwoman."

"Correct. Let's hope it doesn't come to that, but we have to be ready to use troops in pressurized suits. If necessary, I'm going to hit that place with every Ban-shee and special operator we have."

CHAPTER 5

Looking out the shuttle's open rear hatch at the brown water just below, Ayliss was no longer enjoying her Banshee fighting suit. Despite having gone through this mission numerous times in the ship's simulators, she was having trouble believing her armor wasn't going to pull her down into Stygian depths where she would quickly drown. The suits were designed to handle missions just like this one, and the waterway was under a mile deep, but the sight of the enormous lake filled her with dread.

She tried to concentrate on Tin, who stood closest to the opening and swayed in an abiding fashion with the lurching shuttle. The square shoulders of her suit faced the waiting ramp, which jutted out and down at a forty-five-degree angle. Ayliss was behind her, one hand grasping the red canvas webbing that hugged the shuttle's bulkhead. Normally at ease inside the Banshee rig, at the moment she was struggling just to stay on her feet. Her leg muscles were already tiring from the unnecessary strain, but the nearness of their entry into the forbidding liquid made it almost impossible for Ayliss to relax. Seeking a distraction, she turned her head inside her helmet until the rear cameras engaged, showing the looming figure of Dellmore. Like Tin, the seasoned Banshee stood with arms lowered, knees bent, armored hips rocking back and forth.

Somewhere in the back of the squad was Cusabrina, but Ayliss was no longer paired with the reinstated corporal. Bullhead and Lightfoot had both been assigned to five days of sentinel duty outside the ship's bridge, and so Plodder was now partnered with Zuteck, and Ayliss, to her dismay, was working with Dellmore.

"Stop looking at me, rookie," Dell growled. "I know I'm pretty, but you need to concentrate on your job."

The canted armor of Dellmore's helmet hid her features completely, and the comment would have been funny if it came from anyone else. Shifting her view back to the ramp, Ayliss discovered that focusing on the mission wasn't a bad idea. In her mind she saw Captain Breverton giving the briefing, and trying to recall specific details helped to distract her. Breverton was short, with red hair cut so close to her scalp that her head appeared to be rusting, and she'd radiated both competence and confidence.

"Sam's been getting bolder, now that he knows we're short-handed out here. On UC-2147 he set up three phony settlements, complete with actual space-dromes, in terrain that left only a few spots for cofferdam deployment." The Banshees seldom used the cofferdams, which were enormous energy tunnels generated by ships in orbit that cut through a planet's atmosphere all the way to the ground. "The Sims ambushed the touchdown sites, forcing the deployment of an entire division to fight what was later determined to be two brigades."

That detail triggered a memory. Jander and the Orphans had participated in the assault on UC-2147. His platoon had survived the initial chaos, only to be attacked by hundreds of wolf-like creatures late the first night. Jan had almost been killed by one of them, and Ayliss had dreamed of the event during a Step voyage soon afterward. She shuddered at the image of a large dog attacking a very young Jan, biting him in the same leg which the wolf on UC-2147 had almost ripped clean off.

"So we're going to make sure Sam is home this time. Our company will be inserted by stealth in multiple locations, moving to jump-off points where our separate teams will wait while cofferdams are generated in the vicinity of the Sim emplacements. The cofferdams will be real, but the vehicles and troop rings descending inside them will be electronically generated decoys.

"If Sam moves toward the touchdown points in force, we'll know this is a genuine colony. In that case, you will strike your assigned targets in an effort to blind the enemy and take pressure off the cofferdams." As part of that effort, Tin's squad had been ordered to destroy several concealed antennae on top of a winding ridge not far from the lake. "If the enemy doesn't respond to the cofferdam generation, Force troops will be inserted by shuttle to check the ground around the touchdown sites. Once that ground has been cleared, the main body will come down.

"Regardless of what happens, you will destroy your assigned targets when ordered to do so. After that, you will support the attack as it develops—which means be ready for anything." Breverton had grinned in anticipation. "Banshee suits are the perfect combination of optics, communications, and weaponry. We bring speed, armor, and firepower right where it's needed. I expect you ladies to make the most of that."

The memory of the skipper's enthusiasm had reduced Ayliss's anxiety a notch when a glowing number appeared in her face shield display. She gasped, even though the countdown had been part of every simulation.

"Ten seconds," Tin called. "Relax your bodies, but clench your teeth until you hit. Here we go."

The words had clearly been for the rookies, but Ayliss had no time to consider them before Tin was shuffling forward, toward the ramp and the miles of

water below. Not believing her own motion, she released her handhold and followed the squad leader.
When Tin reached the angled ramp, she jogged down
its length and disappeared.

Heart racing, shrinking backward inside the suit
while her legs took her forward, Ayliss started down
the incline with shorter and shorter steps.

"Pick it up, rook!" Dell shouted behind her, but
then the shuttle bounced. A giddy flutter rose in Ayliss's stomach as her right leg came up off the deck and
she started overbalancing to the left. Terrified by the
notion of falling over with Dellmore watching, she
raised the right leg high and slammed it down hard.
Overbalancing to the right this time, she gave off a
desperate peep and ran off the end of the plates.

Gravity seized the suit like a chain around her
ankles with an anchor at the end. Coming to the position of attention as she fell, legs together and arms
tight against her sides, Ayliss shot downward like a
brick-shaped arrow. Her eyes saw the bright sky and
the endless blanket of brown water and she was falling, accelerating, bracing, and yet the water wasn't
there, *where was the water why wasn't she hitting yet?*

The heavy boots absorbed the jolt of the impact,
and momentum sent her driving straight through the
murk. The lake water near the surface was a choco-
late brown, but mere seconds of racing descent took
her down into blackness. Her mind screamed that
this was exactly what the simulator had shown, and

all the readings said she was upright and almost at the bottom, but the blackness enfolded her and she wasn't slowing down and she couldn't see and she was encased in a huge armored box in a giant lake and she was just about to scream when she hit.

The training modules hadn't prepared her for the force of the landing, so one instant she was upright and the next she was on all fours. Despite the darkness, she saw a plume of silt blossom all around her and realized that a large boulder was inches from her face. Cold air blew all around her body, the suit's systems programmed to cool her at that moment so that runnels of perspiration wouldn't be mistaken for a leak. The frigid air was almost as delightful as the readout saying she had full suit integrity, and Ayliss unclenched her aching jaw. Relief arced through her muscles, and she reached out to pat the stone before standing up.

"Now *that* was something." Legacy's voice, awe-filled yet calm, came to her ears.

Standing still, letting her heart settle down, Ayliss watched as the optics adjusted to the depth. Her suit could see through heavy smoke and even certain vegetation, but she'd been warned that the lake's water would thwart much of that. The featureless void gradually resolved into a light brown, allowing her to see several other rocks and the gently waving tendrils of tall aquatic weeds.

"I see we all made it," Tin said. "That's a good start."

The comment set Ayliss's tongue in motion, calling up the display indicating the positions of the entire squad. They appeared as circles of light forming a ragged line with Tin at one end and Cusabrina at the other. Turning in place, Ayliss saw the azimuth that would take them to shore appear before her eyes. The simple functioning of her suit calmed her even more, and she looked around in amazed freedom. All her fears, all her worrying, and yet everything had turned out just as she'd been promised.

"Move out." Tin ordered, and the row of individual submarines started walking across the lake's trackless bottom.

The squad was weaving its way through a grove of kelp-like pillars when it regained communication. Just as the water had prevented them from seeing properly, it had also imposed a form of radio silence that would only be alleviated by shallower depths. The aquatic vegetation swayed around them with the eddying current, but their attention quickly went elsewhere. Tight voices pushed through the water to them.

"—kicked over an anthill!"

"Fire control, I have enemy troops in the open! Request—"

"Mark positions! Show us who's who!"

Flashes of satellite imagery flickered across Ayliss's

face display, overhead shots of the ridge just beyond the lake. It was covered with a forest so dense as to be almost jungle, but the ground on the other side of the escarpment wasn't as thick. Settling into scattered trees surrounded by tall grass, it eventually opened up into clearings large enough for the cofferdams. The troop-delivery energy beams had flattened the undergrowth in several spots, but she ignored them because they were supposed to be decoys.

Heavy smoke rose from the green blanket on top of the ridge, and she caught brief glimpses of explosive light as rockets impacted under the canopy. The feed cut out just as she saw hundreds of moving dots heading for the cofferdam landing zones.

"Push through this shit, and get into the woods!" Tin hollered. "If one of those rockets lands in the water, we're gonna get pureed!"

A hulking shadow appeared several yards to her right, Dellmore swinging her arms and pumping her legs. The grass pillars jerked and twitched and then rose back up to the surface, so Ayliss didn't reach for them. With her arms swinging tight at her sides, she fought the brown wall that pressed in on all points of her suit.

Another flash of imagery, this one obscured by heavy smoke clouds that were being pulled across the battlefield by the wind. Missiles detonating all around the cofferdams now, amid a cacophony of frenzied voices.

"'There's *thousands* of 'em! Send the reinforcements! Send the reinforcements!"

"Contact right! Hit 'em! Hit 'em! *Hit 'em!*"

"Get down! Rockets inbound!"

A concussion wave rippled the surface over their heads, oscillating wrinkles stuttering away from them in frightened rows. Ayliss felt something grab her from behind, arresting her desperate motion, and swatted over her shoulder as much as the suit allowed. She came up with several twisted tendrils of vegetation, and tried to shove them away while pistoning her legs. The grasses refused to release her, and she twisted around to see they were hung up where her Fasces was stuck on her back.

Seizing the shoots with armored hands, she shredded them in fury before drawing the weapon and pushing forward again. She was only a few yards from the shore, but now the lakebed was covered with the rotting logs of long-ago-fallen trees. The decayed torsos collapsed under her weight, and she longed for the surface as if drowning.

A sheet of flame passed over, yellow and orange, and then she was sinking into the pulpy debris and starting to go over sideways.

"Fuck this!" she shouted, using the rifle to right herself before squatting down and kicking off as hard as she could.

The suit's titanic power blasted her right through the surface and into the air. The bright sunshine blanked out her vision for a long heartbeat as her optics adjusted, and then she could see the towering slopes covered with green, the gray fog that steamed up out of the foliage at different points, and Dellmore's back as she disappeared into the woods.

The water had impeded her leap, and so Ayliss landed knee-deep from shore. Something exploded behind her, slapping the suit and sending her lurching forward while a torrent of brown water doused her. Running after Dellmore, she tongued the display to show the rest of the squad.

They were all there, scattered across five hundred yards at the base of the ridge, and she was pounding up the slope to catch up with Dell when Tin spoke. The squad leader had cut off the communications feed from any ground element that wasn't Banshee, and so her commands came through as if the squad was on the planet alone.

"Hold your positions. Pair up and watch each other's backs. The rockets have already blasted the antennae." Booming explosions sounded from the top of the ridge, as if in agreement.

Ayliss located Dellmore on the display, and was at her side moments later. The veteran Banshee knelt behind a wide tree wrapped with vines, facing uphill.

"Get away from me, Mortas!" The arm of Dell's suit came up, pointing. "Get over there and face the lake. You don't have to be up my ass to watch my back."

Red-faced inside the helmet, Ayliss obeyed. Slipping between two trees, she knelt and studied the forest she'd just crossed. The wall of green and brown blocked her view of the water only fifty yards away, so she called up an overhead shot in one corner of her face shield. Drone gunships had joined the fight, and their cameras added definition to the composite imagery.

"Okay, here's what's happening." Captain Breverton spoke calmly. "Somebody on high jumped the gun. Instead of recon coming down in shuttles to check out the ground around the cofferdams, they inserted entire battalions."

"Jump the gun?" Ayliss recognized Legacy's puzzled tone on the squad's internal band. "Wouldn't it take hours to do that?"

"Pipe down," Cusabrina growled. Then, as if reconsidering, "And yes. They were supposed to wait."

Studying the fight on the far side of the towering ridge, Ayliss focused on the knobs of high ground that had been identified as likely sites for Sim heavy weapons. The Force units inserted by shuttle had formed defensive rings on the small hills, but judging from the volume of rocket and gunship fire, they were surrounded by large numbers of assaulting enemy.

"Our people on the ground are taking a beating, and support fires are limited by proximity to Sam." Ayliss remembered the veterans talking about the Sims' favorite way of defeating the humans' advantage in orbital and aerial firepower. Running straight at a Force unit until they were so close, or actually intermingled, that rockets or gunships were as much a threat to the humans as to the Sims. "Command won't send troops down the cofferdams until this is decided."

"Prepare to move." Tin grunted, making Ayliss wonder what Breverton had said that suggested they were about to displace.

"I'll feed you your boundary lines as we go." Breverton's words were mixed with heavy breathing, telling Ayliss that the company commander was already in motion. "Up and over the ridge, ladies. Sam's focused on those small hills. We're gonna kick him right in the ass."

Running up the slope, Ayliss felt a familiar sensation blossom inside her. Dellmore was ten yards ahead, the Fasces clutched across her chest so she could bull through the undergrowth. She'd ordered Ayliss to follow in her footsteps, breaking trail for the newer Banshee in order to cover the ground faster. Despite the thunder from the nearby battlefield, Ayliss quickly settled into a rhythm that allowed her to slide along through the corridor cleared by Dellmore.

The booms and blasts grew louder as they ascended, calling, promising. The enemy was there, armed, attacking, and the vibrations of the explosions sang through the fibers of her muscles as she moved.

She hugged the Fasces, feeling the rush of joy and expectation, and so was almost completely unprepared when they ran into the Sims just short of the blasted summit.

The rockets had felled many of the trees, and one moment Ayliss was watching Dellmore hop over a shattered trunk and the next she was twisting to identify the flurry of movement from the corner of her eye.

"Dell! *Sims!*" she yelled, just as the devastated vegetation came to life. Startled eyes turned in her direction, so many, so human, but they wore the flanged helmets and camouflaged smocks of the Sim infantry. Crouching or kneeling in a tight cluster, their reactions showed they were even more surprised than Ayliss. Diving, turning, raising weapons, they were a blur as she turned the rifle and then she was firing.

Two of them went flying, struck by the heavy rounds, and then she saw the muzzle flashes as at least a dozen of them shot her. Ayliss shrieked in alarm, feeling the impact as the bullets slammed home, forgetting that she was safely encased in armor until the slugs ricocheted away. The momentary terror was replaced with a flood of joy mixed with anger, so she planted her boots and started shooting again. Several camouflaged smocks were already fleeing through the brush, but more of them were hopping and rolling uphill and down, still shooting at her, and she concentrated on killing them.

The sounds of Dell's Fasces rose above the cacophony of Sim weapons, and then a patch of the woods twenty yards to her front erupted in flame as the veteran launched a grenade. Ayliss considered doing the same thing, but then heard more Fasces gunfire not far away and decided against it, fearful of hitting other members of the squad.

"This is Tin! We have engaged some kind of reaction force near the summit! Estimate one hundred of them!"

"We've got the same thing over here!" Ayliss recognized Sergeant Pelletier's voice, with a completely different squad a mile down the ridge. "Watch out for shoulder-fired rockets!"

"This is Breverton. Wade into 'em, Banshees!"

The exhortation send an electric pulse through Ayliss, and she charged into the Sims. Most were on their stomachs, firing madly, but one was standing behind a broad tree and shooting at something farther up the ridge. Skidding up next to him, she crushed his helmet with the butt of the Fasces. Now among the prone enemy, she lengthened her strides and kicked the one closest to her. His arms were raised in futile defense, and her armored leg threw him five yards away.

A multicolored sleeve passed in front of her face shield cameras, and a dirty hand was clawing for a hold. A furious chirping was in her ears, as if a canary had somehow gotten inside her helmet, and then she was jabbing up and back with the rifle barrel, trying to dislodge her passenger. He must have been calling to the others, because several figures pushed themselves up from the soil and rushed toward her. Ayliss was swinging the Fasces around to shoot at them when a muddy boot kicked it downward, the Sim around her neck trying to help his buddies.

Something heavy bumped into her left side, and Ayliss thought she'd been boarded a second time when the body on her shoulders abruptly flew through the air. It smashed against one of the trunks, and dropped in a way that said he wouldn't be getting up again. Turning, Ayliss saw that Dellmore had joined her. The veteran's weapon was clipped to her back, and she stomped straight into the fray.

"This is Tin! Converge on my marker on the summit! I'm bringing in gunships!"

Somehow the command sent a stab of disappointment through her, and Ayliss stepped up next to Dellmore just as the mass of Sims ran into them. Swinging her arms side to side, she scythed them down with the enormous rifle without firing a shot. Each time she connected with a helmet or Sim flesh, the suit's power magnified the blow and sent the target instantly to the ground. Only yards away, Dellmore was grabbing individual soldiers, raising them bodily into the air, and heaving them at the rest.

"This is *incredible*, Dell!" Ayliss shouted, every ounce of her being singing with adrenaline and destruction. The Sims were now running off through the trees, and she raised the rifle over her head in exultation just before Dellmore dived in her direction and knocked her flat.

Machine-gun rounds tore bark and shards from the tree directly behind them, and then they were both crawling across the forest floor to escape its wrath. Ordinary Sim rifles could do little harm to a suited Banshee, but concentrated bursts were another matter. Getting another tree between her and the automatic weapon, Ayliss raised the Fasces and tongued the selector for a grenade.

Her cameras showed a shimmering cloud of heat at the base of three trees close together, and the grenade reticle appeared in her face shield display. Shifting the weapon until the reticle was on target, knowing the Fasces had already calculated the arc, she squeezed the trigger. The boxy rifle kicked upward just a hair, and then the machine gun found her again. Slugs tore splinters just above her head and then chewed the dirt to her front, but the grenade was already in flight and so she rolled to the other side.

The explosive went off in the middle of the emplacement, killing the machine gun's crew, and then Dellmore was calling, "Come on! Let's get to Tin and the others!"

They rushed toward the crest through lingering smoke, sputtering fires, broken trunks, and smashed bodies, but Ayliss saw none of it. A boom sounded from down the ridgeline, a noise she recognized from the simulators as one of the man-packed Sim rockets that Pelletier had warned them about. Dellmore heard it too, and picked up speed as they raced through steadily opening ground marked with the shattered bases of what had once been tall trees.

"This is Dell! Approaching the summit! Tin, I'm to your east! Tabes, don't run into us!"

Ayliss checked the squad's positions while searching the area for more enemy, noting that Tin and Cusabrina were already on the summit and that Tabor and Plodder were coming toward her from the right. The sun shone brightly as Ayliss and Dellmore reached the top, where a field of blackened, splintered trunks pointed at the sky. They cut to the right, heading east, staying in relative cover and moving away from Tin and Cusabrina to start forming a perimeter. On the very edge of the smoldering clearing a hundred yards ahead, Ayliss saw an armored Banshee emerge from the woods.

"This is Tabor! I see you, Dell! Plodder 'n me will take the north side until—"

Ayliss jumped inside her suit, jolted by the nearness of the explosion and the unmistakable boom. A fiery arrow appeared in front of her for a moment, dipping toward the dirt before rising slightly and smashing into Tabor's chest. The huge figure left the ground, Fasces spinning away, and crashed back to the surface ten yards away.

"Rocket! Get down!" Ayliss heard Dellmore yelling, but not at her. The two of them were surging forward, called by the blast that had emerged from inside a tiny grove of trees to their front. Pushing too hard, Ayliss rose up in the air just long enough to see the entire awful panoply.

Three camouflaged Sims knelt in the grove, one lowering the empty tube of the discharged rocket while another sighted in with a fresh missile. At the edge of the clearing, Tabor's smoking suit was sprawled and lifeless, but another Banshee was at her side. Bending, grabbing, trying to pull her partner to safety. Plodder.

Ayliss let loose a scream of rage and despair as the rocket launched, swinging the Fasces around to fire even though she was still in the air. Just long enough to see the missile strike Plodder in the side of her helmet, a starburst of fire and smoke and blood.

Dellmore had also kicked off too hard, and so they both came back to the ground in the middle of the grove and the Sim rocket team. They were still stomping and tearing when Tin called in the fatalities.

Many hours later, Ayliss sat alone in a quiet part of the ship. Large machines hummed in the space below her unshod feet, and she rested her head on the railing that kept her from falling into the abyss. The humans' advantage in firepower had prevailed in the fight on the planet, and the Banshees had been with-drawn once the Sim assault had been broken.

She'd lingered with the maintenance personnel once they'd removed her suit, not ready to discuss Plodder's death with Bullhead or Lightfoot. She and Legacy had embraced for a long time, but there had been no need to explain what had happened because Legacy had been there. Bullhead and Lightfoot would want to know the details, and Ayliss wasn't sure she could explain them. She gently swung her feet, enjoy-ing the sensation after such a long time in the suit, and an immense weariness started setting into her muscles.

A hand rested on her shoulder and then applied pressure as her unwanted visitor sat down. Ayliss expected to see Tin or perhaps Cusabrina, but the face next to hers belonged to Dellmore. The big vet-eran had washed and changed into a fresh uniform, making Ayliss aware that she'd merely pulled a set of fatigue pants over the undergarments she'd worn on the mission.

"Spill it." Dellmore said in a voice that was only slightly louder than the murmuring machines.

"I'm okay," she replied defensively, unwilling to give Dell additional leverage over her. "I'm just not ready to talk with the others about Elliott."

"I thought her name was Plodder."

"It was." Ayliss considered the question. It reminded her of something Jan had told her, about the passing of a Spartacan Scout he'd known. "But not anymore. She's done with all this. She's Elliott again."

"You know, of your entire batch of replacements, I had her figured as the best. Big, tough, not afraid to speak her mind."

"She was the best. She proved that today."

"She did at that. But she also screwed up. Tabes was gone, and if she'd taken a second to check her readout she would have known that."

"If Tabor was only wounded, she wouldn't have had that second to lose." Ayliss shook her head, recalling Blocker's commentary on randomness. "Doesn't matter now, anyway. So why are we talking about it?"

"Because if I ever get nailed, I don't want you running out to get the same medicine." Dellmore looked into her eyes. "Believe me, if it's you lying out there, I'm gonna make sure you're alive before I go."

"I didn't think we'd be paired off again."

"Well you're wrong there. I asked Sergeant Tin to make us a team. Permanent."

Ayliss frowned in confusion. "Why?"

"When you showed up here, I had you pegged as a rich kid who needed some combat time on her record before running for office. I figured you were gonna be worthless in a fight." Dellmore grinned. "But I was wrong about that, wasn't I?"

She felt her face redden. "I do my part."

"Yeah." Dell laughed. "I saw you. You enjoy it."

"I don't dislike it."

"It's nothing be ashamed of—I'm the same way. I like it. I like it a lot." Dell gave a short nod. "Besides, Sam is trying to kill our friends. That's always pissed me off."

"Pisses me off, too."

"Then we'll work out fine." Dellmore reached for the top rail and pulled herself into a standing position. "Come on. You need to get washed up, and then we'll get some chow."

"That sounds good."

Dellmore stuck out her hand, helping her up. The big woman smiled at her warmly. "You got a good nickname there, Rigor Mortas. It fits."

"It's Rig. Call me Rig."

CHAPTER 6

When it got dark, Mortas stopped walking. He found a large irrigation pipe, sat down, and looked out over support base Mound. He'd been there for hours, and still couldn't make any sense of it. A tall anti-personnel fence ran all the way around the installation, but instead of a defensible shape such as a circle or an oval, it more resembled a heart. One of the heart's two bumps ran around the large hill where he was now sitting, and he suspected that this piece of high ground was why the crowded place was called the Mound. The nearby terrain stretched away for miles, flat and empty and orange.

The perimeter's other bump, and the pointed base of the heart, enclosed many acres of the level expanse on two sides of the hill. Unlike the ground outside the defenses, almost every inch of that territory was hidden. A hodgepodge of maintenance sheds, interconnected tents, vehicle parks, and tall stacks of supplies covered it all, making it hard to see where the roads and footpaths passed around them.

The one open space was a small airstrip where he'd been deposited hours earlier. He'd been dismayed to learn that no one from his battalion, or even the brigade, had preceded him to the Mound. No one he'd consulted upon landing, and no one he'd buttonholed since then, had any idea where First Battalion's supply apparatus was supposed to set up.

His new handheld contained none of the current codes in use at this base, so he couldn't call up a schematic of the Mound's layout or communicate with anyone. He'd poked his head into several different headquarters-type tents, but in each case had been rudely told no one could help him. Annoyed, Mortas had decided to walk all over the site in an effort to find an unused portion where he could direct the convoy when it arrived. The troops he'd encountered in his sojourn had been generally friendly, but he'd been surprised to discover they knew little more than he did about the Mound's most basic organization.

He'd grown even more uncomfortable going up the hill. Jander felt naked with no weapon, body armor, or helmet, but that sensation had shifted to genuine concern when the incomprehensible layout of the perimeter became clear. Bunkered fighting positions dotted the fence line, and combat troops were manning them, but even a casual glance revealed several blind spots where infiltrators could approach unseen. A surveillance drone puttered by somewhere in the darkening sky overhead, and he tried to convince himself that the Mound was important enough for rocket or artillery assets if the rebels decided to pay a visit.

Having learned not to trust those systems with his life, he drew some measure of comfort from the obvious fact that the Mound's occupants weren't in any way worried about being attacked. The entire base was lit up like a small town back on Earth, and he spotted clusters of off-duty soldiers waiting outside tents that he assumed were serving meals or providing entertainment. Their voices rose up the slope toward him, loud, carefree, and he was sure he heard music somewhere.

"Where is that convoy?" he breathed out into the blue-gray night, trying to fight off a genuine feeling of depression. The brief encounter with the familiar Sergeant Strickland and the engaging Sergeant Leoni had buoyed his spirits, but that had faded away with every strange face and sight at this new place. He was an infantry soldier, not a supply jockey, and it was hard not to resent his current surroundings. Erica's face appeared in the shadows, and he slipped into that pleasant memory until it too became painful.

"Okay, enough moping." Mortas stood, brushing dust from his fatigues while looking at the small plateau at the top of the hill. He was mildly surprised to see that the red two-story building on its summit had light streaming from every window; the structure was such a tempting target that he'd assumed it would be empty.

At that moment a quartet of soldiers, three men and one woman, came tromping down the gravel road in his direction. Their fatigues were dark green and recently pressed, their black boots shone even in the darkness, and they all wore jet-black caps with bills. He'd seen a few soldiers in that rig during the day, and had decided they were part of the same security force he'd seen guarding Asterlit's throne room earlier. Like the other green suiters he'd already encountered, this bunch talked too loud and moved with an aggressive confidence that he recognized as pure show.

"Whatcha waitin' for, buddy?" one of the men practically shouted at him as they passed. "Get on up there. The Red House is open for the night."

They were gone a moment later, with a chorus of nasty sniggers hanging in the air like a bad smell. Mortas stared at the road where the dress soldiers had disappeared, beginning to understand their comments and hoping to be wrong. He felt his jaw thrusting forward even before he left the trail and headed off through the hill's sparse cover.

A new fence ran around the building, with anti-personnel wire rolled across its top on supports that formed a Y—a configuration meant to keep people from climbing the fence from either side. He'd watched the Red House's only gate for a few minutes from the cover of the woods, and observed several different troops from various units come up the road on foot. Most of them carried the waterproof yellow bag of Force field rations, and once those had been handed to the green-clad guards they were granted admittance.

Music thumped inside the structure, which Jander had decided was once a farmhouse. Circling around to the rear, he found a spot that was hidden in shadow and walked right up to the fence. He was studying the Red House's stone foundations when a timid voice came from the other side.

"Got any food?"

Rumors of refugee abuse had circulated across the Force ever since the beginning of the Celestian slave rebellion, and he thought he'd prepared himself mentally. The words sounded like they'd come from a beaten child, but the figure that approached the barrier was a teenaged girl. Her hair had been cut short, and she was wearing a set of fatigues that were much too big for her. Fearful eyes rose up out of the gloom, and he stepped up to the obstacle.

"What's going on here?"

"Don't you know?"

"No. Tell me."

She sighed just a bit, obviously thinking he was toying with her. The eyes went to the ground, and two pale hands began undoing the buttons of the uniform blouse.

"One ration gets you a half hour. Two get you an hour." She held the fatigue top open, exposing two small breasts and far too many ribs. For an instant he was somewhere else, looking at the taught skin of starvation on a different woman. "A whole case—"

"Stop it!" he barked, fury rising. "I'm not here for that."

She'd already covered up, and cast a worried glance behind her before hissing, "Then what *are* you here for?"

A harsh male voice called from the corner of the building, and she disappeared like a ghost. Mortas stood there, adrenaline humming through him while his hands clenched and unclenched. The anger was real, and it felt good.

"Not this," he answered the air. "*Fuck* no."

Mortas had passed a carpentry shop at the base of the hill earlier in the day, and so that was where he headed. His injured leg had been sore from all the walking, but it felt strong and ready as he strode down the incline.

He'd checked his handheld on the way, hoping that the convoy had arrived but not willing to wait for them.

Reaching the woodworkers' area, he sorted through several barrels of cut lumber before finding a four-foot dowel that seemed sturdy enough for the job. Instead of diminishing with the passing time, his resolve had hardened into a living thing that now glowed in his core and egged him to go right back up the hill. He'd taken the first steps when his handheld activated in his pocket. The message made him smile.

Any Orphans here? We're waiting near the hospital tent. What a jug-fuck this place is.

He stepped out at a fast pace, swinging the club to get a feel for it. Though much heavier than his lacrosse stick from university days, it reminded him of warm-ups during the first practices of a new season. The Mound's hospital was one of the elongated tents, with tubes connecting different segments, so he found it again in no time.

Someone had created a small picnic area nearby, with wooden tables and bench seats. The whole space was occupied by a platoon of Orphan infantry, most of them stretched out on the dark ground, resting against their rucksacks. The sight of their dirty armor and worn boots warmed Mortas, even though he didn't recognize any of them at first. Seeing a backpack radio set up on one of the picnic tables, he walked over.

"Still can't raise anybody, Sergeant." The words

were in a field whisper, despite the growling of generators all around them. "I think we're the only Orphans here."

"There's at least one more." Mortas rested the tip of the club on the ground, recognizing the nearest man at the table. On his first day with the brigade, seemingly a lifetime ago, he'd seen this NCO leading a squad on a conditioning run in body armor. The veteran was much older than the average Orphan, and Jander had seen the scar around his left leg that indicated it had once been amputated. "I'm Lieutenant Mortas."

The sergeant stood up, disapproving eyes sliding over the unarmed and unarmored officer. "I know who you are, sir. You musta just got back. How's the leg?"

"Almost healed, but they made me the battalion supply guy anyway. You're from C Company, right?"

"I'm Sergeant Drayton, and this is Second Platoon. Our lieutenant got promoted, so I'm in charge. We're supposed to secure the supply area tonight, whenever the convoy gets here, but so far nobody knows what's going on. You in contact with them?"

"No. Could be hours." Mortas pointed up the hill. "See that building? They're selling women up there."

"Just a second, *sir*." Drayton raised his voice, and several of the reclining forms sat up. "Colonel Watt has given clear orders regarding abuse of the locals. You might not have heard yet, but no Orphan is to exploit any refugee in any way. We call it Watt's Law."

"Well tonight we're passing an amendment. I call it Jander's Law." He raised the club and rested it on his shoulder. "No civilian is abused in my presence, no matter who's doing it. That place is run by a bunch of assholes in green uniforms and black hats, and I'm going up there to shut them down. How'd you like to come along?"

The C Company troops were coming to their feet, hulking forms in armor pressing in on the table. Drayton's lips cracked into an evil smile, the same leering smirk he'd fixed on Mortas when he'd jogged past the brigade's newest officer over a year before.

"Those assholes in the green suits belong to Aster-lit. CIP. Celestian Internal Police. Basically his private army. Makes no difference to me, but you're pullin' the tail of the biggest tiger on the planet, sir."

"I don't care."

Murmurs of approval sounded all around them. Drayton nodded, the smile still there.

"Saddle up, Second. Let's get a little exercise."

"**G**ate Team, once you take out the guards, peel to the west so you're out of the way. Assault Team, blow right through the front door and then take your as-signed floors. Ground Team, surround the building with Gate Team." Drayton repeated the plan while hunkered down in the tree line. Business at the Red House had slacked off in the time it had taken for the platoon to sneak up the hill, ground their rucks with a guard trio, and then creep into position. Two new clients were at the open gate, negotiating with three CIP green suiters. Jander added his own commands.

"Anybody in green gets beat down, and so do the customers. Try not to hurt the prisoners, but do what you gotta do. We'll get them medical attention as soon as it's over. We're not losing anyone here tonight, so if anybody green raises a gun, shoot them." A borrowed pistol hung on Jander's hip, but the club was his primary weapon. The troops were fully armored, half carrying their rifles and the rest having produced a range of close-quarters combat weapons. They were almost as keyed up as he was. "Let's go."

The branches vanished as the wedge of men crashed forward, the slight rise making Jander kick hard. Several hulking forms outran him easily, slamming through the narrow opening as one, carrying the customers and the guards with them. The entire mass sailed forward a good five yards before collapsing in flailing arms and angry cries. An armored man bumped Mortas as they went through the gate, but he was running too hard to notice. A short flight of steps appeared in front of him, and light shone through the door when someone opened it to investigate the commotion.

The lead troop lowered his helmet, driving it into the silhouette's nose. The head snapped back, and then the opening was clear. Three more got through ahead of Mortas, all of them charging into a small room with sofas and chairs. A mix of proprietors and clients were seated there, and they didn't have time to rise before the wall of armor was on them.

Another flight of stairs, this one narrow with walls on both sides, and Mortas took the steps two at a time. A loud crash chased him up the passage, accompanied by yelling and the sound of gun butts on flesh. A tall figure materialized at the top of the stairs, potentially blocking the way for the others, so Jander turned the club diagonally across his chest and slammed into the obstacle. Driving hard with both legs, he jammed the shouting figure against a wall while a sensation like a typhoon wind passed behind him.

The upper floor was one big open room, with heavy drapes separating it into cubicles to either side of a central passageway. He saw the fabric coming down like sails on a broken mast, just before a swarm of angry bees stung his abdomen. Still holding the club with both hands, he punched upward so that the wood connected with nostrils. Only then did he realize his opponent was a large woman in a black T-shirt and green CIP trousers, and that she was jolting him with a shock baton that she no doubt used to discipline her charges.

She shrieked in pain, but was still shocking him, so Jander stepped back and brought the club down hard on her wrist. The baton dropped, and he turned sideways before hammering the butt end of the dowel into his adversary's stomach. She made a sound like a seal's bark and then collapsed, clutching her middle and fighting for air.

The floor was entirely opened by then, and a maelstrom of violence had replaced the drapes. A dozen Orphan troops were beating figures on the floor, several in green and some half-dressed, while nude forms cowered under overturned cots. Rifle butts, fists, and a long black sap rose and fell in a frenzy, punishing the bodies while the sounds of breaking glass rose from the floor below.

The soldier wielding the sap had lost his helmet, and he stopped swinging the weapon long enough to come to his full height, breathing hard with exertion. The shattering glass noises seemed to inspire him, and he yelled to the others, "Don't be selfish! Give the Ground Team some work! *Throw 'em out the fuckin' windows!*"

Human forms quickly became battering rams, and Mortas watched in elation as the Orphans tossed their victims through the openings. He laughed out loud, finally noticing his own labored breathing, and reached down for the woman who'd attacked him. That motion stopped the mirth, because he came face to face with a teenaged girl curled into the fetal position in the corner. One of her wrists was chained to the wall, and she stared at him in a paralyzed daze.

Next to her was a naked boy the same age, biting both hands and trembling all over.

Mortas tossed the club away, pulling the CIP woman to her feet and then grasping her neck with one hand. She hadn't caught her breath yet, but her eyes blazed with an insane anger. Feeling his legs driving again, he rushed her across the floor, over the wrecked support bars and torn drapes, and hurled her out the shattered window. He was moving so fast that he almost went out as well, and ended up hanging halfway through the opening in the cool night air.

Below him, the beatings continued with wondrous thuds and rewarding spasms. Drayton and some of his troops were already sorting through the bodies, and Jander was about to call for the medics when headlights surged up the road and then swung away on both sides, bathing the yard in near-sunlight. He'd left a message on the brigade emergency channel instructing any arriving Orphans to come to the top of the hill, and so he wasn't surprised to see Sergeant Strickland hop out of the lead truck.

The convoy wound back down the trail until it disappeared, the trucks lurching to a halt almost bumper-to-bumper. Members of Sergeant Leoni's FITCO came running up to join in, male and female, and Mortas marveled at the assortment of personal weapons and their willingness to use them. Sergeant Leoni walked through the gate at a leisurely pace, watching his charges with pride until seeing Mortas in the window.

"Hey there, El-tee!" He waved, surveyed the ongoing carnage, and then looked up again. "You weren't lying, were you? You really *are* a troublemaker."

"**S**ir. Major Hatton's coming up the hill."

The announcement was accompanied by a gentle nudging of his boots, and Jander's eyes opened to broad daylight. After the abuse victims had been evacuated by the medics and the prisoners had been handed over to a reluctant military police squad, he'd curled up against a low wall in back of the captured building. He now saw that it ran all the way around a rectangular plot that had probably been a garden during the peace. As he sat up, aching muscles in his shoulders berated him and his injured leg burned.

"Here." Sergeant Strickland held out a canteen cup of coffee. "You need this."

"That I do." He inhaled the steam, surprised to realize the coffee was of very high quality. After taking a long sip, he groaned in appreciation. "If I'd known this was the kind of brew I'd get as a supply guy, I would have applied for this gig a long time ago."

"Oh, there are a few perks to this job, sir." Strickland turned, waving at the activity on the slope. "Me and Leoni walked around at first light, making friends as usual. This place is loaded with goodies, if you ask nicely enough. The engineers will be by this afternoon to help us clear the trees and start digging in bunkers."

"Did you find out who's in command?" Jander stood with effort, and sat on the wall. The base spread out before him, disorganized as ever, but the hill itself was already transformed. The fence was gone, and many of the convoy's trucks were now parked on a lower plateau that he hadn't noticed the night before.

"You already guessed it. This base is too small and too nasty for the bigwigs. It grew up on its own, and no one's been interested in taking charge." He grinned. "Your name got suggested to me and Leoni more than once while we were taking our tour. You wanna be mayor?"

"No way. Who's securing the perimeter?"

"That's a composite company, a mixed bag of combat troops who were physically unfit for field duty."

"Wonderful." Jander massaged his leg. "Who's their commander?"

"They don't have one. Their most senior NCO is a broken-down Celestian from one of the outfits that went over to the Rogers. Says he's one of the few who stayed loyal, but I think he figured he wasn't up to life on the run."

Mortas saw the large form of Major Hatton walking up the trail, accompanied by Captain Pappas. "What about the building here? Can we use it?"

"Nah. Too tempting a target. The residents here say that Sam—excuse me, the rebels—have never bothered them, but now that the brigade's operating in this area, I don't expect that to last."

"What should we do about it?"

"Knock it down and build a launch site for the resupply darts."

"I'll coordinate that with the battalion commander."

"Don't bother, sir. It's already in the works." Strickland smiled tolerantly. "The engineers are gonna give us an estimate when they're here a little later."

"Settling in nicely, I see." The bear-like figure of Major Hatton approached, and his voice boomed across the hill. Seeing the body armor, helmets, goggles, and rifles carried by the battalion commander and the intelligence officer, Mortas felt out of uniform. Hatton didn't seem to notice. "I hear you evicted some squatters last night."

Jander came to attention, unsure of how the challenge to Asterlit's enterprise was going to be handled. "Hello, sir. I found twenty Celestian citizens being abused here, and put a stop to it. If there's any heat over this, I want to state for the record that Sergeant Drayton and the members of his platoon were acting under my orders."

"I got here at the end of the action, sir, but I supervised the evacuation of the abuse victims." Strickland spoke formally. "I fully support Lieutenant Mortas's decision."

"Relax, the both of you. Nobody's mad about this. In fact, Colonel Watt has adopted your 'Jander's Law' as his own." Hatton suppressed a chuckle. "Yes, we heard the name. So Watt's Law has been adjusted accordingly. From now on, no Orphan will tolerate any abuse of civilians, no matter who's doing it. Even Asterlit's green suits."

"I met him just after I landed yesterday, sir. He is a complete psycho."

"True enough. But he runs what's left of the government on this rock, so let's not go too far out of our way to poke him." Hatton shook his head. "You've been grazing wild for too long, Jan. Time to rejoin the herd."

"It's good to be back, sir."

"You're gonna be plenty busy, anyway. The Rogers have been doing their own thing around here for a long time, but that's going to change. The brigade's running patrols all throughout this sector, mostly squad- and platoon-sized elements. We've got plenty of orbital and aerial fire support for them if they run into anything big, but resupplying them is on you and Sergeant Strickland."

"Any truth to the stories about the hogs, sir?" Strickland asked, causing Jander to wonder if he'd heard him correctly.

"It's all true." Pappas stepped forward. "There's a species of feral pig that was already here, and somebody thought it would be a good idea to import several thousand more of them. They propagate like you wouldn't believe, and they're destructive as hell. Apparently they'll eat just about anything, but luckily one of the things they don't eat is humans. Live ones, anyway.

"They'll root up any structure they come across, and once there's enough of them they may even threaten places like this."

"But in the meantime they're already disrupting ground resupply." Hatton refocused the discussion. "Convoys smaller than ten vehicles are reporting attacks if they stop anywhere for more than a few minutes. We're maximizing the shuttles right now, but once this sector gets hot, the rebels are going to start shooting those down. Sergeant Strickland."

"Yes, sir."

"I thought those resupply darts of yours were a waste of time until now, so you have my apologies. We're going to be needing that capability soon. How's it coming along?"

"We can deliver chow and ammo wherever you want it, sir. We're still figuring out how to pack the water so the sloshing doesn't throw off the ballistics, but we'll get there. I only brought fifty of these with us, but there's a whole yard of 'em back home. Can you get those sent out to us?"

"Colonel Watt's already given the order. You'll be sharing this capability with the supply folks from Second and Third Battalion, so be prepared to train them up."

"Yes, sir."

"Don't let me keep you." The words were respectful, but obviously Hatton had something to discuss with Mortas in private. Strickland nodded, and headed off down the hill. Jander looked up at the battalion commander, knowing what he would say.

"Jan, Hugh Leeger is leading one of the biggest bands of the Orange out here. I'm leaving Erlon with you, and I want you to tell him anything that might help us beat him."

"We won't get the chance to do that, sir."

"And why is that?"

"Our patrols will pick off some of the other bands, but Leeger's too smart to lock horns with an outfit like ours. He'll see we've got our shit together, and then he'll let us wander all over this wasteland without ever engaging us. If he sees a good opportunity he may take it, but it will have to be a lucrative target—nothing small-time. Leeger's always looking for the knockout punch." Mortas looked at Pappas. "You figure out what that is, and you'll know what he's up to."

"Thanks, Jan. I know you were close. It can't be easy, telling us how to stop him."

"That's not what I said. I said if you figure that out,

you'll know what he's up to. Stopping him is another thing entirely."

"We can talk all you want, but I've already told you everything I can about Hugh." Mortas spoke to Pappas while watching Hatton's lumbering stride as he went down the trail.

"I'm going to need to work up a profile on him that I can share across the brigade, but actually I wanted to ask about something else. A rumor I heard."

Mortas smiled, thinking of all the different stories currently circulating about his recently completed, allegedly failed, mission to meet the alien on Roanum. "Tell me what you've heard."

"This isn't military scuttlebutt. It's high level, and nobody here is involved."

"Now you've got my interest."

"You know I've made a study of the Sims, matching their combat actions to the sounds they make. Trying to gain some kind of understanding of their language." Mortas nodded. "There's supposed to be an audio tape out there somewhere, no video, of a secret meeting where humans communicated with the Sims through a translator."

Jander's pulse quickened, remembering the single encounter with the Sim delegates and their leader, the graying veteran with the face scar. He and Varick had gained considerable rapport with the enemy leader. "Have you listened to it?"

"Of course not. I don't even know if it exists. But I understand your question. Whoever shared this tape edited it heavily. It's a long exchange, and the humans and Sims involved are clearly combat vets discussing their experiences in the war. The human voices have been removed, so what they said appears as text. But the bird-talk is all there, with an exact translation. *Hours* of it."

Jander exhaled without showing it. Unless Elder Paul had hoodwinked him and Varick, which was unlikely, only one recording of the meeting had been created. Heavily encrypted, it had been given to the captain of the *Ajax*, who had personally delivered it to Reena. So if an edited version of that tape had been disseminated, it was probably at her direction.

"I imagine that would be very helpful, to people trying to decipher the Sims' language."

"Immeasurably."

"Level with me, Erlon." Mortas had never addressed the captain by his first name. "You've marched with my platoon and fought beside me. I'll tell you everything I know, but you have to do the same. You're not really with the brigade by chance, are you?"

"I'm surprised that story has held up this long. No, I'm not here by chance. There's a loose circle of linguists and scientists, in and out of uniform, who have been working on the Sim language for years. Originally I got myself sent to the Orphans because this outfit gets up close and personal with Sam and it sounded like a good opportunity to gather information."

"But you got hooked on the brigade."

"Don't laugh; if it happened to a fat ass like Merkit, why not me?" Pappas pointed at him. "It happened to you, too. Otherwise you wouldn't have come back."

"Okay, you got me. I'm one of the humans on that tape. I was there." Mortas sat down on the low wall. "What do you want to know?"

CHAPTER 7

"General Merkit. It's good to see you." Reena Mortas stood in one of the most secure rooms in Unity Plaza, warmly shaking Merkit's hand. Ridiculed as Olech Mortas's throne room, the two-story chamber could generate amazingly realistic imagery of locations across the galaxy.

"It's good to see you too, Madame Chairwoman. It's been a long month, as you know."

"It's been the same way here. I've been forced to grant Zone Quest access to several planets that my husband promised to the veterans. It hasn't been well received."

"I know. Between the Bounce and my sources, everyone seems to think you've been reduced to little more than a figurehead." Merkit grinned. "Luckily, they're wrong."

"Not completely. Part of this is a cover story, but part of it's very real. And the more members of the Emergency Senate who buy the cover story, the less influence I wield."

"I've brought something that's going to change that, ma'am."

"I expected there was a reason for this visit." Reena looked past the general, to the room's only other occupant. "Nathaniel, are we sure that we're completely secure here?"

"The room's been swept within the last hour. Nothing detected, as usual. The three of us have been scanned, as has the file the general brought with him. All links outside the room have been temporarily severed. We can proceed."

"Very good." Reena sat on a large, boxy chair with deep leather cushions while Merkit and Ulbridge stood to either side. "Please begin your briefing, General."

"As you already know, we've made great strides in surveilling the target planet Omega." Merkit clicked a button on a remote control, and the lights dimmed in the tall room. "Long-range scanning detected no unnatural emissions from Omega, and nothing electronic at all. We were encouraged by this, and took it as a sign that whatever is building the Sim ships inside the planet has opted to forgo defensive scanning so as not to attract attention.

"Honestly, this sector of space is so dead that without your specialized intelligence I doubt we would ever have found this place." The lights died completely, and were replaced moments later with the darkness of space. "The lack of electronic defenses encouraged me to authorize a stealthy establishment of robotic surveillance close enough to Omega to gain observation of its surface."

The gray planet materialized in the room, first as a head-sized ball and then as a glowing sphere. Reena leaned forward, enraptured.

"As you can see, there are forms of vegetation on Omega despite its status as a planet not habitable by humans. Although the planet has gravity and a thin atmosphere, that atmosphere is not breathable and we have not yet determined the nature of the vegetation.

"However, that became a secondary concern when scanning revealed a series of miles-long, foundation-like rock formations buried at different locations across the planet. One of these formations is located close to the launch site of the only ship that has so far been observed emerging from Omega's interior." A blinking marker appeared on the gray surface, indicating the launch site. "Directed surveillance revealed that every one of these foundation-like formations has a similar large surface opening somewhere nearby."

"What do the analysts say about that?"

"They're the ones who realized that the rock structures were not natural. Once we discovered that they were purposely crafted, we tried focusing different kinds of cameras on them. We were successful with a variety of imaging used to locate ancient ruins on Earth."

"They're cities?"

"That's what we've come to believe. Have a look."

The planet expanded, filling the room like a stone ball rolling forward to crush them. The blinking marker occupied the center of the new view, which now showed canyons and miles of vegetation alongside vast, empty plains. The picture resolved even more, and a maze-like circle took shape next to the marker. Reena studied it, seeing rings formed around an empty center.

"This isn't visible from space without augmentation?"

"Correct. Without those special cameras, none of these remains would have been spotted. They're buried under the soil, often concealed by surface overgrowth. We have no way of estimating their age, but the analysts believe these used to be cities."

"And every one of the launch-capable openings located so far has one of these near it?"

"Yes, ma'am. So far we've identified roughly one hundred of the openings—it wasn't hard, once we had the original to study. The atmospheric flow in and out of the openings is uniform, and we suspect it's the result of activity under the surface."

"What else have you learned?"

"As directed, we've been extremely careful to

avoid detection. We have personnel reconfiguring the smallest existing recon robots to actually enter the planet atmosphere—and ultimately the tunnels themselves. However, we recently observed an event that was so significant that I knew I had to bring it to you personally."

He clicked another button, and the connected lines forming the circular ruins grew even larger. The cavernous crater nearby appeared to be as dark and dead as ever, but then it took on a rosy tint.

"It doesn't actually look like that, but this is a representation of what the scanners were picking up. We thought it indicated another ship launch, so you can imagine our surprise at what came out."

The rose-colored aperture took on a grainy texture, as if the feed were breaking up, but the rest of the surface remained clear. Reena craned her neck, watching as the red-hued crater appeared to start bleeding. Wisps of color began to run from the hole in all directions, moving with excruciating slowness.

"What you're seeing is recorded in real time." Merkit answered her unasked question. The crater had now sprouted spider legs, but Reena noted a difference.

"The ones farthest from the city site are turning toward it."

"Yes, ma'am." Merkit's voice took on an undertone of wonder. "What you're seeing is the heat signatures of an enormous cloud of tiny, flying creatures. We scanned the entire event with everything we had, and our systems immediately found a match."

"It's the alien, isn't it?" Ulbridge asked. "I mean, did the scans match the readings from Glory Main, when the alien was in the tube?"

"Yes. It also matched the data collected by the Holy Whisper when the latest alien appeared at Gorman Station. And what the *Ajax* detected from orbit, when the thing would vanish in the desert." Merkit's voice came to Reena from a great distance. "It's a perfect match. What you're seeing is a cloud of millions, if not billions, of the tiny moth-like creatures that the original alien burst into on Glory Main, just before it was incinerated."

The runnels of red had picked up speed, the closest ones heading straight for the ruins while the others peeled off in perfect symmetry.

"So that's what they actually are?" Reena asked, as if speaking to herself. "Those flying specks that filled the decon tube when the thing disintegrated?"

"There's no reason to believe otherwise. They don't know we found Omega, and they're not trying to fool anyone by appearing to be something else. It makes perfect sense; as a shapeshifter, the alien had to consist of particles, infinitely small, that possess the capability to join together and function as the organisms they imitate."

The aerial ballet continued, with the first line

of heat signatures reaching the dead city's center. They reformed into a circle, flying clockwise while the other strings joined them. The trio of humans watched in silent amazement as the center circle was replicated numerous times, each one larger than the last and all of them rotating in the same direction.

"They're following the layout below them." Ulbridge offered.

"That's right. It's not visible to the naked eye, but somehow they know it's there and what it looks like." Merkit raised the control. "Here's the best part."

The planet shrunk away from them, back to its original appearance as a head-sized ball in space—but with a difference.

"My God," Reena whispered. "Am I seeing this?"

"I had the same reaction, Madame Chairwoman. But it's true."

The hemisphere of the enormous planet facing them was speckled in red dots. Merkit enlarged the image, taking them away from the circular formation to one that resembled a diamond. The flying creatures performed an intricate dance, crossing over the city center while also outlining what appeared to be its buried boulevards. Another ruin was a spiral, and the red lines formed a stationary tumbleweed. In every case, the nearby surface crater glowed a rosy red.

"The event lasted just over three hours, and then they all went back where they came from. They hadn't done anything like this the entire time we'd been watching Omega, so we're intrigued to see if they do it again."

"What do you think it was, General?"

"Our experts have a range of theories. Some suggest the creatures lived in those cities ages ago, and this is their way of honoring the memory. Others are searching the readouts to see if the cities are a power source of some kind, in which case the creatures might be soaking it up. One of the analysts believes the creatures fly by sonar, and that they have to emerge every now and then from the confines of the tunnels to calibrate their internal systems."

"You don't seem to buy any of that."

"It's impossible to tell at this point, Madame Chairwoman. I'm hopeful it means that there is some kind of event going on in those craters that forces them out for a period of time."

"In which case, we could kill them in the open."

"That is my earnest hope." Merkit raised the lights, and Omega vanished.

"What's the status of the recon robots?" Reena asked without looking at either of the men.

"Almost ready to go. Needless to say, if we approach Omega we have to be prepared for the aliens to attempt to bug out. Something in there is building the ships the Sims are using to fight us, so they may have spacecraft in readiness for their own escape."

"You've worked up a plan?"

"Yes. It will require substantial commitment of fleet assets. A cordon at a great distance, ready to move in on a moment's notice."

"I'll do you better than that, General." Reena stood, her eyes on the spot where the enemy planet had been. "We can't do this remotely, and the recon 'bots will only be able to tell us so much. It is *vital* that we determine what's going on inside that rock, and for that we'll need human eyes."

"My plan includes an emergency contingency involving nuclear weapons, ma'am." Merkit spoke darkly. "We know very little about this civilization, and the aliens may respond to our intrusion in an unexpected fashion. They may leave us with no other choice but to nuke them, with little time in which to do it. Under those circumstances, any personnel on Omega . . . would have to be sacrificed."

"Understood. But we can't just guess at what's going on there. We have to know." Reena turned to Ulbridge. "Work up a selection of options that will allow us to secretly reassign Banshee units, spacesuit-capable special operations forces, and any other assets that normally work with pressure suits so they can train for this mission."

"It's a very big planet, ma'am." Ulbridge intoned.

"I know." Reena blinked, hard. "Make sure you give me an option that sends them all."

Olech returned to consciousness feeling bruised, his eyes opening to look directly into the shattered irises of a dead soldier. That image had haunted his dreams for years after the war, but somehow he'd managed to lock it away in the recesses of his mind and hadn't thought of it in a decade. Now, awaking from whatever suspended state Mirror consigned him to between sessions, Olech immediately knew where he was.

He lay on his back, age fifteen and trapped in the wreckage of the craft that was supposed to be taking him and a batch of replacements to their first units in combat. A fragile helmet had prevented his brains from being beaten out when they'd been shot down, the stricken airship bouncing off the ground and rolling for what seemed like an eternity. It hadn't been a troop shuttle, because those weren't developed until later in the war. No, this one had been an ugly, fat-bellied cargo beast with rows of seats welded into its hold.

Those welds had shattered on impact, the belted-in teenagers tumbling inside the cartwheeling hull, vocal cords screeching, each additional impact breaking off more and more seats, Olech screaming right along with them through the forearms pressed over his face. He'd screamed for a long time after the ruined vessel had finally come to a halt, its fuselage cracked wide open to let in the cold wind and the night air.

Blood dripped onto his fatigue shirt, and he looked without wanting to. The boy hanging upside down over him had been impaled, skewered by a shattered stanchion, and his bodily fluids had run over Olech's pinioned torso. He now remembered the pain in his lower back, just above his right hip, that he'd feared was a serious injury but had turned out to be merely the snapped-off end of a seat cushion spring. He'd been struggling to get his hand back there when the wind had brought the first loud, imperious string of caws.

Bird sounds. Coming toward the downed craft, just outside the gaping fracture in the hull. It was the first time he heard Sim speech, and it flooded him with fear and disappointment. Fear because the enemy never took prisoners and mutilated the bodies of Force soldiers, and disappointment because it wasn't supposed to be this way. Not his first moments in the battle area, not handed to the Sims like a sacrifice, not helpless. Like the rest of the Unwavering, Olech had accepted the likelihood of his violent demise trying to turn the tide of the losing war, but not like *this*.

More caws, answered by chirps and peeps that he interpreted as the acknowledgments of a superior's commands. His eyes frantically darting around, seeing nothing but broken metal and tangled wires and dead bodies. Not a weapon in sight, even though he couldn't have reached it anyway. Feeling another breeze, this one closer, and seeing the smaller tear in the bulkhead not three feet away, sure he could wriggle his boy's body through it if only he could free himself.

A sound like a tropical bird tittering in a jungle, and then fragmented beams of light sweeping across the scene of destruction. The lights flashed from the big wound in the hull, and then he'd heard the weak voice, a child's voice; the Unwavering had been little more than an army of children.

"Help me." It sounded like a squeaky hinge, somewhere close to the lights. "I surrender. Don't hurt me."

An automatic weapon turned the lights into a strobe, clattering like a broken machine and sending bullets rebounding all over with a thunder of echoes. More caws erupted; Olech could sense the anger over the ricochets, and the shooting stopped but so did the pleas. The lights returned, and vibrations thumped into his back as boots stomped on the fuselage and enemy soldiers started climbing aboard. Pushing the debris aside, making sure all of the humans were dead.

Feeling his heart revving, his lips curling in a terror-stricken grimace, they were going to find him, he was going to die right here, right now, and then he was reaching for the dead boy hanging in his face. The body slid off of the skewer, landing on him with a ringing crash that set off another long series of bird calls but no shots.

Now truly trapped, having only bought himself

as much time as it would take for them to pull the corpse off of him, more blood and fluid soaking into his uniform, the tiny breeze calling to him to crawl that way, to live, to escape, if only he could move, but he couldn't. The cracked hull was rocking slightly with all the activity, the beams were more distinct, the trills and caws burning into his brain as they struggled with the bodies that were trapped like he was, they were almost to him, and he'd grabbed the boy's belt, meaning to hold the body in place no matter what.

Peremptory caws, from the vicinity of the breach, and then the whole wreck was bouncing as the enemy rushed to leave. The beams swinging wildly, his would-be killers fleeing, and then all he could hear was the receding squawks as if a flock of birds had been chased from a familiar perch where they'd been resting.

He'd never learned what made them leave, as no rescue party had ever arrived. Lying there, listening to his heart gratefully slow, Olech watched himself reach into the pocket of the dead boy where he knew he'd found a folding knife that took forever to slice through the harness that held him. Knowing that he'd crawled through the small crack into an alien land of cold air and darkness and miles of ground shattered by the war, that he'd wandered that dead place until the sun had risen, proving that he wasn't a blood-soaked ghost.

He'd linked up with a Force unit a day later, but it would be weeks before he learned that everyone on that ship had died. Fumbling for the knife, pondering Mirror's absence, still the teenaged Olech yet aware that this was not reality, he was only mildly surprised when the scene shifted as if he had never been anywhere else.

Pinned yet again under a body whose blood ran over him, but this time facedown on the floor of the great hall that had belonged to the Interplanetary Senate. Confusion mixed with fear, as Olech knew he'd visited this experience with Mirror already. The gunfire roared yet again, the different security details blasting away at each other in the maelstrom that had erupted when President Larkin had made his fateful announcement. Olech knew that Larkin was already dead, one of the first to fall, riddled with bullets near the rostrum only ten yards away. He'd been trying to reach the man, hollering over the bedlam for Larkin to get out of the chamber, when the first shots had been fired.

The chief of his security team, a giant named Faldonado, had plunged through the mob and thrown him to the carpet, diving on top of him. The action had saved his life, as Faldonado had absorbed several slugs and died right there. He was collapsed on top of Olech now, trapping him along with the other bodies, half of the Senate had been wiped out in the insane gunplay, and he remembered now that through the shock and the terror he'd thought back to that moment twenty-five years before when he'd hidden from the Sims under a corpse.

The confusion departed just then, as did the roaring reports and the screams and the yells and the whimpers. This was unfamiliar, and Olech half expected Mirror to appear to offer an explanation. He was mistaken in that belief, because something completely different happened instead. In every one of the experiences he'd re-lived, Olech had taken the form of the boy or the student or the politician that he'd been at the time of the event. At this moment, however, he found himself sharing the experience of someone else.

He knew that was the case right away, because he was witnessing the slaughter from the back of the room and couldn't identify with any of the sensory input at all. It wasn't the violence or the carnage; sadly, he'd seen and done worse in the war. No, it was the personality or the psyche or simply the viewpoint of the man whose memory of the event he was now experiencing fully.

Olech's mind balked at the mismatch, the gears grinding as he fought to connect with something he recognized. An awesome level of concentration gripped the witness, but a cold detachment filled the rest of him. Receiving the sensations of the short rifle as it fired, the thrum of the reports vibrating through heavy body armor into his chest, shooting specific targets according to a prearranged kill list while the others, the man's helpers, were fighting the security troops who were trying to intervene.

The rifle jumped slightly, but the witness was an excellent shot and was able to place the rounds so that his victims appeared to have been hit at random. Near the doors, a gray-haired senator jumped up and tried to flee, only to be recognized by the gunman and cut down. Then, a pile of bodies had shifted enough to show the round torso of yet another designated victim and he killed that one too.

Olech, disembodied but somehow riding inside the assassin's head, fought to escape the inexplicable absence of emotion. It was like pushing against a glacier that wasn't there, a bone-rattling cold that nonetheless had its origin in a space that was completely empty. The shooter continued his work, methodical, focused, but experiencing no internal reaction to the murders other than a weak pulse of disgust at how pitifully his victims were dying.

The mechanism inside the assassin's brain shifted, giving Olech the impression of a switch having been thrown, and he realized that the first phase of a planned operation had just been completed. There was more to do, and little time. He felt a foreign hand reach up and press a throat mike against the flesh that housed his vocal cords.

"'This is Asterlit. Sterilization team, sweep through

the room. Remember, body shots from different angles."

Hulking forms in fatigues and heavy body armor moved forward in a crooked line, roughly shoving through the piles. Lifeless arms and legs sliding and rolling away, smoke smell choking the room, and Olech now saw that Asterlit and the rest of Horace Corlipso's security force were wearing tactical goggles and gas masks. Watching the killers as they searched out the targets that had only been wounded or, amazingly, left unharmed. Feeling Asterlit's clinical response as the different senators were dispatched.

Revolted to find that the strongest emotion the assassin experienced was a swell of satisfaction that he had so ably managed the task assigned to him by his benefactor, Horace Corlipso. Repelled by the cavity that should have been filled with rage or hatred or shame, Olech pushed as hard as he could and abruptly found himself in the empty gallery outside the Senate chamber. He was himself again, down on his knees, shivering when Mirror walked up and knelt in front of him.

"Why did you do that?" he shouted, grabbing his twin by the arms and shaking him. "Why did you put me in that diseased mind?"

"His mind isn't diseased." Mirror seemed not to notice the shaking. "He has no empathy for the members of your race, or any living thing, but he was born that way."

"Are you trying to excuse him? *He murdered half the Senate!*"

"Explaining and excusing are two completely different things. Regardless of what he lacks emotionally, Asterlit isn't blind or deaf. He is completely aware of the suffering he causes, and he has known the fear that comes from being physically dominated or nearly killed. He knows what he is doing is wrong, but he doesn't care. He doesn't relate to the other members of your species as anything but tools or victims."

"You've studied him closely."

"So many Step voyages, so many different experiences, his is not the only personality that matches that profile. Fortunately, his type is not common among humans."

"There's more of them than you think."

"You're wrong, Olech. Most of your fellow humans have natural empathy in varying degrees. Unfortunately, every one of them seems capable of ignoring that when it gets in the way. It is a major source of your race's troubles." Mirror stood. "You yourself know all about that."

Mirror walked away, leaving him intact but alone. The former Chairman of the Emergency Senate slid to the carpet, where he rolled into a ball and wept until he vanished.

CHAPTER 8

Jander Mortas blinked as he emerged from the command bunker into the bright sun of midday. His helmet and goggles hung from the canteens attached to his torso armor, but he made no effort to don them. The familiar Scorpion rifle swung easily at the end of his right arm as he walked, enjoying the strength that had finally returned to his left leg and taking in the sights of Camp Resolve.

The site was the only refugee camp inside the Orphan Brigade's sector, and its management had been taken over by an HDF mechanized infantry battalion three weeks before. That had been shortly after Colonel Watt had proclaimed his refugee abuse law to be in effect wherever Orphans went, and someone had seen the wisdom of removing Asterlit's thugs before the brigade did it for them. The place had been a hellhole without even a name, but the mechanized commander had done a lot to clean the place up.

Looking around, Jander recognized that it was still a hellhole, but at least its tenants weren't being mistreated anymore. He'd just brought up the latest supply convoy, and watched with satisfaction as Sergeant Leoni supervised the unloading of badly needed rations. Leoni jokingly scolded Trimmer, a lanky driver standing up in the back of one of the trucks, and the youngster responded with a mischievous smirk. Like so many of the FITCO troops, male and female, Trimmer was always spoiling for a fight. In ambushes, he was usually the first to bail out and charge at the rebels still stupid enough to try and stop them.

"Hey." Captain Pappas came out of the bunker behind Mortas. "I'm going to walk around a bit. Don't leave without me."

"Getting desperate, sir?" Jander grinned. Orphan combat units had racked up an impressive number of kills over the past weeks, mostly from the Flock and even a few of the Orange, but Pappas's efforts to gain intelligence on their opponents had all fallen flat. "Gonna poll the noncombatants to see what they know?"

"You'd be surprised by what they know." Pappas removed his helmet and hung it from a canteen, but kept the goggles. Producing a brimmed cloth hat from a cargo pocket, he put it on. "The Rogers come and go here at will."

"You're kidding." Jander looked around at the stout wire fence, the menacing watchtowers, and the anti-hog moat recently dug by the engineers. "How?"

"This place is too big for a single battalion to secure. They've done a good job adjusting the perimeter, but there was only so much they could do with what they inherited. The green suits only pulled enough guard to prevent a general breakout, so apparently there are hundreds of little tunnels and blind spots.

"The rebels are smart. They smuggled food in while these people were starving, and slowly siphoned off recruits in return. See all those faces?" Pappas pointed at the interior fencing that separated the HDF command area from the long, low refugee barracks. A dozen figures, all ages, stood watching them. "The tenants observe everything that goes on, and they pass that to the Rogers when they visit."

"We're feeding them, and they're helping the guys we're fighting. This place gets crazier by the day."

"You been here a month, so you must be certifiable by now."

"You been here a lot longer than I have, and with a lot more frustration. Me, I spend my time handing out goodies and occasionally shooting my way out of an ambush, but your job's the one that sucks. The Rogers sure picked up on your spies fast."

"And staked the bodies out where we could find them. That was not a good day."

"So what's the plan now? You hoping to get intel the same way the rebels do?"

"Exactly. My mistake was sending people down into the mines. I should have realized there's plenty of information to be gained right here, from people who never leave this place."

"If they watch our every move, how are you going to make contact?"

"Sick call starts in fifteen minutes. Lots of opportunities to talk one-on-one."

"Good luck." Mortas looked over at the line of movers. "My guess is we won't be done unloading for at least two more hours."

"Thanks. Don't leave without me."

"I heard you the first time." They exchanged smiles, and Pappas walked off across the orange soil.

Jander watched the unloading for another minute, finally deciding that Leoni's FITCO troops didn't need his help or supervision. It was a familiar feeling, and one he didn't mind; Strickland had been running the battalion's supplies for so long that he usually had very little to do. Intrigued by the faces at the wire, Mortas slowly walked toward them as if merely killing time.

"Hey, Lieutenant." A middle-aged woman greeted him from the other side when he got close enough. She wore a clean set of mechanic's overalls, the standard replacement for the rags they'd been wearing when Asterlit's green suiters had departed. "Thank you for all you're doing."

Remembering Pappas's words, he approached with caution. "You're very welcome. How long you been here?"

"Oh, I was in two camps before this one. They were all the same, until you soldiers took this one over."

"What did you do in the peace?"

"I was a factory worker. Not as rough as slavery, but still pretty bad. I came to this planet for work, but didn't know the whole thing was rigged so I'd never be able to pay off my passage." It was a common story, and Mortas was beginning to wonder if he'd misjudged her when she blew her act. "Your people are from the Orphan Brigade, right?"

"A little bit of this, and a little bit of that." He replied honestly, and started walking away. She didn't shadow him, which was another giveaway. Someone had taught her not to be a pest when probing for information. They must have developed some kind of signal, because the other watchers drifted away from the fence before he reached them. With an unobstructed view, he looked into their part of the camp.

The doors and windows in the barracks were open, and tenants of every age and description were out and about. A long stone sink was being used to hand-wash the garments they weren't wearing, and he spotted a diagonal series of scratches in its side. At first they looked like Xs etched into the sink by idle hands, but then he recognized that they were crude representations of birds in flight, rising higher. The symbol of the Flock.

The Flock had been behind every ambush he'd encountered on the roads, and Jander had seen plenty of their face tattoos. Some were quite artistic, ranging from single large birds that covered half a head to the more common image of a flock lifting off into the sky. It was insane, the way the former slaves marked themselves that way, but that was the Flock in a nutshell. They had no intention of being taken alive.

Shaking off the dark thought, Mortas noticed that the refugees were tending several small gardens in different spots. He stopped to study that, noting with disappointment that the crops were small and sickly. The soil in this part of Celestia had never been good for farming, as he was discovering in the small plot he'd planted up on the Mound. At first it had been a way to combat the boredom between convoys, but after a while his small garden had become a memorial to his predecessor, Captain Follett, and his obsession with discovering new food sources. It also reminded him of the peace-loving colonists he'd gotten to know on Roanum, and for a moment he was back there, with them. With Erica.

"Lieutenant Mortas?"

A child's voice interrupted his daydream, and he looked down in startled bewilderment. Many of the refugees had the orange tinge, and so he wasn't surprised to see the pigmentation and the matching hair.

His consternation came from recognizing the face of the child soldier who'd walked next to Hugh Leeger in the video Asterlit had shown him weeks before.

"I know you."

"I've never seen you before." Yellowed teeth cracked into a wide smile, suggesting the bare-chested boy was playing with him. Mortas decided he didn't like that.

"So what are you? His gun bearer?"

"I was his sponsor. I found him not far from here. If I hadn't spoken up for him, he probably would have been killed."

Jander looked around, aware that the refugee lookouts had left the two of them alone. He lowered his voice. "How is he?"

"He's free. Maybe for the first time in his life."

"Believe it or not, I'm happy for him. He was more of a father to me than anyone I've ever known."

"I do believe you. He's the same thing to me."

A stab of jealousy, followed by a deeper cut that said the fence wasn't the only thing separating them. "So he sent you to see me. Is there a message?"

"Yes. Your brigade has picked off so many members of the Flock that they're getting desperate."

"And yet we almost never see the Orange."

"That's his plan."

"So what's the message?"

"You Orphans are in danger, and you don't even know it."

"Stop talking tough, you jaundiced little jerk. You

see that bunch offloading supplies? They're mine. Criminals and brawlers, every one of them. I give the order, they'll run straight through this fence, drag you out by your balls, and laugh the whole way."

"I'll be long gone before they even hear you. Done it before."

"So give me the message and fuck off."

"He wants you to know that your brigade's made some powerful enemies. Asterlit's one of them. Here on Celestia, it's all about money. You Orphans have disrupted that."

"We're only one brigade, in a big army."

"No, you're not. Other units are adopting your Colonel Watt's Law, shutting down the brothels and the black market."

"I call that the power of good example. I would have thought your people would support something like that."

"We do. *They* don't." The child began to back away, without haste. "So that's his message, for you especially. Asterlit's going to find a way to hurt you."

That night, the stars were out in such abundance that Jander was able to tend his garden without his goggles. The darkness was transformed into a blue-gray bowl overturned on top of the Mound, and he duck-walked among the rows of tiny plants without fear of crushing them. A cooling breeze caressed the top of the hill, unimpeded by the infamous Red House that had been torn down weeks before. The spot had been deemed unfit for a launch pad due to its small size and its exposure to enemy observation, so the old walled garden was all that was left.

Finishing his inspection, Mortas stood and stretched. The base had been transformed, and he looked down on it with satisfaction. Gone were the blazing lights, replaced by blackout entrances and mandatory goggle use at night. Many of the tents and temporary structures were also gone, having been dug into the hill and the surrounding terrain. The base itself had been expanded dramatically, in order to decrease the size of individual vehicle parks and to create several shuttle pads. The disjointed perimeter was now a proper defensive belt, with camouflaged bunkers, interlocking fields of fire, anti-personnel wire, and a wide anti-hog moat.

He was pondering the increasing problem of the expanding pig population when a shadow emerged on the trail. Helmet, rifle, goggles, and body armor made it almost impossible to tell who it was, but something about the wraith's gait suggested he knew the visitor.

"Emile? Captain Dassa?"

"You know, I didn't believe it when I heard you'd turned gentleman farmer on us." The stars reflected off of the circular lenses just under the helmet's brim when Dassa looked up. "What a sad end to a good infantryman."

"Just trying to feed the troops, sir. Following in the steps of First Battalion's legendary supply officers."

"Stop it. You're embarrassing me."

"I was actually referring to Drew Follett." Jander carefully walked over, taking Emile's hand warmly. "You barely had the job for a month, if I remember."

"And they promoted me, just to keep the battalion from starving." Neither man continued the story to its true conclusion, when the brigade's enormous losses on Fractus had left B Company's top slot open for Dassa to assume. "Major Hatton's pleased with the job you're doing."

"Sergeant Strickland does all the work. I just go to coordination meetings with the higher-ups. Officer stuff."

"Sounds awful. But I brought you a gift. First Platoon's spending the night here, and I thought you might like to visit them."

"I dunno. I was planning to spend the evening watching my plants grow."

"Come on. They're eager to see you."

They headed down the trail, which took on a greenish tint once Mortas had donned his goggles.

"I gotta hand it to you, Jan; I have never seen a supply base showing this kind of light discipline."

"The trick is to start by beating the living hell out

of a gang of criminals on a high hill where everybody can see it. After that, you've got their attention." Dassa laughed, and Mortas corrected himself. "Honestly, I've got this one truck NCO named Leoni who made all the support types toe the line. He's got the touch. Friendly where friendly works, but rough when it doesn't."

"So who's in command here? Nobody I talked to seems to know."

"We've got a rotation going, if you can believe that. Three different colonels who own the biggest outfits on the Mound. They really don't like this place, but when they heard that an infantry lieutenant had basically taken over, they couldn't leave it alone. Each of them spends a week here before running back to showers and air-conditioning."

They passed a line of troops in the darkness, maintenance personnel by the look of their outfits. All of them wore goggles, and almost half had torso armor. Several muted greetings reached out to Mortas, and he returned them by name.

"I heard you'd been elected mayor. I didn't believe it until now."

"Strickland and Leoni again. They know how to find things people need, like the body armor you saw. Most of these troops want to do things the right way—ready to defend themselves if necessary, not attracting the bad guys' attention with all those lights—but a lot of them didn't have the training or the basic equipment." Jander paused. "Listen to me, telling you about life in the rear. How's it been going out there, sir?"

"It's just really strange. On the one hand, we've hit the Flock hard. They had this whole sector basically under their control when the sun went down, but we changed that. Aggressive patrolling, heavy use of snipers, and quick reaction teams. Wyn Kitrick came up with the idea to run phony supply convoys loaded with hidden troops, and that really scored some points until Roger changed up on us.

"There are so many deserters among the rebels that they've got an answer for most of our standard stuff. So we switched to old-fashioned groundpounding. Humping enough ammo and water to survive a fight, but not so much that we can't move quickly. It's a tough balance, but your old platoon does it well. Wolf seems to have a sixth sense about where the bad guys are headed, and before you know it First Platoon has caught up with them or even got in front."

"That doesn't sound so strange."

"That part isn't. The weird part is the way it's all changing. The Orange have hunkered down inside the mines, and nothing we've done has brought them out. I heard they sent a platoon of Spartacans underground, a special tunnel rat outfit, and that we lost every one of them. Robot recon hasn't done any better, and Erlon's spies . . . well you know what happened to them."

"That's all Leeger's influence. I told Pappas he was

too smart to fight us. The question is, what's he been doing all this time? He's not just waiting down there."

"Neither are his troops." Dassa stopped next to the sunken opening of a large bunker. "We think the Rogers are still getting around on the surface pretty well."

"How? Every truck and mover has been chipped and entered into the system. They can't pull any of that nonsense of pretending to be Force units anymore."

"Maybe it's the hogs. Everybody assumed the rebels spoofed Victory Pro into releasing new herds here so they'd have something to eat."

"That wasn't it?"

"Come inside. Ringer's got an interesting story about this."

The two men clomped down a short flight of wooden steps set into the ground, and Mortas heard noisy laughter as they entered the first set of blackout drapes. He removed his goggles before following Dassa into a well-lit dugout with a low ceiling and a prefabricated floor.

He stopped just inside, a wide smile spreading at the familiar sights. The walls lined with rucksacks, weapons, and body armor, with ground mats spread out in front of them. Dirty infantrymen in rows to either side, most of them in T-shirts and camouflaged trousers, engaged in the full range of stand-down activities. Pulling a soiled bandage off of a purple blood blister. Cleaning weapons. Eating chow. Peering at handhelds, getting the latest censored news or re-reading the most recent messages from home.

"Hey, Lieutenant." A hard voice, young, from the corner behind him. "What you doing here?"

Anger flared up in Mortas, even after he saw that the challenge came from someone he didn't recognize. Late teens, shaved head, cleaning part of a grenade launcher. The troop stared at him insolently, and Jander decided to play with him.

"Not much. Just taking it all in. You know?"

"Well take it all in somewhere else. This is First Platoon, and if you ain't First Platoon, you can go—"

"Well look who it is!" A figure rolled up in a field blanket had lifted his head to view the confrontation, and he now sprang to his feet. "Shut up, Greeber. This was our last platoon leader."

The thin frame of Private Prevost approached on bare feet before hugging Jander's torso armor. "Good to see ya, sir! How's the leg?"

"Better than ever. How's the head?" Prevost's helmet had been cracked in half by a flying rock at the end of the wolf attack.

"Gettin' there. I still see double sometimes." Prevost pulled at his nose. "But I make it work for me. Whenever things are going to shit, I tell myself it's not half as bad as it looks."

The two friends laughed, and other familiar figures started rising. Remillet and Bernike shook Jander's hand warmly, both experts with the grenade launcher that the troops called a chonk.

"Looks like we got all the chonk men sleeping in the same spot." He turned this over in his mind before turning to Prevost. "They finally give you some authority?"

"Nah, this is one of those unofficial things. Lieutenant Wolf lets me take charge of the chonks when we're fighting, just like you did." Prevost grinned. "Kinda makes you wonder why we have platoon leaders at all."

"You said it." The surly words came from Greeber, still sitting on his ground mat, but just a little too loud.

"Greeber, I will kick your ass," Prevost snarled. "You know who this is? This is Lieutenant Jander Mortas. You see that Spartacan knife he's carrying? He *killed* a Force major with that, when the guy flipped out on him. And he *fucked* that alien shapeshifter, before he found out she wasn't human."

Mortas couldn't decide how to react to the cascading exaggerations, but Prevost saved him.

"You *did* think she was human, right, sir?"

The group laughed heartily, and Prevost took Mortas by the arm. "Come on, say hello to the rest of the platoon."

Moving forward, Jander looked at the end of the room. Dassa was pointing at something on a wooden table, surrounded by the platoon's senior NCOs and a stranger who was no doubt Lieutenant Wolf. Medium height with a shaved head, the platoon leader's muscles showed through his T-shirt. He brought an index finger near Dassa's, and the men around him nodded when he spoke. A flush of envy went through Mortas, but then a tall soldier was in his path.

"Hey, sir!" This was Ringer, the man Emile had mentioned. "Good to see you again. Listen, you're friends with Captain Pappas, right?"

"Oh, not this again, Ringer," Remillet said gently.

"Nobody believes me, but I know what I saw."

"Captain Dassa said I should talk to you, so he believes you enough for that." Jander touched Ringer's arm. "What did you see?"

"Craziest thing. I was pulling security for a sniper team, on top of this rocky knob near Supply Line Orpheus. They were watching the route, so I was keeping an eye on the plain behind us."

"What, did you hear something?" The joke came from one of the new men, and Ringer's normally placid features froze in a cold stare. His nickname came from the constant sound in his ears, the after-effects of too many explosions.

"It was what I saw." Ringer looked at Mortas. "You know those hogs we got runnin' wild around here?"

"Yes."

"They don't come together in big bunches unless there's a lot of food, or something big to tear up. So what I saw was probably a group of families, a few big males, a bunch of females, and a whole lot of young ones. Nothing special."

"Go on."

"Except there were these other shapes. Dark like most of the pigs, just a little taller than the males, moving with them. On two legs."

"Now tell him what their heat signatures looked like, Ring."

The veteran pursed his lips and twisted his head to look at the floor. "I know what I saw. Those were *men*, Lieutenant. Bent over, camouflaged, but moving with the hogs."

"I believe you. But you did check their signatures?"

"Yes." For the first time he looked doubtful. "I can't explain it, but I figure that's why we got people like Captain Pappas. Their heat readings were almost the same."

"You were droning, Rings." Prevost put a hand on his shoulder, giving him a brief shake. "Happens to all of us. Humping all night to get in position, watching all that great big nothing, the sun beating down, you thought you were awake but you weren't."

"Tell Captain Pappas, sir." Ringer stepped up close to Jander. "I'm not wrong."

"I'll do it. Don't worry."

He was about to clasp Ringer's arm in acknowledgment when the soldiers to his front parted and the medium-sized officer was in front of him. Light green eyes that blazed as they went from his head to his toes.

"Mortas! How's my leg doing?" Wolf demanded.

Taken aback, Jander stammered a response. "Last time I checked, it was my leg."

"No it's not. You were feeding it to a big dog when I saved you. That makes it mine."

Wolf was standing too close, and even though he was shorter he carried his muscles with an aggressive confidence. Jander thought he detected smirks from some of the men around them, even troops he'd commanded, and it rankled him more.

"You rode up in an armored car after my guys had killed most of the wolves. I don't count that as being saved."

"You're right about the platoon." The green eyes glowed, and Wolf spoke to the group. "This platoon don't need help from *anybody*!"

Hoots and howls boomed around the bunker, increasing Jander's annoyance. He'd encountered this type of male before, at prep school, in university sports, and in Officer Basic. Full of bravado and self-congratulation, some of them could deliver but most of them didn't.

"And this platoon ain't afraid of *nobody*!" a voice called from behind him, obviously the second stanza in a well-used group cheer.

"What platoon's got the highest number of kills in the whole brigade?" Wolf shouted, and through the forest of heads Jander saw Dassa watching in bemusement. When he made eye contact with the company commander, Dassa raised his arms in a gesture of helplessness.

"First! First! First! First!" The chant went on for ten seconds more, and then died out. Mortas noted the way every eye was on Wolf, waiting for the next prompt.

"Sorry to cut this short, Mortas!" A hand slapped his torso armor. "But Captain Dassa just gave us tomorrow's mission, and we got infantry stuff to do."

He turned and headed back for the table in a gesture of dismissal, and Jander was standing there alone when Dassa walked up. Most of the men had stopped to say goodbye, but they were now busying themselves with their gear, and Jander knew he'd been forgotten. Wolf was bent over the table, working out the details with Dak and the men who had been his squad leaders, and he barely felt Dassa's hand on his arm.

"Come on. I'll walk you back."

Jander didn't move, staring at the green eyes as Wolf outlined his plan for the next day's operation. Dassa spoke quietly.

"I know he's a handful, but he wasn't lying about the stats. The platoon's in good hands."

Mortas turned and headed for the blackouts. Dassa went with him, and they stood together outside as their goggles adjusted to the night.

"No need to walk me back, sir. I'm gonna go check

with the security company, make sure they're on their toes."

"Never a bad idea. And don't worry—I'll talk to Pappas about what Ringer saw."

"Thanks." Jander looked down the steps, seeing them now as a void. He raised his goggled eyes to Dassa, and pointed at the bunker. "I don't like that guy."

"That's okay. Roger the Rebel doesn't like him either."

Mortas didn't reach the bunker where the Mound's security force maintained its command post. He was walking past a covered garage where mechanics were working on a mover when the first explosions rocked the base. Diving for the ground, he scrambled up against a pile of lumber and raised his Scorpion rifle into firing position, but there was nothing coming at him. Bodies raced past, but they were Mound personnel heading for protection underground. Somewhere out on the perimeter, more blasts sounded.

Still watching for danger, he slipped an electronic thimble onto his finger and used it to put aerial imagery in one lens of his goggles. The camp appeared as a collection of orange-to-red heat signatures from the various machines and collections of personnel, but he was familiar with that. Small fires had sprouted at three points on the wire, the largest right at the main gate and another one near the main shuttle pad. A heavy machine gun started up somewhere out in the darkness, and was soon joined by rifle fire.

"Security, this is Mortas!" Working so closely with the force that protected the Mound, he had a direct link established. "What's going on?"

"We got breaches in three spots!" The answer came from the command bunker. "How the hell did they get so close?"

Jander spun the thimble in the air, enlarging the image of the base. A constellation of white dots was rapidly moving away, and he recognized them as the signatures of the hogs Ringer had mentioned. His warning that the rebels were using the animals to conceal their movements echoed, but it was no time for explanations.

Out on the perimeter, the gunfire rose to a steady roar. Focusing the picture on the main gate, he now saw tiny flecks of light, incoming and outgoing bullets, alongside the flames that had once been twin watchtowers guarding the entrance. Concrete fighting positions had supported the wooden structures, and he watched in surprise as bright flashes streaked toward them from just outside the wire. The unmistakable boom of shoulder-fired HDF rockets came to him moments after the bunker busters slammed home.

"They're through! They're at the entrance! They're throwing grenades!" the voice from the command bunker screamed, and then the transmission ended in a thunderclap.

Jerking his head around, Mortas debated where to go. If the rebels were inside the perimeter, it would be foolish to run around presenting a target. His thoughts went to FITCO and his own supply people, up the hill.

"Sergeant Strickland? Sergeant Leoni? This is Mortas."

"Hey Lieutenant!" Leoni sounded buoyant. "You in a safe spot?"

"Not really. Where are you?"

"I got my boys and girls on the slope just above our truck park, armored up and loaded for bear." A marker blinked into life, showing the bunkers that overlooked FITCO's vehicles. "Anybody tries to damage my wheels is gonna be sorry."

"Sounds good. You seeing any movement?"

"Just a bunch of chickens with their heads cut off. You'd think people would know where the shelters were."

"Roger just nailed the command post, so stay put and try to coordinate air support. What about Strickland?"

"I'm with the battalion's stuff," the supply sergeant answered, and another marker appeared on the slope close to Leoni's. "Rigging charges on the medicine and the ammo. Just in case."

"Don't waste any time on that," Leoni advised. "This isn't a smash-n-grab. They're here to kill. Hey, Lieutenant?"

"Yeah."

"I already called for drones, but there's a problem. Since we haven't had any customers here until now, they reassigned our support. They say we can have orbital rockets if things get bad enough."

"Fuck." Mortas tensed up, bringing the Scorpion rifle tight against his armor before recognizing the shadowy figures as more troops trying to find shelter. "Listen, I'm gonna head for the perimeter. Looks like most of the positions are still intact, and they're fighting it out. You're in a good spot to coordinate everything, so see what you can get us, short of those rockets."

"Understood. Be careful, El-tee."

He laughed at the absurd advice, and was about to rise when Dassa spoke inside his helmet. "Jan, you should head up to your sergeant's location and take over the command post's job. I've got First with me, and we're headed for the gate."

Despite the confusion of the surprise attack and the wisdom of Dassa's suggestion, he still felt resentment at being excluded from the fighting. Wolf's mockery rang in his ears, goading him. Besides, Dassa didn't know that Leoni was more than up to the task of bringing in aerial assets without blowing the whole camp to pieces. Jander was about to tell his former company commander that he was coming to join him when someone called out from nearby.

"Lieutenant Mortas! Lieutenant!" It was hard to locate the sound over the booms and growls of the distant battle, but a rapidly waving hand caught his eye. Twenty yards away, kneeling among stacks of palletized supplies, was a small group of Mound soldiers. Most of them wore body armor and helmets, but some only had goggles and weapons. He looked left and right, and ran over.

Skidding into the dirt next to the waving hand, he looked up to see a woman's face under helmet and goggles. Hands pulled him to a knee, and grim expressions pressed in.

"Tell us what to do, sir." The woman ordered, and Jander's mind flipped into platoon leader mode.

"What's your name?"

"Corporal Easterbrook, sir. Ordnance."

"How many people you got?" he asked, checking the imagery again. Firefly dots were moving through the breach near the shuttle pad, and a yellow bud blossomed when one of the aircraft exploded.

"Fifteen total!" she hollered above the noise. "Three from my section, plus some cooks, a few clerks, and a couple of I-don't-knows."

Mortas switched the goggle view to a communications schematic that showed all of the individual torso radios closest to him. Punching the air with the thimble, he created a quick network that patched them together.

"If you can hear me, raise your hand."

Roughly ten palms came up, all of their owners helmeted. "Okay, pair up—anyone without a headset is gonna need my commands relayed to them."

He went back to the imagery, spotting First Platoon moving on a diagonal route for the fighting at the gate. More fires were sprouting on the shuttle pad, but it was hard to see how many of the enemy had broken through. Thinking quickly, he tapped the thimble on each of the heat signatures around him, marking them as friendlies.

"Okay, listen!" He raised his rifle across his chest, with the barrel pointed at the sky. "While we move, hold your rifle like I'm doing. It's safer. We're headed for the airstrip. The bad guys are through the wire there, and they're wrecking the birds. We're going to kill them."

Heads bobbed tightly, and a few dry throats murmured assent.

"Follow me."

Weaving through the rest of the camp, trying not to trip over tent ropes, warning the neophytes not to bunch up time and again, inhaling the smoke and the sickening odor of burning fuel, but hearing no shooting from the airfield. Machine guns and rifles roared from the bunkers on the hill, tracers passing over the sheds and maintenance bays to their right as they ran, while the dim booms of chonk rounds sounded from the distant gate where Dassa had taken First Platoon.

Finally reaching the end of the temporary structures, seeing the strip alight in orange and yellow and the black dots that ran in front of the flames like some kind of fire-worshiper dance. Knowing that a long irrigation ditch faced the field on that side, and that it had been dug deeper to serve as a shelter if the base got attacked.

"Cut to the right!" he shouted, sweat pouring down his face. "Get in the ditch!"

Bumping into the figures closest to him, herding them toward the trench, and then seeing them pull up in confusion. Standing there in the firelight.

"Get down! Get in the trench!"

Bulling his way through them and then stopping in the same stupefied manner. Looking down at the long gash in the ground and seeing it had been filled in with a writhing mass of humanity. Fatigues, coveralls, and what he believed was a set of bare buttocks all struggled at his feet, fighting to get lower as the gunfire raged overhead.

"Down! Flatten on the ground!" He barely got the words out when a volley rattled at them from the strip. Light winking in the fire and smoke, something plucked at his sleeve, and then they were all down on their stomachs. Legs squirming, boots sliding until they were at the edge of the ditch, and then the rifles barking as one.

Sighting into the flat ground, the goggles adjusting so that the enemy figures appeared as human silhouettes inside the billowing smoke and backlit by the fires. A knot of them rushing forward, had to be the ones who'd fired at them, and then he was calmly sighting in on the surging shadows and knocking them to the ground.

"Single shots!" Mortas called out. "Take your time! They're not as close as they look!"

They didn't hear him, of course. A frenzied howl rose up from their front, the occupants of the trench made hysterical by the popping roar over their heads. One instant Jander had a clear view of the strip and the burning shuttle hulks and their wilting, wavering opponents and the next his rifle was crushed into the mud and so was his face and it seemed that hundreds of people were jumping up and down on his back.

The occupants of the ditch were gone a moment later, terror giving them wings, and he pushed himself up onto his elbows. Turning, Mortas watched their flying backs. They hit the nearest tent like a stampede, running so hard that it simply billowed for an instant and then disappeared under their assault. Not believing what had just happened, Jander broke out in laughter.

"Look at 'em go!" Easterbrook was yelling, and he thought she meant the fleeing Force soldiers until the troop next to him in the dirt jostled his arm. The man was struggling to stand, and then he was leaping, not into the cover of the empty trench but across it, they all were, animal yells filling his ears as they charged. Left alone, Jander fought his way to his feet and straddled the ditch as well, still laughing.

His goggles now showed his small command charging through the hell-world of the strip, and he churned his boots on the melting surface in an effort to keep up. Somewhere near the opposite end of the strip one of the shuttles blew up in a tower of flame, and the hot wind that rushed over Mortas reminded him of the fuel and ammunition that was alight all around him.

Ammo. Regardless of their enthusiasm, his hastily gathered troops weren't carrying the standard load of infantry soldiers. His armor was loaded down with magazines, but some of the support personnel appeared to lack even canteens. Still running, now alone, he darted his eyes around until finding the grisly scene of the rebels who had been caught in the first volley. Sprawled across a small space, surrounded by flame, they lay still.

Mortas bent low when he came to the first fallen Scorpion, scooping up the weapon and then another. Dropping to a knee to sling both rifles across his chest, scanning the corpses to see which ones might have been carrying extra ammunition, shocked to see that most of them had no body armor. Black Xs and

Vs stood out across their faces like ash, the tattoos of the Flock. The heat billowed around Mortas, forcing him to move.

Rushing off through the fire, hearing the scattered shots beyond the breach in the fence, knowing that his people had gone through and were chasing the rebels who had survived.

Hours later, just before the sun came up, Jander sat exhausted with his back against the slanted wall of a bowl-shaped crater. His face was smeared with dirt and soot and dry sweat, and he longed for a drink of water. All around him, bodies rested on their stomachs with their weapons pointed over the rim of the depression, while two wounded soldiers were resting in the middle. The medics in the group had taken charge of their care, and pronounced the wounds minor.

It had taken him two hours to finally round up East-erbrook and the others, and he was exhausted from chasing them down. Jander had been running all over the battlefield like an incompetent nanny, catching up with one group only to lose control of another. They'd been like children on a scavenger hunt, running after the heat signatures that appeared in their goggles and scooping up rebel weapons when their own had emptied. The gunships had finally arrived, and that had put an end to the pursuit. Once the drones had started churning up the ground with mini-gun fire only a few hundred yards in front of them, they'd asked Jander about a safe place to hole up.

Amazingly, none of them had been killed. Mortas listened to the engine of a drone passing overhead, while viewing the imagery of the surrounding plain provided by the air assets. The rebels who had survived were long gone, and in his goggles he watched as an arrowhead of vehicular heat signatures approached his position from the direction of the Mound.

"That you, Sergeant Strickland?" he rasped.

"That's right, Lieutenant." He heard the truck motors along with the words. "Tell your gunslingers not to fire us up."

"That would be hard—we're almost empty."

"Tell 'em just the same."

"You got it." Sand ran down his pants when he stood, now seeing the outlines of the trucks and armored cars. "Everybody stay cool on the perimeter. Those movers are our resupply. And our ride."

He needn't have bothered. The night's adrenaline had worn off, leaving the newly blooded support personnel spent and quiet. They'd managed to stay awake, but the approaching sign that the battle was truly ended sent many of them sagging to the dirt. Mortas smiled, looking at them with affection as the armored cars passed to either side. The trucks rolled to a stop, and he recognized several members of FITCO as they hustled over the rim carrying rucksacks that bulged with water, ammunition, and food. His stomach rumbled at the idea, and he was about to ask what they had in the way of chow when Strickland was standing next to him.

"Some night, huh?" Mortas asked.

"Some night." The supply NCO sounded tired, but an undertone of remorse floated along with the words. "I got some bad news, sir."

"What? We lose somebody back there?"

"Us? No. We fought from the bunkers; we were fine." He sighed heavily. "I'm sorry, sir. Captain Dassa got killed in the fight at the gate."

CHAPTER 9

"Madame Chairwoman, I am going to become a suspect if I don't keep feeding them new information." Timothy Kumar almost hissed the request, his face drawn with strain. "I need something more."

Reena Mortas looked past him, through the one-way glass of Olech's personal underground train. The decorative tiling of the private tunnel system leading to Unity Plaza should have been a blur, but instead it leveraged the train's motion. A blend of light green and dark blue surged together in a rolling, cresting wave without end, and she smiled at the effect. She'd designed it herself, in happier days.

"Madame Chairwoman?"

"I heard you, Timothy. It seems your friends are quite greedy. I ceded them control of three very rich planets in the war zone, planets my husband had given to the Veterans Auxiliary. Now you're saying they want more."

"That's not it." Although the car's only other occupant was Ulbridge, busily tapping on a handheld in the corner, the physicist still glanced over his shoulder. "Of course they want me to pressure you for more concessions, but I'm fearful they . . . suspect something."

"I see." Reena leaned back against the padded blue seat. Most of the car's walls were lined with them, and she momentarily remembered other trips, with the compartment loaded with happy staffers and guests. The dead echoes of those gatherings gave way to the empty space, reminding her of Olech's absence, and she took it out on her unwilling agent. "So when you're not bringing them more dirt on me, or another gift, they notice that you don't contribute much to the conversation."

"Zone Quest has spies *everywhere*," he answered through clenched teeth. "They believe you're plotting something, something big, and I can't give them even a hint of what that might be."

"Perhaps you should remind them that you pulled my fangs a long time ago. It was petty blackmail, and of course you forgot I might have something much worse on you, but as far as ZQ and the other members of that dirty cabal are concerned, you're my boss."

"They've come to doubt how easily you rolled over, especially now that you've blamed Horace's murder on Leeger. They don't see the leverage anymore."

"The leverage is still there." Reena decided to stop torturing him. "No one's forgotten that Leeger worked for us."

"But when he joined the rebels, it passed the guilt onto him." He exhaled, as if not believing the words he was about to utter. "And very few people in the settled worlds would believe that Reena Corlipso would murder her own brother."

"Even if she believed he had a hand in her husband's disappearance?"

"That's too complicated for the masses."

"But not for your friends. They're as devious as you are, and they understand the power of deep, dark secrets."

"It's not enough." It was Kumar's turn to sit back, but he wasn't relaxing. "And the planets you gave them are out of reach. They can't exploit them because the Sims are on the offensive, and it's driving them crazy. You should have seen their faces when I told them what you were giving up—on two of those rocks alone they could make up almost half of the minerals they used to get from Celestia."

"I imagine Asterlit's not unhappy about that."

"Of course he's not. He's got half the Force holding off the rebels while he's repairing the recaptured mines. ZQ is just as beholden to him now as . . . before."

Kumar almost didn't finish the sentence, realizing he'd been tricked.

"That's something new, isn't it?" Reena asked sweetly. "Asterlit's direct involvement with your friends."

"It shouldn't be surprising," Kumar answered weakly. "He controls Celestia's delegation to the Emergency Senate, he's still one of ZQ's biggest suppliers, and like it or not he's Celestia's new ruler."

"A great many people don't like Asterlit at all. And that's useful to me. From this point on, I want you to tell me whenever his name is mentioned."

Kumar's face fell. "I'm not sure I can keep this up much longer."

"I feel the same way myself, these days." Reena made eye contact with Ulbridge, who lowered the handheld. "I'm getting pilloried on the Bounce because we're losing ground in the war, and because nothing's getting resolved on Celestia. I'm spending more and more time fending off questions about those planets I ceded to Zone Quest, and not just from senators. Functionaries from the Veterans Auxiliary are beating on my door, in a way they never would have dreamed of just six months ago."

Kumar gave her a doubtful look, and Ulbridge matched it from behind him.

"Makes a girl yearn for a quieter life."

"Are you actually thinking of quitting?"

"My husband's still missing, a lot of people think I'm doing a poor job, and frankly the hours are just too damned long."

"Is this the truth? Or is this what I should tell them?"

"You'll be more convincing if I don't answer that. Why don't you go practice?"

Kumar stood uncertainly, and Ulbridge released the locks on the door leading to the next car. A uniformed security guard scowled at the physicist as he passed, and the passage closed. Ulbridge approached, and sat.

"Was that wise, ma'am?"

"Certainly. Just think of how distracted that crowd will be, arguing about my successor."

"There is a danger that they might not argue for long."

"Even better. If they start lobbying for my removal, they'll have a hard time opposing me when I announce my plan to resign, to dissolve the Emergency Senate, and hold real elections."

"They'll oppose you anyway. They'll have to."

"You're going to make sure they're too busy for that—and Kumar just gave us the evidence. Zone Quest is conspiring with the one man the entire galaxy blames for perpetuating the suffering on Celestia."

"Asterlit."

"Kumar was hiding that involvement because he knows Asterlit is very unpopular. Despite his best efforts, Celestia's new ruler hasn't been able to keep the atrocity stories from getting out. You see, organizations like Zone Quest know it's much better to present a nameless, faceless front to the people. It's hard to fix the blame when decisions are made by boards and committees. Asterlit is the name and the face of a great deal of suffering—and you're going to tie him to Zone Quest and their cronies."

"That task just got a little easier, ma'am."

"How so?"

"An unexpected source. There's a story gaining traction that Jander has gone on a bit of a crusade. Apparently he led some Orphans on a raid of a particularly nasty brothel run by Asterlit's security people—and his stance was then adopted by the Orphan Brigade's commander. It's gaining momentum with other outfits there as well."

"That is surprising. Finally one of Olech's children did something to help me."

"It's even got a name. They call it Watt's Law."

"The boy has no political sense. He should have put his own name on it. Doesn't he understand the power of the name Mortas?"

"He's always tried to avoid using it, Madame Chairwoman."

"It was a joke, Nathaniel. You've given me some encouraging news." The train glided to a stop at the heavily guarded station under Unity's main tower, but Reena made no move to rise. "Tell me about the

Banshees. How are they responding to the new training regimen?"

"They're good soldiers, ma'am. They're giving it their all."

"No, I mean the cover story. Are they buying it?"

"Apparently they find it as credible as any other explanation ever offered by Command."

"That's hardly encouraging."

"They're buying it, ma'am."

"No matter how many times they brief us, I will never understand what we're doing here." Elaine "Bullhead" Bontenough remarked to no one in particular. Paired off with Zuteck, she was roughly a mile away from where Dellmore and Ayliss were concealed.

"What's not to understand?" Cusabrina asked in a conversational tone. She and Lightfoot were another mile away, also hunkered down. "We've got this high-speed equipment that monitors what's going on inside a giant crater, and Command wants us to practice with it."

"Yeah. That's the part that confuses me," Bullhead continued. "If we're supposed to be training to monitor a great big hole somewhere, how come the practice crater is nowhere near us?"

Hidden under a slab of rock that formed a shadowy ceiling overhead, Ayliss chuckled at the banter inside her helmet. The squad had been deposited on a captured planet far from any Sim activity, and the break had loosened their tongues.

"What, you thought we were gonna set up right on the edge?" Legacy was paired with Tin, and the normally strict squad leader wasn't stopping the bull session. "If we did that, we wouldn't need the gear, would we?"

"And we might fall in," Zuteck offered. "Don't forget we're stupid. Too stupid to be told the truth. Right, Sergeant Tin?"

"I cannot believe what I'm hearing," Tin answered in an airy tone. "All that bitching about the back-to-back missions and we-never-get-a-break, and what happens when they put you in a warm, safe spot with nothing to do? More bitching."

"I just don't buy the explanation, is all."

"It's simple enough. Sam's a big digger, always has been. You saw one of his ships launch from inside a mountain."

"It was a shuttle, not a ship."

"Correct. So what if Sam sets up on a rock with great big craters and decides to take advantage of it? He could launch all sorts of things, from missiles to fighters, right out of prepared openings that our intelligence folks are bound to overlook."

"But that's not what these things are supposed to detect." Bullhead rejoined the discussion, causing Ayliss to sit up and examine the device again. She moved quietly because Dellmore was asleep next to her, the suit making her look like a deactivated robot. "In the briefing they said we were on the lookout for transport-sized craft. Big things. Ships."

The desiccated ground dropped away from Ayliss at a modest angle, a spread of tan sand, whitened rocks, and emaciated trees. An enormous cavern opened in the middle of the square formed by the squad's four positions, but that was too far away to see. Instead, she focused on a barrel-shaped pod with three extended legs sitting under a brown camouflage net. Her suit told her the device was emitting modest electronic signals directed down through the soil, and she could just make out the hard probe sticking into the ground beneath it.

"So Command's let their imaginations run away with them," Tin responded. "It's not the first time that's happened. Be thankful it gave us a rest."

"We're not the only ones." Lightfoot entered the conversation. "I was talking with First Sergeant Blocker's commo guy Ewing. He said there are teams all over this rock, doing exactly what we're doing."

Cusabrina laughed. "Ewing? Isn't he a doper?"

"Not anymore." The words came out before Ayliss could stop herself. For a moment she saw Ewing's raging face, his shirtfront doused with blood from having cut Vroma Rittle's throat. "He quit right after the fight on Larkin Station."

"So it's true, then?" Cusabrina asked. "He's the one who killed Rittle?"

"Yeah. Rittle's people shit all over him and the other vets on Quad Seven before I got there. I didn't realize how much he hated that guy. Or that he carried a knife."

"Hey, I don't care if he's a druggie or a murderer. Can we stay on topic?" Lightfoot's annoyance sent a ripple of laughter over the net. "Ewing knows a lot. He takes all the late radio watches, and he knows how to comb for data."

"What did he tell you?" Tin sounded interested.

"He can't put his finger on it, but something big is on the way. He said requests for Banshee support are being turned down, and that the excuse is that we're too busy."

"I don't feel busy."

"Right. So there's a bunch of us here, doing this, and the rest of the sisters are committed somewhere else."

"You sure he isn't doping again?" Tin asked. "Back on Quad Seven, he told me about hearing this eerie space music while manning the radios with the fleet. He said he only heard them on the late watches."

"Go ahead and ask him, when we get back aboard ship."

"Of course, you could always ask First Sergeant Blocker." Dellmore yawned audibly, and Ayliss turned to see her stretching the arms of her suit. "I hear you have a way with him, Sergeant Tin."

A subdued flutter of giggles rode the airwaves, but Tin didn't sound concerned when she answered. "Never a bad idea to be on good terms with the guy who runs our entire support company."

"Good terms." Dellmore laughed warmly. "I never heard it called that before."

"Nothing wrong with it. I checked with the skipper."

"Hey Rig," Cusabrina interrupted. "Did *you* approve this? Didn't Blocker used to work for you?"

"He worked for my father. I was just a child." Ayliss strained not to laugh. She'd suspected Tin was attracted to her former bodyguard, but the tumult of the past weeks had kept her from learning that the pair had acted on their feelings. "But that does raise an important question. Sergeant Tin, aren't you and I almost the same age?"

"Careful, Rig," Dellmore growled in fake admonishment while the radios soared with laughter.

"What's that got to do with it? Most of the guys my age don't know shit. Give me a combat vet who's served two complete tours any day. And he sure does have that support company humming, now doesn't he?"

"Got *something* humming."

The laughter died out slowly, followed by a silence indicating that the squad had taken Tin's interrogation as far as they dared. Ayliss decided to walk around a bit, but there wasn't room under the rock overhang to stand up. Rolling on her side, and then onto her stomach, she did a push-up with the aid of mechanized arms. Bending her right knee, she planted her boot on the dirt and pushed off. Lurching forward, she jogged a few steps before regaining her balance.

"Gotta work on that, Rig," Dellmore muttered. Ayliss looked over at the motionless suit, and Dellmore activated the cameras inside her helmet so that her partner could see her face. It was merely a projection, but it was a completely accurate depiction of the scene inside the bell-shaped top of the suit. Dellmore gave her a half-critical look and then shut her eyes again. The image dimmed and vanished, replaced by the armored face of her helmet.

Ayliss chose not to respond, well aware of the skills the more experienced veterans displayed in operating their suits, as if the outfits were merely a second skin. She also knew that those skills only came from months of experience in the suits and that she would acquire them in time.

Time. The previous months were now a blur, loaded with training and combat. She started ticking off the operations the squad had been involved in, growing amazed at their number. The Banshees all across the Force had been in great demand, with the Sims attacking or popping up in so many places, and there had been little opportunity to reflect on any individual fight before they'd been preparing for the next.

Looking out over the tan slope, Ayliss imagined what it would be like to simply lie there in the sun, no suit, no weapons. The planet was a Hab, so she could actually have done this. Nothing stirred on the open ground or in its few trees, and she enjoyed the unfamiliar sensation of being on an operation with no fear of being detected by the enemy.

The feeling didn't last long, because a dull vibration came up through her boots and ran along the entire inside of her suit. Like an electric pulse, it warbled against her skin while growing in intensity. She was just about to ask if anyone else was experiencing a similar sensation when an HDF shuttle lifted off from inside the crater hundreds of yards away. It shot straight for the sky, its engines operating at maximum capacity, and then disappeared from view.

Wearing a look of bemusement, she studied the monitoring device to see if it had responded in any way. A tiny red light near the top of the cone blinked at her, once, and when she called up the readout on her face shield there was no record of the launch or any other activity.

"I think these things need a little more field testing." she remarked, and a chorus of similar comments came back to her.

"Just another piece of Force space junk," Dellmore stated with equanimity, appearing at Ayliss's side.

"Seen it before. Once, I don't know, probably three years ago—"

Tin overrode the entire communications net. "Looks like we're cutting this one short, ladies. Just got the word. Turn off the devices and get ready for transport."

When the radio net returned to normal, Legacy asked, "Are we sure they were even on?"

CHAPTER 10

"We're dug in on a knob west of Supply Line Orpheus. Marking position."

The report was accompanied by the noises of a battle so distant that it couldn't be heard on the Mound. Rockets were impacting not far from the speaker, and Jander thought he heard the long belch of a drone gunship firing up a target. The unit was a platoon from A Company that had been tracking a Flock raid party for hours. Aerial reconnaissance hadn't been able to find the fast-moving outfit, and the enemy had delayed their pursuers with two doomed ambushes. The Orphans had handled the close-in fights easily, and finally got close enough to direct rockets onto the fleeing rebels. Darkness had just fallen, and they needed resupply.

"I see your marker." Mortas opened his right eye

while closing his left, shutting out the darkened imagery of the battle position in order to see what was happening right in front of him. One of Sergeant Strickland's resupply darts pointed at the night sky at a forty-five-degree angle, and a team of FITCO troops was securing supply containers inside the open hull. A rolling platform stood next to the rocket on its launcher, both manufactured by Sergeant Leoni's people.

"We're short on machine-gun ammo and chonk rounds. That's the priority."

"Understood. The darts have plenty of room. I'm sending you a basic load for the crew-served and the grenade launchers, a med pack, extra batteries, and bags of water." Hearing the words, Sergeant Leoni gave Mortas a thumbs-up from the gantry. Like the rest of the workers, he was stripped down to a T-shirt and fatigue trousers. The new commander of the Mound's security company was much more active than his deceased predecessor, and the base hadn't been approached by rebels since the night Dassa had died.

"Bags? Did you say bags?"

"Yes. Water in the standard drums and cans sloshed around too much, and it threw off the dart's flight. But if we line the inside with these canteen-sized bags, it spreads out the effect."

"If you say so. You sure this thing's gonna land safely?"

"Don't worry about a thing. Pick out a landing spot twenty yards by twenty yards, with lots of dirt in the middle, and mark it for me."

"And Roger can't change the flight? They've done that to missiles, you know."

"That's the beauty of outdated tech. The darts were never meant to be used this way. My people fitted them with the rockets, so Roger doesn't have a clue how to stop them. It's not a guided flight like a missile; we compute the whole trip, and lock it in. We can even reverse thrust just before it hits, so instead of burying its nose in the dirt, it lands on its side."

"I'm gonna move my people away from that spot, all the same."

"Doubters all around me. No faith in anything anymore."

"If you're that confident, how about you pack some goodies for us? We been out here humping for five straight days on nothing but rations."

"Already done." Mortas watched as insulated containers were strapped into the center of the load. "Got you a nice hot meal, straight from the mess hall."

"Outstanding. Remind me to repay the favor next time we're on the Mound."

"No need to thank me. Thank Drew Follett."

"Who?"

"Oh, nobody. Just a guy who enjoyed seeing people eat."

The dart's hatch had been sealed shut, and everyone except Leoni had climbed down. Standing on the platform, he peered at the load through a hardened observation window that was another one of FITCO's improvements. Satisfied, he swung down and stepped over to Mortas while the gantry was wheeled away.

"Ready to launch," Leoni reported, and then called out to the shadows of the troops nearby. "Give it plenty of room. I know we've done this a lot, but when you been around bang-boom stuff as long as I have, you don't take anything for granted."

The dark silhouettes disappeared, and Leoni took the control device from his pocket. Flipping off its double safety, he turned to Mortas. "Go for launch, sir?"

"Make sure you don't hit my garden." The flat-topped hill, now minus the infamous Red House, loomed up in front of the launcher.

"Garden? That's a little generous for a patch of weeds."

"Patch of weeds? I've got a nice row of carrots, and two of string beans."

"The hell you say, sir. Nothing good grows here."

"You remember that package you got through quarantine for me?"

"Yep. I had to trade half a pallet of toilet paper for that clearance, and almost got in a fistfight with the chief NCO at the airhead. He insisted on seeing what was in that box, until I told him it was pornography."

"And he didn't want it?"

"Oh, I also told him you were an officer. He figured it was sick fetish stuff, and told me to take it away. So what was it? Magic beans?"

"A little gift from the Holy Whisper colony on Roanum. You remember that mud munition Sam used to destroy Fractus? He first employed it on Roanum, and the Whisper found some samples. They developed this capsule, part mud-maker and part fertilizer—"

"Excuse me, sir. I'm sure you think that's interesting, but I do have to fire this thing sometime tonight."

"I just assumed you weren't listening. Fire when ready."

The words were barely out of his mouth when the rockets mounted next to the dart's fins gave off a brief hiss and then flared into fire. Mortas's goggles had just adjusted to the intense light when the torpedo-shaped craft shot up into the night sky. He tracked it for a moment, the engines propelling it up over the hilltop, and then it was gone.

"Your package is inbound." Mortas radioed the waiting platoon. "I'll give you a warning ten seconds out."

"Got it. Waiting."

FITCO soldiers were already scrubbing down the launcher, and Mortas saw Trimmer leading two other troops in a shuffling dance as they stamped out a small ground fire started by the engines. An acrid smell hung in the air when they were done.

"Those were some nice words you said about Captain Dassa the other night, by the way." Leoni spoke while tracking the dart's progress on the controller. "Always tough to lose a buddy like that."

"He was the best officer I ever met. Our company got stranded on Verdur, deep in the jungle, Sims all around us, and I never once doubted we'd come out on top. Because of him." Jander paused. "Thanks for arranging the ceremony, by the way. It was something we did in the infantry, but I wasn't sure about you rear-echelon types."

"If this is the rear, I'd hate to see what the front looks like. Twenty seconds, sir."

"Ten seconds to arrival," he relayed to the waiting troops. "Get your heads down."

"And . . . it's there." Leoni shut off the controller and put it away while Mortas waited for confirmation.

"Wow!" A pleased voice spoke in his ear. "That was *right* on target. Landed on its side and slid to a halt. Perfect."

"We aim to please. Be careful opening it—the hull's gonna be hot."

"No shit. Thing's practically glowing."

"Just imagine riding one of those down through the atmosphere."

"I'd rather not. You guys gonna come get this thing?"

"Affirmative. It's important Roger doesn't get his

hands on any of these, so if you have to leave it for any reason, make sure you blow it in place."

"Hey, if it keeps the hot meals coming I'll chop it up with my bare hands. You have a good night there, Mound."

"You too, groundpounder. Enjoy the food. Stay safe."

Later that night, Jander sat on the wall surrounding his garden. He'd shed his armor, helmet, and goggles, allowing the breeze to cool him. The base flowed down the hill and onto the flat, its perimeter greatly strengthened after the sneak attack he'd helped defeat. A shuttle was preparing to lift off from the repaired airstrip, but apart from that the camp was quiet.

After the hustle and bustle of long days running supplies, he'd found he enjoyed the peace at the top of the hill. The gray plain spread out and away, to the spot where it mated up with the star-winking sky. Not far away, patrols from the Mound's new security force were waiting in ambush along likely avenues of approach. Packs of the feral hogs moved around as well, and somewhere out there Pappas was studying them to see if they could indeed shield rebel troop movements as Ringer believed.

Pondering Ringer's theory reminded Mortas of Dassa, and he suddenly felt tired. Despite the hostility and violence of their first meeting as teenagers, Dassa had been a living link to Jander's life before the war. So many of those links were now gone, or altered forever. Dassa and his father were dead, Reena was more or less an enemy, Leeger was working with the enemy, and Ayliss was with the Banshees.

Thinking of the all-female strike force always brought memories of Varick, and that brightened his mood for a moment even though he hadn't heard from her in weeks. Correspondence on Celestia was heavily censored, but he'd received several messages from her once he'd been established in his new job. Apparently her re-entry into the Banshees wasn't as certain as Erica had believed, but she was working her way through it. She'd been re-certified in all the tasks of an armored suit, but hadn't received orders to a new unit yet.

As always, his mind shifted to the warm memories of their nights together. The blissful weeks when they'd been held up on the *Ajax*, not knowing if they would be rewarded or punished for their actions on Roanum— and not caring. Varick's indifference to possible censure had drawn him even closer, as did her insistence on returning to the fight. That was some woman. She'd jumped into the water with him, though aware of the horrible snakes, without a moment's hesitation. And she'd jettisoned the evil shapeshifter even as he'd offered to take the blame for the justified decision that could easily have gotten them both court-martialed.

Movement on the trail interrupted his reminiscence, and Mortas squinted into the gloom. The approaching shape was tall and thin, not wearing body armor or even a helmet, but he recognized the walk and tried to connect it with a name.

"I can still take you two falls out of three, even at my age." Hugh Leeger's voice jolted him, but Jander forced himself to stay seated. His rifle was ten yards away, as was the communications rig in his armor.

"What are you doing here, Hugh?"

"Can't visit an old friend?" Leeger stopped a few yards away, dressed in a worn set of fatigues and boots. "I'm not armed, if you're worried."

"I'm not worried, but neither are you. I bet you've got some help hidden, just short of the crest, watching us. Am I right?"

"I'm alone." The tall man closed the distance, and sat down with a sigh. He seemed to be admiring the view, and so Mortas studied him. His skin didn't seem to have turned orange yet, but it was hard to tell in the dark. It did appear a bit sallow, and his childhood bodyguard had lost considerable weight.

"How'd you get in here?"

"In the back of a truck. You'd be surprised, how many of the people on bases just like this one are helping us."

"I would have hoped those helpers would have seen the error of their ways when we got attacked the other night."

"That wasn't us." It was Leeger's turn to study him. "But I heard all about it. Big base like this, loaded with people with guns, and you ended up leading what? Fifteen of them? Not a ringing endorsement."

"Most of the types here aren't combat troops—but those fifteen fought like pros."

"That leaves a whole lot more of them, wearing the same uniform as you, who didn't help out. Your army's divided, even the ones who didn't come over to us."

"No one's happy about being here. But some of us remembered our oath."

"And what oath was that? The one about defending humanity?"

"Yes. And that's what we've been doing here—at least the Orphans, anyway. You might not have heard this, but we've got a policy."

"Watt's Law?" Leeger chuckled. "Don't look so surprised. As I said, we've got helpers everywhere. And with the way Asterlit keeps the Force in the dark, I guarantee I know more about what's going on than you do—here, and off-world."

"You get good Bounce reception down in those mines?"

"Better than the censored junk you get. Did you know that Watt's Law—and what you did on this hill—was a story on the Bounce?"

"Just another Mortas family puff piece, probably."

"Oh, somebody's pushing it all right. But it's got

legs of its own. Lots of politicians, especially the ones trying to look like they didn't know there was slavery here, have taken your stand and made it their own."

"Just what I always wanted. A bunch of corrupt liars teaming up with me."

"You may be needing those corrupt liars. What you did here, saving those poor kids, is all it takes to tip things over. Asterlit's feeling the heat, and he blames your unit."

"Well let's hope he doesn't send us to some god-awful wasteland, to chase orange mutants and tat-tooed fanatics."

"Did you notice anything about those tattooed fanatics the other night? That a good percentage of them were women and children?"

"I was a little busy. They were shooting at us and setting fires. They killed my best friend from the war zone, too. I don't much care what they looked like."

"But you did notice. So what's that tell you?"

"That we've killed so much of the Flock that they're sending women and children on suicide missions."

"You really think that? Pappas is slipping." Hugh gave a short whistle. "Tell him that instead of looking for snitches at Camp Resolve, he should try doing a head count."

"That's impossible. I should know; I run supplies to them. New refugees keep coming in, and old ones keep sneaking out."

"Not anymore. There hasn't been a refugee convoy

to Resolve in three weeks. And all those camps that Asterlit still controls? They've been emptied."

"What are you saying?"

"Asterlit was never anything but a weapon wielded by Horace. He has a certain animal cleverness, sure, but he only knows what he learned from his master. To stay in power, the minerals have to come out of the ground. Asterlit controls a number of mines in the undisputed zones, but there's nobody left to work them."

"No." The import of Leeger's words chilled him. "That can't be true. No way they'd pull that, after everything that's happened."

"Sadly, yes. All those good Celestian citizens who thought slavery was all right as long as it wasn't happening to them, the ones who ended up packed inside those camps fighting for scraps, are seeing just how easy it is to get reclassified as a slave."

"Somebody once told me that the Celestian term for orphan was the same as the term for slave."

"Well, refugee has the same meaning now. They've kept it quiet, but every camp Asterlit controls has been relocated to the secured mining areas. It's a simple arrangement. You want to eat, you better meet your daily ore quota." Leeger's tone had flattened. "Lots and lots of folks wishing they'd run off and joined the rebels when they had the chance."

"How come I don't know this already?"

"The same reason slavery was allowed here in the

first place. Zone Quest, the Force, and the Emergency Senate need that ore."

"All this suffering, for a bunch of rocks."

"Don't forget there's a lot of money involved."

"So is that why you're here? To tell me this?"

"I want you to come with me."

"You know better than that."

"Jan, quitting your family was the hardest thing I ever did. But it wasn't really a choice. I just couldn't be a part of that anymore, knowing all the misery I was helping create."

"So sending women and children into machine-gun fire makes you feel better?"

"At least they die free, with weapons in their hands. Better than leaving them to this." Leeger pointed to the spot where the house had stood. "As you well know. And I already told you that wasn't us. The Flock's a strange creature, almost a cult, you can't reason with them."

"But you've tried."

"Why wouldn't we?"

"What aren't you telling me, Hugh? What are you planning?"

"Come with me, and you'll know everything."

"I'm piecing it together just fine on my own. It isn't like you, to just hide underground. You're cooking something up." When Leeger didn't respond, he continued. "Just understand something. If the Orange start killing Orphans, the gloves come off."

"Your outfit's been hunting us since you got here. You're not any good at it, but I'd say the gloves are already off."

"You know what I mean. Asterlit asked me how to beat you, and so did my entire chain of command. So far I haven't given them the answer."

"I doubt you could."

"You remember what my father used to say about conflicts? He said people mistake the prize for the key, and that throws off their planning. The key is the thing that gets you the prize, and you have never confused the two. You're not just waiting us out. You're maneuvering for the knockout punch—and I'll figure out what that is."

"Maybe that's why I want you with me. It'll be safer."

Jander stood, slowly. "I don't know how you got in here, or how you plan to leave, but my people have bunkers all over this hill. If I start yelling, you'll be in irons by sunup."

"And handed over to Asterlit by noon." Leeger didn't move.

"I wouldn't give you to that prick."

"You wouldn't have any choice. Command would make you. Just like they're going to make the Force give up the remaining camps."

"They're going to move all those people to the mines?"

"The ones that are left. We've been taking more

and more of them to safety, right under your noses, and nobody noticed."

"Somebody noticed." Jander sat back down. "The pigs were never meant to be food, were they? The refugees you're smuggling out just walk off with them."

"Very good. Even I didn't see that one coming. A guy who used to work for me realized we could defeat overhead surveillance by moving among the hogs, if we smeared their fat on us." Leeger chuckled lightly. "It's a little limited. You gotta keep the numbers down, and you can't direct these beasts for shit. So you go with 'em until you're out in the open and then you just split off, moving the way they do."

"The Sims on Verdur defeated our surveillance by gluing pieces of heat shielding on their smocks. Tough bastards." Jan pondered the news. "So is that how your little orange messenger gets around?"

"His name is Sunlight. He was born in the mines. Hates it down there. He goes wherever he likes, running with the hogs."

"He thinks highly of you."

"No more than I think of him. He's a lot like another kid I raised."

"You only raised me until I went to prep school."

"And what did you do at that school, the first time somebody pushed you?"

"I kicked his ass."

"I rest my case."

A breeze rode the slope, fluttering the leaves in the remaining trees. Jander broke the silence in a whisper. "I'm tired, Hugh. I've never been this tired."

Leeger laid a hand on Jan's shoulder and gave it a squeeze. "So tell me about your friend, the one you lost the other night."

CHAPTER 11

"This is bad," Zuteck warned between bites. "Whenever they're too nice to us, something awful is on the way."

"For a meal like this, let it be bad." Cusabrina responded. Most of the squad was seated around a table in a crowded mess hall, enjoying a meal of steak with every side dish they could name.

"Look at this place." Lightfoot craned her neck. "Everything's brand new. It's like we're the first ones to ever eat here."

"So who are all these other people?" Dellmore asked. Although the Banshees were wearing newly issued olive-colored flight suits, they didn't stand out in the sea of coveralls and fatigues. The mess hall was a kaleidoscope of uniforms, many of them wearing work belts and equipment monitors. "Never seen any of these faces before."

"Well, First Sergeant Blocker is sitting right there with the skipper, and there's Pelletier and her squad." Legacy chimed in, pointing.

"That's not what I meant," Dellmore said, cutting her off. "Who are all these strangers? And why'd they fly us straight inside this place from the field, without letting us see it from the outside?"

"I'd say they were more concerned with keeping us from being *seen*, not from seeing." Sergeant Tin answered in a tone laced with misgiving. The shuttle that had picked them up at the crater had shut down the surveillance feeds to their suits, and they'd disembarked inside a large hangar with sealed doors. Their suits had been taken away for maintenance, and they'd been escorted to a comfortable squad bay to shower up and guess at what was afoot.

"It's official—something's up." Bullhead slid into a seat next to Tin, leaning in. "I sneaked out onto a loading dock and got a look around. This is one big complex. The part we're in right here, it's a dome connected to a much bigger dome by a covered tunnel. I saw two other domes the same size as this one, and I'd guess they go all the way around the one in the center. There isn't a single window anywhere, and there are a *lot* of MPs patrolling the perimeter fence."

"I knew it. Place is like a jail." Zuteck shoved her

empty plate aside, and started on a bowl of ice cream. "This is *bad*."

"I know her. That's Carlisle." Dellmore spoke to the squad from a seat in an auditorium that was quickly filling with Banshees. "Breena, see the one that just walked in? That's Carlisle, right?"

"It is," Cusabrina answered. "And the one behind her looks likes Uplaster. Remember her?"

"Bet she's still a bitch. Walking with a limp, these days." Zuteck answered. Sitting next to her, Ayliss was trying to make sense of the gathering. The squad's veterans were spotting numerous Banshees from units that should have been far away and, judging from the greetings, hugs, and middle fingers being exchanged all over the room, they weren't the only ones.

"Hey, look at the back." Bullhead called in a low voice, and the squad made a show of stretching as they obeyed. A line of MPs had blocked the three rows at the top of the seating area, and a hatch in the rear of the auditorium was now admitting their occupants. Men in camouflaged fatigue trousers, chest-hugging long-sleeved tops, and black skull caps mutely filled the two top rows, leaving the third one empty except for the MPs facing the new arrivals. To a man they were below average height, with wiry frames and expressionless faces.

"Spartacan Scouts. Best recon there is, and Command treats them like criminals. Unbelievably brutal training. See that thing they're doing? Looking all bashful, eyes darting around a few seconds and then back to the floor? They just mapped out the whole room, all the exits, and all the weapons," Dellmore whispered in Ayliss's ear. "*God* I love those guys."

"Rig!" Lightfoot hissed from several seats down. Ayliss turned to look, and immediately saw what had caught her eye. She exchanged a wide-mouthed look of surprise with Legacy and Bullhead.

"What is it?" Dellmore asked.

"See that dark-haired sergeant, the one with the electronic eye? That's Sergeant Stempful. She was our chief trainer in Banshee Basic. And the ones behind her? All her NCOs."

"My, my." Dellmore giggled, sliding down in her seat. "Ol' Zuteck is right. If they're cleaning out the Basic Training cadre, this one's gonna be big."

The seats were almost filled when the lights were lowered and a large monitor flickered into life in front of them. For a moment, Ayliss believed a clip from a horror movie had somehow been projected by mistake, but then the entire throng surged to their feet without a sound or an explanation. Inured to military protocol, she popped to attention along with the others, standing rigidly with her eyes fastened on the face looming over her.

Seen from the shoulders up, the figure wore the dress uniform of a general in the Human Defense

Force. However, it was the head that held Ayliss's attention. No hair, no nose, and skin that looked like sandpaper. The eyes glowed with terrible intent, and even when the voice came through the speakers it was impossible to determine the gender.

"Take your seats, please." The Banshees almost threw themselves down, and Dellmore took the opportunity to lean in close to her. "General Immersely."

Ayliss stared in wonder at the highest-ranking Banshee of them all. Although Banshee units were assigned by fleet and space sector, and therefore commanded by admirals or generals, Immersely was their ultimate superior. Looking out of the corners of her eyes, Ayliss saw that the entire room was transfixed.

"I chose to address you without my facial prosthetic because I wanted to mark this occasion. As some of you may have already guessed, for the first time in the war every active service Banshee will be committed to a single operation. You have been gathered together to prepare for a mission that I believe will bring this war to an end."

Inwardly, Ayliss frowned. Raised among a political elite who used soaring phrases like that one with abandon, she had a deep suspicion of such lofty pronouncements. So many propaganda campaigns had been designed to give the impression that volunteering for the Force, donating to the latest cause, or even voting for a certain politician would hasten the day when the conflict with the Sims would be finally brought to a victorious conclusion. Born into the war, into the very family that ran it, Ayliss had ceased long ago to believe it would ever end. That it *could* ever end.

"What I'm going to share with you right now is information that is so highly classified that it should explain why you've been sequestered. You will remain under a condition of total lockdown until this mission is completed, but only because it is vital not to tip our hand.

"Thanks to the efforts of a wide-ranging team of scientists and Force personnel, we have located the planet that is the origin of the Sim enemy we have faced for so long."

Despite her pessimism, Ayliss joined a collective gasp from the audience.

"We have identified the entities that are making the Sims." The skull on the screen moved its nerveless lips into a grimace of hostility. "And you are going to exterminate them."

"**G**ood afternoon." The Banshee captain was tall, with strawberry blond hair and a burn mark on her right cheek that stood up like an exclamation point. Wearing pressed camouflage fatigues, she stood in front of a large wall monitor. "I'm Captain Erica Varick, and I have the dubious distinction of having met both of the shapeshifting aliens that humanity has encountered so far."

Seated in a briefing room just large enough for her Banshee company, Ayliss straightened up in her seat. Jan had mentioned Varick several times in a heavily censored message, and Ayliss had already deduced that she'd accompanied her brother to Roanum on what was publicly labeled a hoax.

"You all know this clip." Varick waved a hand at the monitor, which activated to show the image of the original shapeshifter just before it was destroyed. Standing in a vertical tube with transparent walls, the thing appeared to be a naked human female with rust-red hair. Alarm lights flashed all around her, and a mechanical voice warned that an alien presence had been detected on the station.

Foamy chemicals splashed down on the figure in the tube, burning its flesh and removing its hair. It propped itself up against the cylinder's unbreakable wall, glaring at something outside the video frame. Its arms began to tremble after a time, and then it disintegrated into a swirling cloud of tiny, moth-like black dots.

"Stop video," Varick ordered, in a prearranged presentation that she was delivering personally to every Banshee company in the complex. "As you know, the shapeshifter had taken the form of Captain Amelia Trent in order to infiltrate the Twelfth Corps headquarters known as Glory Main. It was incinerated inside its decontamination tube, but not before being scanned completely—including the specks into which it resolved when it abandoned its human form.

"I was present at this event, and as a result I was assigned to investigate a second contact with the shapeshifting alien race. One of their members was reported to have contacted a Holy Whisper settlement on Roanum, asking to meet with representatives of our government. You may have heard that this contact turned out to be fraudulent, but I've been cleared to tell you it was not."

Varick seemed to be looking directly at Ayliss, who leaned forward with her fingertips resting on the seat in front of her.

"It was another shapeshifter, and it had taken the same form I saw on Glory Main. It not only resembled the entity that impersonated Captain Trent, but it also demonstrated detailed knowledge of the previous shapeshifter's sojourn among us humans— including its demise. It maintained that the members of its race are indeed shapeshifters, that they are all telepathically connected, and that they infiltrate new species in order to learn more about them.

"That last part was a lie. In an unguarded moment, the alien revealed that it—and its predecessor—had one goal in contacting humanity. They want the Step. That *thing* told me that once they gained the Step they would send a Sim invasion force to all of the settled planets and wipe out humanity."

Varick paused, to let her audience absorb the implications of that statement. The seated Banshees remained silent, so she continued. "Our contact with the second alien took the form of several meetings over a number of days. At the end of each encounter, the shapeshifter would walk off into what was essentially a barren desert. Orbital and aerial tracking attempted to determine where it went, but failed every time. However, on one of those occasions the heat signature given off by the alien—which matched a human heat signature—disappeared in a burst of specks very similar to the particles scanned on Glory Main."

Varick waved again, and the monitor changed to the forbidding gray surface of the unidentified target planet introduced to the Banshees the night before.

"Long-range surveillance of the planet believed to be the source of the Sims revealed an important piece of data some time ago. After observing the latest Sim ship launch from inside the planet, scanners identified roughly one hundred more craters which could perform the same function. Those openings received special attention, and so this behavior was recorded."

The monitor played an assortment of different tapes showing the clouds of moth-like specks emerging and then performing their arcane aerial dances over the ruins of Omega's lost cities.

"For reasons unknown, extremely large numbers

of these moth-like things left the craters simultaneously all over the planet, and then flew around in precise formations. Earlier scanning had detected the ruins of ancient cities just beneath the target planet's soil, and each of these clouds took on the dimensions of those ruins while flying over their locations. They performed this ritual for almost an hour, and then returned to the inside of the craters.

"While we have not yet determined what they were doing, we were able to conduct detailed scans of the particles. They are an exact match for what was observed at Glory Main."

The reaction this time was more vocal. The assembled soldiers gave off an assortment of utterances ranging from brief whistles to animal grunts and one comment from Captain Breverton that made her troops laugh.

"*Got* you, motherfucker."

"Motherfucker is right. I spent a fair amount of time speaking with the alien while it was in human form, and it was exceedingly clever. It seemed reasonable and very human, until it felt it could drop the mask. It expressed a deep-seated hatred and contempt for humanity, and an intense desire to destroy us."

"What did it say it wanted originally, Captain?" Tin called out. "Before it dropped the mask?"

"It offered to broker a peace between us and the Sims. The aliens are still the only entities that can communicate with both sides in this war, which is why it was so important to meet with this thing." Varick raised a hand, silencing the obvious question. "I've been ordered not to reveal anything more about the contact with the shapeshifter, but I promise you this: I have shared every bit of information I have that has bearing on this mission."

"**M**ortas." Erica nodded at Ayliss when she joined her on the low stage. The rest of the company was leaving the auditorium, but Captain Breverton had relayed Varick's request to speak with Jander's sister. "It's nice to meet you. Your brother was the other half of that mission to Roanum."

"I'd guessed as much, from the Bounce stories and the parts of his messages the censors let me see. He's on Celestia now, and I hear they're even worse about controlling what gets out."

"They are at that. I got a couple of messages from him early on, and think he got my responses. Once they pulled me into the planning cell here, it's been a total blackout."

"You were corresponding, ma'am?" Ayliss cocked her head to the side, smiling in insubordinate insinuation. "He didn't tell me that."

"I suspect there's a lot he didn't tell you." Varick returned the smile. "That's why I called you over. It didn't seem right to be in the same room and not introduce myself."

"How is he?" Ayliss asked, and then reconsidered her words. "I mean, how is he doing?"

The two women burst into muted snickers.

"I'm worried about him, on Celestia. Your brother's rebellious streak could get him in hot water in a place like that."

"If even half of what we've been hearing is true, he'd have good reason. But he loves the Orphans, and respects his commanders. That should keep him in line."

"I'm not sure of that." Varick looked past Ayliss, making sure the remaining Banshees were out of earshot. "You know that second alien I mentioned? We had it trapped in a Transit Tube, and it was laughing at us because it believed we were too junior to decide what happened to it."

"What did happen to it, ma'am?"

"Jan was going to jettison it, tube and all, to burn up in Roanum's atmosphere. He knew the thing would outsmart the bigwigs if it got to meet them."

"Did he do it?"

"No. I did."

"You've got a bit of the rebel in you too, eh, Captain?"

"I'm starting to see that as a Mortas family trait."

Ayliss looked at the exit, seeing that the remaining

Banshees were all gone. "I've got to catch up with my squad, but I'd like to continue this. Come eat with us tonight."

"Love to. Listen, so far the attack plan hasn't solidified—"

"Surprising, seeing how well those ground sensors were working."

"Hey, at least Command recognizes those things are junk. Most other times, they'd say we weren't using them properly."

"We, ma'am? I haven't seen many of you staff types out training with us."

"That's my point. They're still deciding how to pull this thing off. One option is to blow the whole place apart, which would be my preference. But with those monitors not working, and our only other data coming from a great distance, I think you know what's coming."

"Somebody's gonna have to go into those holes."

"We have to know what's down there. Right now the idea is to use recon 'bots, but no recon 'bot can get past a locked hatch. The aliens might have gone to a lot of trouble to keep the surface of that planet nice and dull, but I'm betting it's very different, just below the surface."

"Which means humans have to do it."

"Right. That's the reason the Spartacans are here, but they've only got a company's worth trained in suit work. I think the Banshees are going to have to do the rest. And I'm not going to sit this one out up in orbit."

"You sure that's why you're asking to go with my squad, ma'am?"

"What else would it be?"

"My brother asking you to look out for me." Ayliss chuckled. "He does seem to have some kind of influence with you."

"He didn't ask me to do that. In fact, he offered to get me a job with your stepmother."

"And you turned it down? You're a good match for him—you don't know a good deal when you see it."

"I'm Banshee through and through. If my sisters are going into those craters, I'm going with them."

"All right. I'll take it to my squad leader and see what she and the others say. Come sit with us tonight." Ayliss headed for the exit. "My partner Dellmore's gonna like you. I can tell."

Erica shook her head while trying not to laugh. "Fuck you, Mortas."

"Why do I think you've said those words before?"

Ayliss tried not to rush, slipping through the crowded passage that led to the big dome in the middle of the complex. Each of the smaller domes was the home and training area of separate Banshee battalions, but the big work was going on in the center. Most of it was off-limits, as she and her squadmates had learned through seemingly innocent off-duty wandering, but the spaces where their suits were being overhauled were not.

Blocker stood next to a station where the separated halves of an armored suit hung from a dark frame. Deek Orton, another of Blocker's comrades from Larkin Station who'd been forced to flee Zone Quest's wrath, was standing next to him pointing at a handheld.

"See right here? That's the only available space."

"So put it there." Blocker answered.

"But it's gonna interfere with—" Orton squinted down the line, and then nudged the much larger Blocker. "First Sergeant, visitor inbound."

Blocker intercepted Ayliss, guiding her away from the sparks of an overhead welding gun. Once they'd crossed a yellow warning line painted on the floor, he stopped. "This looks urgent."

"We just got briefed on what Command thinks the shapeshifters actually look like."

"Yeah. Big clouds of gnats."

"How did you know that?"

"That tape from Glory Main was distributed all over the war zone almost two years ago. You don't need a degree in astrophysics to see the connection." Ayliss glared up at him, and Blocker relented. "Okay, I got the same briefing. So what's wrong?"

"I talked to Captain Varick, the Banshee—"

"I know who she is. What did she say?"

"They're cooking up a plan where Banshee teams are going inside the craters on the target planet."

"Got to. We can't afford to guess here. And it won't just be Banshees. We got a specialized Spartacan outfit, and every suit-wearing special ops team, too."

"Okay, but what about this?" Ayliss leaned in. "So far, fire is the only thing that we're sure can destroy the shapeshifters. The only thing we know about those craters is that they make great big ships down there. So when we go poking around inside those things, something unexpected is going to happen."

"It always does."

"If it's a big enough surprise, the higher-ups are gonna freak out and thermo-nuke the place. With us inside it."

Blocker beamed at her with affection. "Look who's developing some good strong paranoia. My Little Bear."

"I'm fucking serious."

"Don't worry about a thing. If you thought of this, so did a lot of other people. Now get back to your squad."

"Bear!" she barked. "This is *Command* we're talking about. They're stupid as hell, and they don't give a shit. My sisters are not going to die for no good reason . . . like that doe that got killed because it ran the wrong way."

Blocker nodded, looking solemn. "Leave it to me. And focus on your training. Concentrate on the role they give you."

Ayliss cast him a doubtful look, and then hurried off. Blocker watched her go, and then returned to Orton.

"She onto us, First Sergeant?"

"No. It was something else." Blocker paused, and then raised his eyes to the cavernous ceiling. "But it did give us an additional job. Where's that thief Jerticker?"

CHAPTER 12

"**C**ome on over, Jan." Major Hatton's voice spoke inside his helmet, calling Mortas away from the activity that surrounded him. First Battalion's A Company had shuttled into a new position the night before, and he stood on a low hill in its center. All around him soldiers were digging in, emplacing obstacles, and performing the endless tasks of creating a defensive perimeter.

The location had little to recommend it. Apart from the small hill, it was as flat and empty as the surrounding plain, and all the materials the troops would need to construct bunkers had to be shuttled in. The position was covered by aerial drones and orbital rocketry, but as a spot to fight off a determined attacker it left a lot to be desired.

Mortas walked past a circle of radiomen who always

accompanied the brigade's commander, Colonel Watt. A mobile headquarters, they used the communications gear in their armor and helmets to coordinate with and direct the brigade's other two battalions. Watt had come out to the new emplacement that morning, and Major Hatton had summoned Jander there as well.

The two commanders stood apart from the rest of the soldiers working on the hill, Hatton large and bear-like where Watt was average height and barrel-chested. Both men turned goggled eyes to face Mortas as he approached.

"Major Hatton tells me you received another communication from the Orange last night, Jan."

"Hugh Leeger visited me on the Mound, sir." Jander stood at attention, unsure how his meeting would be taken.

"Now that is interesting." Watt slid his goggle lenses up inside his helmet, leaving the frames pressed against his dark cheeks. He looked around, squinting in the sunlight, and then noticed Mortas's posture. "Relax, Jan. Major Hatton's told me the basics, and you're not in any trouble. I doubt Leeger gave you a chance to take him prisoner."

"He walked right up to my garden, unarmed and alone. I didn't try to capture him because I knew he'd be handed over to Asterlit, sir."

"Not if I could help it." Watt raised his index finger. "I've had to brief that guy several times, and it's like talking to a robot. Hard to understand how someone with so little emotion can be perpetrating so much misery."

"That was one of the reasons Leeger gave for his visit, sir. He said that Asterlit has secretly reopened several of the mines that the slaves didn't capture, and that he's manning them with refugee labor. He said they're forced to work in exchange for their rations."

"Dear God. Just when you think we're getting somewhere with this disaster." Watt exhaled, and for the first time Jan saw fatigue in the man's face. The Orphan Brigade's commander unfastened his helmet, and motioned for the other two men to sit on the ground with him. "I suppose I shouldn't be surprised."

"Sir?"

"History, Jan. As brutal as the war with the Sims has been, we forget how much cleaner it is than the wars fought on Earth. No cities, no civilians, no refugees. Just two armies going at it out in the boondocks. Heck, the way Sam dies in captivity, we don't even have any experience running prisoner camps anymore.

"Some of those ancient conflicts on Earth got awfully nasty when you added in the civilians. Social order was replaced by roving bands of men with guns. As if that wasn't bad enough, you sometimes had hordes of the displaced, completely at your mercy. I'm not excusing any of it, but it's easy to see how monstrous abuse flourished under those circumstances."

"I like to think it takes a certain kind of mindset to commit those crimes, sir." Major Hatton offered.

"So do I. Unfortunately, the galaxy is full of people like Asterlit and the oligarchs who used to run this place. They certainly had that mindset, and the rebellion hasn't taught them a thing. I swear, talking to Asterlit, it's like he sees the people around him as playing pieces to be used up in a game that only he understands."

"Leeger said that several refugee camps under Asterlit's control had been moved to the mining areas, sir. It wouldn't be difficult to confirm that, using our reconnaissance assets."

"The difficulty comes after you confirm it. Every Force unit on Celestia ultimately answers to Asterlit. That's the only way we can legally operate here, the only way we can legally have crossed the CHOP Line out of the war zone. It would do no good to report these crimes to the individual who ordered them."

"If I may, sir? Maybe we tell someone else."

"You remember when you reported to this brigade, Jan? The day we met?"

"Yes, sir."

"I told you that the Purge had politicized the Force, eroding trust where trust is of paramount importance. I also told you that we don't play those games in this brigade. I asked if you were a politician's kid having an adventure in the war zone, or if you were an Orphan."

"I'm an Orphan, sir. No matter what."

"I know that. And you have no idea how much it pains me to say this. Our policy remains the same, but that's as far as it goes. We will not tolerate any abuse in any area we control, or any abuse that occurs in front of us, regardless of where we are. Nothing you've been told by Leeger violates either of those conditions."

"Leeger also said that Asterlit was maneuvering to transfer the remaining refugees from Force control, sir."

"Leeger is leading a rebel force that would like nothing better than to have us lock horns with the Celestian government."

"But what if he's right, sir?"

"I understand your concern." Watt raised a conciliatory hand. "Unfortunately, every refugee in the camps is still a Celestian citizen, under the control of their government. They can move them around as they see fit."

"And if they move them to the mines, sir? People we were protecting?"

"Jan!" Hatton barked, and Mortas went silent.

"It's all right," Watt responded. "You didn't catch up with us until we'd been here for a month, so you don't know what it was like. We were pulling every job except the one we were trained to do. We're a light infantry strike force, and they had us running convoy security and guarding supply dumps. Asterlit tried to have us assigned as security for the SOA three times, and if he'd succeeded we would never have gotten back to what we do best."

Watt looked out over the positions again, and for the first time Mortas was able to imagine him as an old man even though he wasn't even fifty.

"And even that's not good enough. We've racked up some impressive numbers, especially against the Flock and the smaller rebel outfits, but the Orange are our primary targets and we've lost track of them. It's good to know that Leeger is still in the area, but it still leaves us having done little to influence his actions."

"Sir?" Jander already knew what Watt was going to tell him, but feigned incomprehension.

"Look around you. Is this a proper spot to plunk down an Orphan company? No. We're dangling the bait all across the brigade's sector, in the hopes that Leeger won't be able to hold his people back.

"We're doing this because we're running out of time. Asterlit is going to pull us from this mission if we don't get better results, and this time we're going to be manning the walls and gates around that fat-cat playland in the capital. Leeger's waiting us out, so our only chance is to trick him into fighting us, or hope that Asterlit forgets about us."

"Even if it means the refugees from Resolve go to the mines, sir?"

"I cannot let the soldiers of this brigade come under that man's direct control, Lieutenant Mortas. Not if I still want to call myself their commander."

"I want to apologize, sir." Mortas stood with Hatton at the base of the hill, watching a flight of shuttles approach. "I was out of line."

"Actually, you weren't." The major held up a hand, indicating that a message from one of First Battalion's other elements was coming in. He listened to whoever it was, and then answered them. "No. No, we've discussed this before. If you go helping out with the patrols there, you might not be able to respond quickly if A Company needs help. Yes, I know the troops are sitting around doing nothing. That's the whole idea. If the Orange make a move against this place, it's gonna be big and fast. I want you ready to move."

With the conversation ended, he returned to Jander. The incoming shuttles weren't far away, and Mortas was going to leave on one of them. "God do I miss Emile."

Mortas didn't respond, inwardly shocked that Hatton would criticize one of his company commanders. He must have been speaking with Wyn Kitrick, who'd taken command of B Company after Dassa's death, and clearly Kitrick's impetuous nature was conflicting with the overall plan. B Company, including Jander's old platoon, was on standby at a base not unlike the Mound.

"So what was I saying? Yeah. Colonel Watt's just like the rest of us. He's caught between a rock and a hard place, and he doesn't like working for Asterlit any more than you do." Hatton exhaled loudly. "I honestly wish the rebels had wiped out the Celestian government before we could get here. Would have been a whole lot cleaner."

"Sir, Leeger told me that he got onto the Mound in the back of a truck. He said there are a lot of Force personnel who are helping the rebels."

"Not surprising, given how many troops deserted once they got here. And they're not the only ones who wonder if we're killing the wrong people."

CHAPTER 13

"**Y**ou're a complete bastard, Mirror." Olech's words were strained and choppy. "You already know what happened here. Why do I have to re-live it?"

"Knowing what happened and understanding it are two different things, in this case." Mirror walked next to him through a broad corridor jammed with armed men in body armor and helmets. Though keyed-up and alert, the security teams didn't notice the middle-aged twins who passed through them.

"What's to understand?" Olech's eyes were fastened on a sealed door at the end of the hallway. No matter how much he wanted to back away from it, he couldn't stop moving forward. "I'd just been in the middle of a huge firefight, in the Senate chamber no less, and the only reason I lived was because Faldonado died on top of me. Half the Senate was wiped out, and the Interplanetary President was killed in what could have been called an assassination."

"Called?" Mirror stopped in front of a young security man with dried blood on his cheek. For the first time, Olech thought he detected anger in his guide. "You know it was an assassination."

"I mean back then, when it happened. Nothing was clear. I didn't even know who was alive and who was dead, when this meeting took place. It was chaos."

"That is why it is so important to review this episode." Instead of leaving him, Mirror stepped up to the door. He turned with an expectant look. "Are you coming?"

In a departure from previous experiences, the two identical men walked straight through the barrier like ghosts. Olech cringed as the lights of the big room showed him the survivors of the massacre, minus the ones who'd been badly wounded. The room itself was used for classified briefings under normal circumstances, and resembled a smaller version of the Senate chamber. Terraced rows of curved tables rose up from a low stage, and the seats were occupied by a ragged assortment of men and women. Some were slumped on the desktops while others were gathered in tiny, whispering groups, but most of them bore rusty discolorations on their suits and uniforms.

Olech stepped away from Mirror, surprised to be allowed to move freely. Now that he was in the room, the old composure returned. Knowing there was no way to avoid the memory, he walked down the side aisle and stopped next to a man roughly fifteen years his junior. Slumped in the immovable chair, his neck and hands caked with another man's blood, Senator Olech Mortas stared out into the air.

"It's all right." He spoke to the younger version of himself, but there was no response. "Do what you have to do."

"But that's not what you did, is it?" Mirror spoke to him from up close, and Olech was shocked to find they were now standing in the back, looking down on the battered group.

"Shut up, Mirror. You know what's about to happen."

The door opened, and Horace Corlipso rushed through. Dressed in a dark suit with a high collar, he moved with strength and decision. The low conversations ended as he went down the aisle, and even the most benumbed senators raised their heads. Horace reached the stage, and held his palms out.

"Everything is back under control." He spoke as if addressing a skittish animal. "We've suffered through a terrible tragedy today, but I want you to know that you're all safe. Loyal troops have secured the building, and we must remember that we are all that is left of humanity's government."

"He practiced those lines for hours," Mirror commented. "Especially that part about loyal HDF personnel."

"I *know*."

Horace took a step closer. "President Larkin is dead, and the news of this tragedy cannot be kept secret for long. We are a race at war with a powerful enemy bent on our destruction. We *cannot* allow this situation to spin out of control."

Olech watched his own rust-colored back straighten several rows down, and he raised a hand as if to push something away.

"What happened today was just a terrible series of misunderstandings, but no one will believe that, given the bloodshed. Given the death of the president."

Mirror and Olech watched as faces turned left and right, the awful realization dawning.

"We are now the leaders of our entire race. With the president dead, we command our armed forces. We can decide, right here, right now, to take charge of this awful situation. Or we can let this devolve into accusations of plots that will lead to factionalism and possibly civil war."

"No." A senator Olech didn't know uttered the syllable involuntarily, through a dry throat that he then cleared. "No!"

"That's it." Horace pointed at the man, nodding vigorously. "Don't just sit there. We can't just sit here. We have to act."

Other voices sputtered their assent, but the younger Olech didn't join them. From the back of the room, Olech watched himself turn, face confused, as if not recognizing the people around him.

"We have to move now," Horace shouted. "We have to safeguard the highest command positions in the Force, inside and outside the war zone. The top leadership positions must be occupied by reliable officers."

"Amazing, the power of those words," Mirror whispered. "Safeguard. Reliable."

"Stop it, Mirror."

"It would be easy to be swayed by his argument—most of them were."

"So was I."

"Really?"

The young Olech appeared to have recovered his senses. His hands clutched the edge of the desk, and his shoulders rose and fell with his breathing.

"We cannot take the chance that some general out there will decide he's a modern Julius Caesar, lead his troops across the CHOP Line, and plunge us into civil war," Horace continued. "The authority to choose commanders rests with the Senate. Even without this tragedy, what we do tonight is within our purview. We are going to purge the top ranks of anyone whose loyalty is in doubt."

"But, how can we know who's loyal?" shouted a

white-haired senator, his voice cracking. "Who's to decide that?"

"We will. And the only way we can know for certain, is if the men and women in this room provide the names of officers for whom they can vouch personally."

"Stand up," Olech whispered, pained eyes on himself. "You know what he really means."

"Our troops are locked in combat with the Sims this very moment," Horace shouted. "They cannot be put in a position of doubt. They cannot be told one moment that they serve this commander, and a moment later told that it's someone else. The replacement of the doubtful officers will have to be instant, with no warning and no discussion. As if they died in combat, and they were replaced by the next officer in the chain of command."

"What are you sitting there for?" Olech yelled. He tried to move, but found his feet nailed to the floor. "You *know* what's about to happen! You were out there!"

"What about President Larkin?" called a voice from the back. "How do we explain his absence? How do we explain any of this?"

A hush fell over the throng, and Horace nodded again. "You know that today's events were triggered by Larkin's foolishness. Springing his nonsense plan on us, and not expecting a violent response. I'm sorry to speak ill of a dead man, but Larkin bears the responsibility for everyone who died today.

"So let that be his legacy. Once we've purged the command ranks, we'll explain to the people that Larkin had unilaterally ordered those commanders to retreat from the Sims because he believed the war was lost. We'll tell them the truth about how he died, that it was indeed an accident, but they'll know we, their leaders, opposed his defeatist actions with strength and resolve."

"Don't buy it, you fool." Olech wasn't shouting anymore, his voice pleading even as the young Olech appeared to relax. To subside. "He's playing you!"

"We're going to offer a new strategy, one that honors our thousands of fallen heroes, instead of turning our backs on their sacrifice." Horace looked at Olech. "And who better to do that than one of our own, one of our saviors, one of our sacred Unwavering?"

Olech watched his bloodstained hand reach up, touching the red ribbon that Lydia had always insisted he wear. Though she'd been gone for five years, he knew his younger self felt he'd never needed her counsel more.

"Senator Mortas?" Horace reached toward him with an open hand. "Will you take that assignment? Will you tell us how this war *really* should be fought?"

The forty-year-old rose to his full height, and a

hush fell over the room. He squared his shoulders, and pressed his arms against his sides.

"Gladly, Senator Corlipso."

They were back in the hall outside the briefing room, but this time it was empty. Olech sagged against the wall, and Mirror loomed over him.

"The next day Horace announced that President Larkin had told the Interplanetary Senate that he'd ordered the Human Defense Force to radiate every habitable planet outside the war zone, in an attempt to create a firebreak in space. The Force was going to abandon the planets already seized, and use the Step to leap back to the settled worlds."

"Head in the Sand." Olech muttered.

"That's what you and your co-conspirators dubbed that plan—even though it was a complete fabrication."

"I know. I made it up myself."

"It was replaced by the 'Head On' plan, which committed humanity to fighting the Sims wherever they appeared."

"Again, I was its author."

"Horace announced the creation of the Emergency Senate, after explaining that Larkin and the others had been killed in a tragic misunderstanding. It would be some years before the office of Chairman of the Emergency Senate was created, but you won that position on the night of the murders."

"There were more murders. Lots more. The Purge."

"Yes. Shielded by the Head in the Sand lie, Horace and his friends set about assassinating or arresting every officer above the rank of major who wasn't solidly behind them. In many cases they had the new appointees remove their predecessors personally. A bond of blood and guilt."

"I didn't know they'd do that!"

"But you did suspect."

"The president had been killed, along with half the Senate, and *nothing was going to bring them back!*" Olech shouted. "Ever been in a war, Mirror? One night I left my platoon on a hill, going back with a detail for ammo, and while we were gone the Sims bombarded that place for hours. By the time I got back they were all dead. They died, and I wasn't there with them!"

His duplicate regarded him sadly, but said nothing.

"But what did I do? I was just a private, but I reorganized the defenses. They hit us time and again, but we held them off because I didn't sit there crying about the dead." He pointed a shaking hand at the door leading back into the briefing room. "Just like in there. I didn't have the luxury of standing in the back, watching! And I couldn't bring back Larkin or the others. We were in a losing war, and we had to make the best of a bad situation!"

"Horace certainly made the best of it."

Olech brought his index finger up in front of Mirror's eyes. "We held the alliance together. We didn't collapse into a civil war. We didn't leave those troops with divided leadership. And how about that leadership, Mirror? Some of the generals who were removed were the same incompetents who got so many of my buddies killed. Who almost got *me* killed. And you know why Horace was so hot to butcher them instead of just reassigning them? Because they were just as political, just as careerist, just as corrupt as the ones who supported him—they were just supporting someone else!"

Mirror's face swam in front of his eyes, and then Olech found himself standing inside a large bunker made of logs and sandbags. It was filled with soldiers, most of them in combat gear, but all of them bareheaded. His son Jander stood at the front, speaking to the group.

"I met Emile Dassa when he was fifteen and I was seventeen. We attended the same prep school, but Emile wasn't there long. He told me that his father had been an aide to a general killed in the Purge, when my dad and his cronies got rid of the Force officers they considered disloyal. Emile told me that his father had recently died under mysterious circumstances, even though the Purge was seven years earlier."

"Where is this, Mirror? Jan looks so tired."

"He's eulogizing his best friend from the war. This is a memory from a soldier who attended, collected when that man was evacuated for his wounds, using the Step."

Jander looked grim, but he rested a consoling hand on a muscular man with startling green eyes who appeared ready to collapse with remorse.

"Emile said he believed my dad and his friends had murdered his father, after overlooking his connection to that general for several years. We fought that very night, and I broke his arm. He was kidnapped from the school infirmary by people trying to gain favor with my father, and shipped to the war zone. He was assigned to a brutal colonial militia outfit, but fought so well that he gained a commission in the Force and then joined the Orphan Brigade.

"Emile forgave me for what I'd done to him, and we became good friends. He taught me a lot about being an infantry officer, and he was the best commander I've known out here. But he wouldn't have been out here if it hadn't been for me and my family. And that is why I say that Captain Emile Dassa was the final victim of the Purge."

The scene dimmed, and then Olech was back in the empty hallway.

"That was a rotten thing to do, Mirror."

"So was the Purge."

"I didn't know that was going to happen!"

"But what did you do, when you found out about it?"

The raised hand dropped to Olech's side. His lips

puckered, and he slid down the wall until he was sitting on the floor. "I told myself the same thing I told myself in the war. They were gone, and nothing was going to bring them back. I had to deal with the present reality. I had a responsibility to hold it all together."

Mirror squatted down. "And that was your mistake. That rationalization allowed you to tolerate a long string of crimes you should have opposed. And to commit some of those crimes yourself."

Olech shook his head before raising red eyes to Mirror. "Don't you think I know that? Weren't you listening, when my capsule was launching and you grabbed me? I know those were my thoughts. That I'd done terrible things in the name of defending humanity."

"Of course I heard. But you told yourself your heart was pure the entire time, no matter what heinous acts you ordered. And you still believe that."

"Is that what this is all about? Convince me I was wrong?"

"No. I'm answering your original question. You climbed into that capsule to find out why, after giving you the Step, my race never contacted yours again." Mirror touched his cheek. "Our study of humanity in Step sleep showed there was no way for us to ever safely interact with you."

"Because we're capable of such barbarity?"

"No. Because you're capable of committing that

barbarity and then convincing yourselves it wasn't barbaric at all."

"Timothy, for an intelligent man you're being awfully stupid." Reena didn't look at her guest. Her gaze swept out over the grounds of the Unity Plaza campus, from an outdoor pavilion high on the central tower. "I told you to get me evidence that Zone Quest has been colluding with Asterlit."

"You think there's any proof of this?" Kumar cast a worried glance at Ulbridge. "They've discussed it in meetings I've attended, but apart from that there is no way for me to substantiate a thing."

"Your testimony is going to be a bit weak without it."

"Testimony? You never said anything about that. In what proceedings?"

"Why, the senatorial investigation that's going to lead to the dismantling of a much-hated megacorporation that's guilty of war profiteering and other crimes."

"There is no way I'm going to testify against Zone Quest. Even if you managed to break them up, their last act would be my murder. And you're not going to break them up. They're too powerful, their friends are too high-placed, and they'd only appear to be dismantled. You have no idea what you're fooling with there."

"Thanks to Nathaniel here, Damon Asterlit is about to become the face of the ongoing oppression on Celestia. Those accusations are going to cause quite a few of ZQ's high-placed friends to distance themselves. And when you prove that Asterlit and ZQ were joined at the hip, the whole thing will be a *fait accompli*. So get me the proof."

"What proof?"

"The ore is moving again. That's the evidence. So get the data showing the link between the minerals leaving Celestia and the raw materials coming into Zone Quest's hands. I'll do the rest."

"I don't know anything about that industry."

"You were one of Horace's top counselors, so play that up a little. Tell the ZQ board that your knowledge of pre-rebellion Celestia—you might want to suggest you know Asterlit better than you do—puts you in an excellent position to help make sure Asterlit's not robbing them."

"Madame Chairwoman, I cannot approach them that way without creating suspicion."

"Suspicion enough for them to throw you off of a tall building?"

Stone-faced, Ulbridge took a single step forward. Kumar shrunk back from the railing.

"I'll try. But it won't work."

"You're a very devious man, Timothy. I have faith in you." Reena looked at Ulbridge. "Nathaniel, have our guest escorted to the station."

Alone for a moment, Reena looked down on the long shadows stretching across the trees and lawns of the campus. Night would fall in only a few hours, and she would finally be away. Off to a sector of deep space where a specially assembled armada waited.

"Ma'am? I've brought Doctor Harlec." Ulbridge approached, with Dev Harlec in tow. The diminutive genius wore his trademark warm-up clothes and thick-lensed glasses.

"Dev." Reena extended her hand. "I apologize for interrupting your work, but this conversation had to take place in person. How is the translation software coming along?"

"The tape of the negotiation with the Sims has been a goldmine. Until now, our linguists only had intercepted transmissions to work with. They'd been forced to guess at the meanings of the different bird-like sounds, with limited success. However, having the precise translation allowed us to apply a range of metrics that have provided a key missing piece.

"In even the most basic conversations, the Sims appear to repeat the same sounds—the same trills, caws, and chirps—over and over. But we now know that the human ear simply can't detect the different warbles of those sounds—their pronunciation, if you will—which makes all the difference."

"So you've cracked it?"

"I wouldn't go that far. It was, after all, a recording of a discussion that only lasted a few hours."

"A conversation that had never taken place before in history. Sims speaking with humans through an alien translator. Every moment of those few hours was groundbreaking."

"I didn't mean to trivialize the event. We've made great strides in identifying actual words in the Sim vocabulary, and part of our team has started applying what we've learned to the database of intercepted transmissions. But the translation device itself is still a long way from operational."

"I'm going to need something from you in the near future. We're going to be broadcasting an urgent message to the Sims in the war zone, and it has to be accurate."

"Accurate or not, it will serve little purpose if we can't follow it with more communications. And the translation software is simply not up to that."

"Keep at it. Night and day." Reena placed a hand on his shoulder. "I can see you've burned up another set of eyes already, but we must be able to communicate with the enemy within the next month."

"It sounds like you're not telling me everything."

"That's fair." Reena raised a restraining hand when Ulbridge opened his mouth. The security man subsided, and she went on. "I'm about to go on a trip. When it's done, I hope to be able to tell the Sims that they've just lost the war and that it's time to talk peace."

CHAPTER 14

Ayliss wandered the quiet warship, unable to sleep. She knew that the stillness had been ordered from on high, to give the assault troops a chance to rest before the battle. The veterans in the squad had dropped off to sleep at once, but she'd found it impossible.

The tumultuous events of the previous days had ended so abruptly that they all ran together. The notice to cease training at the domes and prepare for immediate loadout. The shuttles taking them to the transports, and the transports Stepping them to the invasion fleet. The urgency and excitement of everyone she met on board, the atmosphere charged with the momentous nature of their mission.

She walked the passageways of the ship alone now, save for the occasional sighting of a crewmember soundlessly going about a task. The difference was stark, and unnerving. The entire vessel had hummed with activity, and she and her squad had moved from update briefings to suit prep to rehearsals and more update briefings as if on a conveyor belt.

Ayliss smiled involuntarily, remembering the delivery of paint tins and long brushes in the cavernous hold where Blocker's people had been running final checks on the suits. Command frowned on the Banshees' practice of painting female genitalia on their armor, an age-old tradition when fighting the all-male Sim combat troops, but General Immersely herself had ordered the distribution of the pigments and tools across the fleet.

Their armor had been colored an ashen shade that would allegedly provide some camouflage on Omega, and so the paint was a dark gray. The markings added by the Banshees had ranged from modest to outrageous, and Ayliss had walked around the bay to view the artistry. Returning to her own simple renderings, she'd burst out laughing to see that the top half of Dellmore's torso sported two demure circles with dots in the center that made them look like eyes. Blocker's man Orton had been standing in front of the rig, confounded by the difference between the symbols and Dellmore's ample bosom.

"Hey mister." Dell had spoken in fake annoyance, pointing at her T-shirt. "My tits are up here."

The joke had caused the squad to erupt in laughter, and Orton had blushed madly. Walking away quickly, he'd been heard muttering, "That's just not accurate. It's downright dishonest."

Ayliss finally reached the compartment toward which her wanderings had always been pointed, and she keyed in her identification before requesting admittance. The hatch opened with a burp, and she stepped inside a small room decorated with monitors and control panels. Its lone occupant sat facing her, a set of headphones down around his neck.

"Hello, Minister." Christian Ewing greeted her with a smile. "I thought you'd be resting."

"Minister." Ayliss snorted, pulling up a chair. "When are you going to stop calling me that? I'm just a private now."

"I dunno. In some way I'm always going to think of you as the governor of Quad Seven. And who knows? If this thing's as big as Command says, you may not be a private much longer."

"I'm going to need a lot more time in grade to get promoted to corporal."

"Not what I meant. If this does end the war, you'll be able to go home."

A sudden memory, of Ewing straddling the body of the Zone Quest manager Vroma Rittle. "You will too, if I have anything to say about it."

"That wouldn't be a smart move. The Guests have long memories, so even if you got me pardoned it wouldn't make a difference in the long run. No, looks like ol' Christian is going to be a deep-space cowboy for the rest of his days." He tapped the headphones. "Not that I mind."

"You still hearing the music that nobody else can? Even without . . . you know."

"You're not offending me. I used to wonder myself if it was the drugs." He seemed sad for a moment. "Honestly, I was a little afraid of that. But I've been straight since re-upping, and I get as much long-range signal duty as I want. It's still out there. I still hear it, and it's even more beautiful than before."

"What do you think it is?"

"It's too intricate to just be background, or bouncing waves of whatever. Somebody or something out there really has an ear for this."

Out there. The phrase brought back visions of the briefings and the footage of Omega and the dread of being stuck on the surface when Command blasted the planet into nothing. It made her heart thud, so Ayliss tried to focus on Ewing's story. "Ever try recording it?"

"Oh, lots of times. Funniest thing. When I'm listening to it, I can hand the 'phones to somebody right next to me and they don't hear it at all. Then, when I put 'em back on, the music's right there. So of course I recorded it, and you know what? I can't hear a thing on playback."

"You're a lucky man."

"That's not the word most people use."

"That's because most people can't see that something out there picked you to hear this. I envy you."

"Everything's going to be all right, Minister."

"Why do you say that?"

"Never seen you this keyed up before. Is it possible that you got your fill of the action, these past few months?"

"Given what we've got ahead of us, let's hope not."

They both laughed quietly, and Ewing reached out to the controls. "Wanna see the latest updates?"

"I've had my fill of *that*, thank you. It's all the same stuff, anyway."

"Ayliss." Ewing raised his eyebrows. "You forgotten my special skill set? I'm not talking about the diluted intel they pass out."

"You're kidding me." She leaned in, whispering, "You snatched the high-level info? Command will crucify you, they catch you with it."

"Nail you up right alongside me, they find out you watched it." Ewing's eyes burned with a crazy challenge, and his index finger hovered over a button. "So what'll it be?"

"Play it."

Ewing activated the largest monitor, showing the gray planet Omega. Colored lines slowly extended through space, indicating probes flying past the target. "Surveillance is getting closer and closer. If the aliens are watching, there's almost no way they could miss this. We're not even disguising the robot recon flights anymore. At first they just flew past at a distance, but when nothing happened they started working in wide orbits."

"Has there been any reaction?"

"Nothing. We'd already established the long-range coverage, concentrating on the identified craters, but there's been no response. It's driving Command crazy. Some of the honchos think it means the aliens are asleep down there, others think they're waiting for us to make a move, and a few even think the bad guys went overboard on staying hidden."

"Meaning what?"

"Even passive defenses can give you away. Scanners, antennae, telescopes, they all emit something. When your goal is to remain undetected, sometimes your best bet is to stay blind."

"But you don't believe that's what's going on."

"It doesn't fit the story. Command assumes that the shapeshifters captured one of the old factory ships a long, long time ago. They altered the human DNA on that ship to make the Sims with all their special characteristics. Then they made a whole lot of 'em, outfitted 'em with ships and guns, and the tools to make more ships and guns, and sent 'em out to fight us."

"You mean they're too smart to just be hiding in there?"

"Yes. When we finally get into those craters, I think we're going to find something that is going to absolutely astound us." They watched the different series of surveillance tracks crossing the blackness near the target, and when Ewing spoke he didn't look at Ayliss. "You know how I managed to kill Rittle?"

"No. I only saw the aftermath."

"Big son of a bitch, stronger than he looked."

"I know. I went straight for him, and he threw me into that bulkhead so hard it almost knocked me out."

"He tried the same with me, pulled me in close." Ewing's lips disappeared, and he shook his head as if to ward something off. "I grew up in a lousy neighborhood, no father, no brothers. Always getting beat up. So I got tired of that and started carrying a knife. Got it taken away from me a couple of times, but that taught me the secret. You want to cut somebody, make sure they don't even *suspect* you've got a blade until after you use it."

He wagged a finger at the screen. "I'm worried they know that."

"What's wrong?" General Immersely had donned her facial prosthetic, but the synthetic skin only moved near her mouth. "What did you see?"

General Merkit was waiting inside a small briefing room aboard the flagship *Aurora*. He activated the compartment's main screen, to show a view of Omega from space.

"We're close enough to detect large-scale motion

on the surface, provided it's not blocked by cloud cover."

"Large-scale motion."

"Very." The planet enlarged until it blotted out the darkness, and then the picture resolved until it focused on a broad plain. "This location is three miles west of Crater Number Ninety-Three."

The view seemed to be miles above the plain, but even from that vantage point a trail of dust was evident. It rose for several hundred yards, forming a cone that bloomed at its far end. At its origin, what appeared to be a freight train was running across the open on no tracks.

"Once we detected the activity, the satellite gave it priority." The view resolved yet again, swooping closer until the eddies of the gray cloud could be seen in motion. The train stormed over the dirt, but it was not a machine.

"It looks like a combination of a worm and a centipede." General Immersely walked up to the screen. "Must be enormous."

"We estimate it's five hundred yards long, and fifty yards in diameter. See the segments? It's like a string of spheres joined together."

"What's its locomotion?"

"Hard to tell, but your centipede analogy seems correct. Look at the tracks behind the cloud."

"Lots and lots of feet."

"Here's where it gets interesting." A shadow grew

on the marks of the creature's passage, and then crossed over the dust plume. It rippled and heaved like a set of rapids, and then caught up with the beast.

"Shapeshifters?"

"Yes. The scans match. We'd only seen them once before, at night, but that there is a gigantic swarm of the moth-things."

The creature became aware of its aerial pursuers, and started weaving in a serpentine gait as if to shake them off. The moth horde spread out along its length, and appeared to touch down on it.

"What are they doing?"

"After running this through a series of filters, our analysts believe they didn't land on it. They seem to be forming a kind of flying cocoon. As you can see, the creature didn't take kindly to that."

The dust storm grew in intensity as the beast accelerated, tearing up great clods of dirt in its desperate flight. With no warning, a tentacle many yards long erupted from one of its segments and swung at the air above it. Moments later it was joined by many others.

The picture widened, and Immersely gasped when she saw that the creature was headed directly for a sheer drop-off that ran for miles to either side in a crooked, broken edge.

"It's going to go over."

"We believe that was its intention all along."

The swarm tightened along the worm's length,

separating as the flailing tendrils sliced through them and then filling back in. The creature's weaving became more pronounced, slowing its progress, and then it began to turn away at seemingly the last second. Dust rose like a smoke bank, continuing over the edge of the precipice even as the beast itself swung to its right. The tentacles still swatted at the sky, but they'd lost their agility and seemed exhausted.

"They took it over," Immersely guessed. "It meant to go off the cliff, but they forced it to come away and to stop fighting them."

"Almost." The tentacles waved drunkenly as they retracted inside the segments, the irises closing as if they didn't exist. The elongated body came to a halt, parallel to the edge, trembling along its entire length. The swarm shimmered all around it, but then the giant worm seemed to slump to the dirt in a mighty crash. Dirt erupted from both sides, and then the beast started rolling sideways.

"See?" Merkit pointed. "It pulled in the feet as well."

The cloud broke free at the last instant before the enormous tube went over. It took thirty seconds to fall, slamming into the rock-covered deck below and exploding in a sickening lake of black ichor.

"There's been no indication that anything like that exists on that planet?"

"None. We reviewed the round-the-clock video of Crater Ninety-Three, and established that the creature did not come out of it. The moths did, and they went straight for it even though it was miles away and there were no tracks until it reached that plain."

"What are you saying?"

"My team believes that the shapeshifters have some kind of telepathic connection with the creature. That's how they found it, and that's how they almost turned it around."

"All right. But why?"

"My analysts have conjectured that there is a missing piece to our explanation of how the aliens created the Sims. Even with the ability to assume the shapes and functions of complex organisms, the amount of labor needed to create the equipment to manipulate human DNA, and then bring millions of Sims to life, would require a gigantic workforce."

"You're saying that those craters lead to caverns and tunnels that could be loaded with things like that beast?"

"We now suspect it could be a wide range of creatures, some like that one, many of them much smaller, with appendages that would allow them to perform the tasks directed by the aliens."

Immersely lowered herself into a chair. "When does the Chairwoman arrive?"

CHAPTER 15

"Maybe it won't be so bad." Captain Pappas sat with Mortas on the wall surrounding his garden. The sun had risen an hour before, and the base below them was alive with activity. "Hot chow, cold showers, real bunks."

"Never-ending guard duty, VIPs refusing to show their credentials, sneak thieves slipping through the wall."

"Life in the big city." Pappas sighed. "Colonel Watt fought it as hard as he could. But let's face it; we did some good work out here at first, but then the whole sector dried up. Your convoys are rolling unmolested, and the patrols haven't made contact in a week."

"So we get turned into Asterlit's palace guard for doing our job too well?"

"I'm not so sure of that. The Orange waited us

out, just like you said they would, but we were putting a nice big dent in the Flock until Asterlit started shutting down the camps. I was there when they took the last refugees out of Resolve; half the movers they brought left empty. I swear most of that camp had already run off to the rebels."

"How is this word not getting out, sir?"

"That's easy. Asterlit gets to block satellite, orbital, and drone surveillance wherever he likes. There are giant swaths of territory that might as well be controlled by the Sims, for all anybody knows about what goes on there."

"But we do know. They took the refugees to the mines, and turned them into slaves. It's like nothing's changed."

"It's worse than that. Any Force commander who questions what we're doing here gets relieved. Command has basically handed us over to Asterlit and his CIP thugs."

"And now we're gonna guard the wall around his little piece of heaven."

"I'm told he needs to send every green suit he can spare to control the mines. Which is funny, in a way. The refugee population in Fortuna Aeternum—outside the SOA's wall—has grown by leaps and bounds because of the forced relocation. They realized the camps were just holding pens, and they found a way into the city."

"He'll round them up next." Mortas shook his

head. "There has got to be a way to send the word out without putting Orphan commanders in hot water."

"The word's not good enough. You need evidence." Pappas tried not to smile, but failed. "Like footage from a manually controlled recon drone."

"You didn't."

"I had to. Friends of mine in one of those drone outfits redirected a couple of flights for me. It's even worse than you think. They've got thousands of refugees in these stinking pens. One flight got footage of carloads of children disappearing into the mine; another showed a food riot. Outside one of the pens they've got this whole row of wooden frames where they hang people up in all kinds of uncomfortable ways. Troublemakers, I guess."

"Did you get it out? To that underground circle of yours?"

"Of course. We've been slipping communications past Command for years."

"When that story breaks, they're gonna figure out who did it."

"My drone pals are covered. Both missions crashed, reported as downed by the rebels."

"What about you?"

"Can't say I'm comfortable with the idea of being inside Asterlit's compound. Which is why I'm gonna tag along with Colonel Watt and his staff this morning. They're visiting the Security Ministry for the first coordination meeting."

"You're not brigade staff—why are you going with them?"

"Because when you're really scared to do something . . . do it right away."

"I still don't get it." Mortas stood with Sergeant Leoni beside the Mound's quiet airstrip. "Why can't we leave the darts with you?"

"Once the brigade goes to Fortuna Aeternum, FITCO's not gonna have a home anymore. I have to find another outfit that needs us, and chances are they won't be in this sector. And I can't take two hundred darts with me."

"You could, if you just came with us. Wouldn't that be simpler?"

"Oh, much. *Too* much," the NCO replied. "First, we wouldn't have a job because the brigade's gonna be drawing supplies from all those nice warehouses inside the SOA. Second, there'd be all sorts of headquarters types asking where I got all these vehicles. Third, those same headquarters types would start looking into the personnel records and finding out half my boys and girls aren't where they're supposed to be. I am never taking this company into that rat's nest."

"We're not going to have this security mission forever, you know. Wouldn't it be better for you to just stay loose, work with some of the units here on the Mound, and then link up with us wherever we go next?"

"It's a bad idea to be an outfit that's just floating free, sir. Somebody notices, and next thing you know, you've been given a new home—like it or not. Always best to choose your own poison."

"I think I resent that."

"Don't. It's been a lot of fun working with you, sir." Leoni removed his helmet and scratched his head. "Tell you what. Leave the darts with me. I'll have my people find a nice shady spot to hide them, behind a big stack of crates that never moves. Hopefully they'll still be there when you come back."

"How will I know where to find them?" Mortas was asking when the noise dampers in his helmet snugged down three times around his ears. That meant an important message was about to come in, and he signaled for Leoni to put his helmet back on.

"All Orphan units. All Orphan units. Red three. Red three. I say again—red three." Jander thought he recognized the voice as one of Major Hatton's radiomen, but he was too busy reaching into a pouch on his armor to give it much thought. Red was the code word to switch to an Orphan emergency band, and the number indicated which encryption key to load so no one else could listen in. Finding the code device, he slid it into a port on his armor and flipped it to the third setting. All around them, members of

FITCO were donning their rigs and slotting the en-cryption key.

"This is Major Lucas Hatton." Jander's heart began to thud when he heard the measured formality. "I am the commander of First Battalion of the Orphan Bri-gade. I have received and confirmed a report that the brigade's commander, Colonel Jonas Watt, has been arrested in Fortuna Aeternum by Governor Asterlit."

Icy rage spread out across Mortas's body as he re-membered his own meeting with Asterlit. His hands curled into fists, and he had to force them to relax.

"The charges are insubordination and unlawful off-world communications. Colonel Watt and most of his primary staff are now prisoners at the Security Ministry. All three of the brigade's battalion com-manders have received orders to stand down and await the brigade's new commander."

"No." Mortas growled. "Not just no. *Fuck* no."

"Fuckin' right, sir." Leoni intoned.

"I can only speak for myself," Hatton continued, as if reading a statement for the permanent record. "I am going to the Seat of Authority. I am going to remove every Orphan from Asterlit's custody. If nec-essary, I will employ lethal force to do so."

Jander's eyes flashed around him, taking in the blue sky, the shuttles parked on the strip, the trucks and movers, and the stacks of ammunition. So much distance, and so many obstacles, between where he was and where Watt was a prisoner. Courses of action rattled through his mind, each one quickly disqualified by the defenses of Asterlit's compound.

"I cannot ask or order any of you to come with me. My actions will unquestionably be seen as criminal and punishable by death."

"Hahahaha!" Trimmer laughed aloud, causing Mortas to turn. While he and Leoni had been standing there, the drivers had already started gathering weapons and ammunition. The lanky soldier seemed thrilled. "Punishable by death? What isn't?"

"Any Orphan who wishes to remain in good standing with Command should obey the order to stand down. I will not think ill of you. But I am going to the city."

A readout in his goggles told Jander that every Orphan had successfully switched to the new frequency and loaded the encryption. Even so, broadcasting on the net was temporarily restricted to the battalion commanders and so no one else could respond. Having made his own decision, he scanned the flight line for signs of military police or anyone else who might prevent them from commandeering the shuttles.

"This is Colonel Marcus Jolip. I am the commander of Second Battalion of the Orphan Brigade. I only speak for myself." Jander recognized the wording Hatton had used. "I am going to the Seat of Authority, to recover the Orphans unjustly detained there. And I will kill anyone who tries to stop me."

The commander of Third Battalion came on, uttering similar words, while Mortas racked his brain for a solution to Fortuna Aeternum's defenses. Rescuing Colonel Watt meant assaulting the Ministry itself, and with the city's defenders already on alert, part of that assault would have to land directly on the building. Unfortunately, every Force shuttle and vehicle had been outfitted with tracking chips to keep the rebels from impersonating loyal troops. Even without the devices, the shuttles would be shot down long before they reached the target.

"Can we drop the barracks lawyer bullshit?" Mortas giggled involuntarily, recognizing Sergeant Major Zacker's voice. The radio net had been thrown open to all ranks, and a chorus of laughs joined his own from many points in the brigade sector.

"There isn't a man in this brigade who doesn't owe Colonel Watt his life. So we're all going." The radio filled with yells of assent and fury, and Zacker waited until it ended. "But none of that means shit unless we come up with a way to get there without having our own ordnance dropped on us. And somebody needs to figure out how to capture the Ministry without giving the CIP time to murder the colonel."

Jander's hands closed into fists again, his frustration rising. His head jerked from side to side, searching the airstrip for the answer, and his legs began to move him. Thoughts of forcing the air controllers to file false flight plans blazed up into glorious light before dying out in the dark recognition that any shuttles approaching the SOA would be suspect.

His anger rose as a living thing, spurred by memories of serving Watt in the war. The brigade commander had taught every Orphan to think for himself and to improvise when needed, and here he was, failing him by not finding the answer. Jander made himself stop, turning toward Leoni and the FITCO troops. Surely these rogues were devious enough to solve the problem.

The thought vanished when his eyes landed on the long rows of darts. Memories shot through his brain in a high-speed calculation. Corporal Cranther telling him how the darts were used to drop individual Spartacans into harm's way. Strickland explaining that the missiles weren't part of any recognized Force tracking system. Major Hatton ordering him to spread the darts across the brigade's supply units. Leoni's people stuffing individual water bags inside the rockets to protect the more fragile cargo.

Himself walking on the long, flat roof of the Security Ministry.

The radio net had fallen silent, Orphans everywhere searching their minds for a solution to Zacker's problem. Mortas tapped Leoni on the arm and pointed at the darts. The NCO seemed confused for a second, and then his mouth opened in a combination of awe and dread. Jander nodded at him gravely, and then spoke to the rest of the Orphan Brigade.

"This is Lieutenant Jander Mortas, Supply Officer for First Battalion. I know how we can do this."

"**L**isten, I don't know how many gantries you have, but I only have two." The supply officer for Second Battalion spoke to Jander on a separate, secured net. The brigade's communications staff had gone into high gear, and coordination was flying across the units. "I can only get two darts in the air at one time. We aren't going to be able to take out the SOA surveillance node with two troops!"

"You don't need the gantries. If you prop a dart against something, it'll launch just fine as long as it's pointed at the sky. I'm using the Mound's pig moat for mine." Jander replied in a calm voice, seated inside the dry concrete ditch and tapping at a handheld. The fencing behind him had been removed for five hundred yards, and the moat's outward slope was lined with darts being prepped for launch.

"The moat. That's brilliant. We'll do that."

"You wanna hurry. I ain't waiting for you." Mortas studied the graphic symbols popping up all over the aerial footage on his handheld. The Orphan Brigade was so used to receiving missions on the fly that the staff work of organizing their assault was cut down to almost nothing. An entire company from Second Battalion happened to be reorganizing at their version of the Mound many miles away, and so they'd been assigned the task of dropping on and destroying the SOA's communications center in the compound. Blinding Asterlit's defenders would hopefully allow the other Orphan units to approach the city without being torn apart by rockets and drones.

"Mortas, I've got my battalion's entire recon platoon, as well as a rifle platoon here with me." The now-familiar voice of Third Battalion's supply officer came to him. "How come we're not assigned to hit the Ministry? You've got no infantry with you at all."

"I've got a hundred brawlers with me, loaded up with breaching charges and hand grenades. We'll tackle the Ministry just fine."

"We should switch. You take the western barricades and we'll go get the colonel."

"The only way to take down the Ministry is to land on the roof. I've got that mission because my people have the most experience programming the darts. One miscalculation, and you'll go skidding right off the edge. You'll fall six stories, and then have to fight your way inside, except the crash will have already killed you. Still want the job?"

"No. No, you're right."

Updates were flashing across the handheld screen, and he was having trouble keeping up. One of them seemed urgent, and so Jander switched back to the brigade frequency.

"This is Wolf, First Platoon B Company First Battalion." Mortas spotted the encrypted marker on the map, and his eyes widened. His old platoon had been five miles from a covered irrigation ditch that would hide them the rest of the way into the city. But now they were much closer even though they were on foot. "Looks like we'll be first in the city, too. Me and my guys are halfway across the flat, and nobody's blasting us."

"They just haven't noticed you yet," an angry voice from brigade responded. "As soon as they do, you're dead."

"Not a chance. We're doing it like Roger. We're spread out in packs, moving in big circles like the hogs do. There aren't any of 'em near us, and nobody's the wiser."

Mortas narrowed the focus, and almost laughed with pride. His former troops were scattered over several hundred yards of open terrain, grouped in threes and fours, and looping around in what at first appeared a completely aimless journey. They must have been suffering terribly in the heat with their full combat loads, but Wolf was right.

"This is DeNapoli." Mortas recognized the gruff words as coming from the commander of Third Battalion's C Company. "I've commandeered a supply convoy headed for the city. My people are jammed inside the trucks, and the chips all say we're clear to the western barricades. The rest of you better get a move on, 'cause when we reach the checkpoints the shooting's gonna start."

All over the brigade sector, units were in motion. The independence of thought cultivated by Colonel Watt was making itself known in his rescue, and Mortas felt excitement starting to rise in his limbs. Shutting down his handheld, he tucked it into a cargo pocket and stood. Fully armored, helmeted and goggled, carrying as many magazines and grenades as possible, he walked toward the first dart with his rifle in hand.

"It's time," he said to Sergeant Leoni. "Keep firing 'em, even if the roof is jammed up with the empties. This is *not* going to be pretty."

Leoni took the Scorpion from him and handed it to one of the troops preparing the missile. He then shook hands with Mortas. "Once we've got the relay going, I'll be coming in behind you. Be alive when I get there, sir."

"I will do my best."

He looked across the first row of darts to be launched, leaning against the hog moat's walls at a forty-five-degree angle. Trimmer and six other similarly pugnacious FITCO drivers gave him a variety of nods and waves, and they all started climbing inside the tubes. Upside down now, his head toward the fins and the engines, squeezing his long legs between two canvas bags containing enough explosives to tear through a reinforced door. Hands began strapping him in while he checked the releases holding his rifle against the hull.

"Here's the latch, sir." A familiar voice echoed inside the dart, and he looked up to see Easterbrook pointing at the handle that would free him from the tube. She cracked a wide smile, reminding him of the grime-covered face on the morning after the Flock attacked the Mound. "You didn't think you FITCO types were gonna have this all to yourselves, did you?"

"You help us, they'll lock you up for the rest of your life."

"*Help* you? I'm in the third salvo, sir. Leave some of those green sonsabitches for us, okay?"

"I make no promises."

Figures loomed up next to the dart, pouring boxes of transparent bags around him. Half gallon in size and only three-quarters full, the water containers would hopefully buttress the shock of landing on the Ministry's roof. More hands stuffed them in around him, and then an additional box was added. The curved door came down, and he was looking out through the chest-sized observation window.

"All the life support stuff had been yanked out of these things when Captain Follett got them, sir." Sergeant Strickland spoke on the radio, his nose almost touching the window. He pointed at several circular holes in the transparent covering. "We drilled these so you can breathe. Can't say what it's gonna do to the flight characteristics."

"We'll find out in a moment." Strickland gave him a thumbs-up, and Mortas called up the imagery of the target on his goggles. Fortuna Aeternum was its usual depressing self, but neither the SOA nor the slums around it showed any sign of alert. No one was on the roof of the Ministry, and the streets around the building were empty except for some foot traffic. "Assault Team, this is Mortas. I will launch first. Once you're on the roof, don't forget your breaching charges. Blow any doors they block, then throw grenades. You know where Asterlit's throne room is—that's the target."

The imagery showed several new markers in addition to Wolf's platoon hustling down the irrigation ditch and DeNapoli's column almost at the outskirts of the city. Orphan elements, some of them as small as squad level, finding ways to secretly close the distance between their sector and the city. He called the support units of Second and Third Battalions, confirming they were ready to launch their darts.

"Lieutenant Mortas, sir?" Trimmer called in a happy singsong.

"Go ahead."

"You forgot to tell us to enjoy the ride."

The net filled with laughter, and he was too busy joining in to respond. The countdown in his goggles reached zero, and then a giant shot-putted him into the sky.

The engines below his head roared and rattled, but the sound was deadened by the water bags. They'd slammed downward at launch, pinning his head and filling his vision with sloshing water. Mortas struggled to get his arms up among them, but finally realized that he wouldn't be able to push them back into position. Sliding a hand across the ammo pouches on his armor, he found the long knife that had once belonged to Corporal Tel Cranther. Careful not to cut himself, Jander started bursting the water bags.

Cool liquid flowed over him, but he could finally move again. A brilliant blue sky filled the observation window, and he felt the vibration as the finned tube sailed through the air. He flipped the goggle view, seeing the same tranquil scene at the target and now feeling the adrenaline. Colonel Watt was somewhere inside that building, and a bizarre chain of events and machinations had put Mortas in the perfect position to free him. He was leading an assault force riding unexpected, undetectable, unstoppable missiles, they were going to land directly on top of the headquarters of everything that was wrong on the entire planet, and they were going to kill the evil men and women who worked there. It was just the Red House writ large, and the comparison fueled his excitement. He wondered where Sergeant Drayton and the platoon from C Company were at that moment, and then remembered he was still holding Cranther's knife.

Sliding it back into its sheath, he thought of an odd comment the jaded Spartacan had once spoken to him. *You just wait until the real story gets out. How we've been used out here.*

Its appropriateness for their current situation seemed to reach all the way from the barren planet Roanum where it had all begun. Cranther had been speaking of the abuses he'd suffered at Command's hands, but Mortas saw how it fit his own reactions to this depraved world of Celestia. He heard the words of different troops, grumbling about having joined to fight the Sims, not to prop up a civilian government. That by so doing, they were aiding the same regime that had enslaved the very people they were fighting. That their mere presence was a crime in itself, in that Force commanders were not allowed to bring their troops across the CHOP Line.

A digital countdown appeared in one corner of his goggle view, the dart's Doppler getting a pingback from the tall structures of the city. He switched to the cameras on the missile's nose, marveling to see the dirty ground racing by and knowing it was below him. After that, a scattered set of small houses and then the river, brown and ugly. The rocket sailed over the slums, over the barricades and checkpoints manned by Asterlit's foul followers, and nothing was coming up to meet them—no fire, no missiles, not even a warning.

The engine grunted, dropping to a lower speed, and the water bags slid toward the nose. The tiny flight passed over the wall surrounding the SOA, and Jander's ears filled with the whoops of rage and relief from the other seven darts. Pulling his eyes from the goggle view, he looked through the window at the bright sky in an effort to burn it into his memory. A tiny crack had pushed all the way across the windshield, but it wasn't important, because regardless of how hard he landed, or who might try to stop them, he was going to fight his way into that giant hall, hold Cranther's blade against Damon Asterlit's throat, and demand his surrender.

Unfastening the harness as the engines died completely, only hearing the wail of the wind, remembering that the Spartacan Scout had been an orphan on this very planet, a runaway from the certain fate of being sent to the mines, and feeling a mystic rush at the way it was all coming full circle, it was all coming together, it was meant to happen, and so it was going to work.

The goggle view showed the long roof only a hundred yards ahead, the missile's flight was almost perfect, the dart was going to land on its side with its momentum spent, and then the latch would release him. The cameras showed the hard surface rushing up, and he braced his arms against the wall.

"This one's for you, Tel!" he shouted, somehow sure the dead man was hearing him and laughing in righteous delight.

The dart slammed into the roof so hard that his helmet bounced off the hull and his goggles went dark. The entire tube went up in the air, still flying, still moving with incredible speed, and then it touched down again but kept racing along as if on ice. The goggles came back to life, the nose cameras showing him the ornate railing, short pillars of gray stone, fifty yards away and then only ten and then none.

The cracked window exploded into a thousand pieces that disappeared in a howling wind, and Mortas's dart went straight through the railing and over the side.

CHAPTER 16

The invasion of the planet code-named Omega started in an unusual fashion. Instead of HDF warships materializing from the Step in a tight siege ring, a large number of small robot spacecraft entered Omega's atmosphere after a prolonged, stealthy approach. They didn't descend very far, and instead began a series of zigzagging movements that allowed them to seed the thin air with thousands of much smaller aerobots.

These in turn maintained their anonymity by falling for miles, gracefully swaying with the eddies and gusts, until they were well dispersed. Their systems activated not far from the surface, wings spreading, and then they too began serpentine circuits that photographed and scanned the ground beneath them. The feed went to their parent vessels high above, who relayed them to waiting satellites that then fed the data to the fleet.

Their small size, coupled with their many tasks, caused the low-level aerobots to run out of fuel not long after that. The 'bots that were closest to the craters and the buried ruins were the first to break off, heading for untraveled sectors where they set down and expired. Not long after that, their mechanical siblings working quieter zones did the same. Their parents continued to cruise at high altitude while the first fruits of their labors were examined on the distant ships of the slowly constricting cordon. Data collected directly from the planet Omega, believed to be the origin of the Sims and the home world of the shapeshifting aliens.

"There's been no response, Madame Chairwoman." General Merkit sat with Reena inside a busy operations room deep inside the flagship *Aurora*. "Either the aliens are extraordinarily well disciplined, or they don't know we're watching them."

"Is that the consensus opinion of the commanders?" the Chairwoman asked quietly. Although she oversaw everything in the HDF, Reena was leaving the actual management of the operation to the admirals and generals she'd hand-picked for the operation.

"It is. We're gaining valuable data, everything from the limited flora and fauna to the composition of the soil, and it's still being processed. However, the important information is inside those craters. If we have tipped our hand, every moment we delay gives them that much more time to hunker down—or initiate their escape plan, if they have one."

"If they try something like that, do we have redundancy on the cordon line? Even if they flood one spot?"

"Yes. We war gamed it to death, and then gave it to the computers. Everything says we're ready to stop any breakout."

"What is the next phase?"

"Another seeding of low-level robots, this time overflying the craters themselves. The commanders recommend that we have the ground troops ready to launch before that."

"Give the order."

On the warship carrying Ayliss's Banshee company, the cavernous compartment holding the armored suits shifted into high gear with little folderol. Having rehearsed the mission until it was second nature, and then having spent several days waiting on the word, the signal to don suits came as a release. Technicians swarmed the conveyor belts the Banshees would ride while being sealed inside their suits, and armorers carefully loaded the Fasces with their special ammunition. Considering the shapeshifters' moth-like characteristics and their susceptibility to fire, three of the rifles' six barrels had been switched to flame configuration. Two of the remaining barrels fired standard rounds, while the last remained a grenade launcher. More mission-specific ordnance and equipment was loaded into the shuttles, including the ground monitors and a wide range of incendiary explosives.

"Whatever you do, don't strike a match." Legacy spoke to the squad while pointing at the squat fire bombs. They'd just entered the bay, and were still wearing fatigues or flight suits. They'd shaved their heads bald, and Tin called them together for one last word before the suit-donning began.

"Circle up." The short woman gazed across their faces, a warm smile spreading. "I know we're just a perimeter team, but I wouldn't be anywhere else, or with anyone else, for this mission. I have total confidence in each and every one of you. Follow the plan until it goes to shit, and then kill everything that isn't human.

"Take a good look at each other." Hands reached up all around, arms across shoulders, the eight women tightening the circle in a special ritual they'd chosen for this mission. "When this is over, we will stand here again. All of us."

"Or none of us." the squad answered.

"I will kill for you." Cusabrina took up the litany.

"I will kill for you." Ayliss recited with the others.

"I will die for you." Dellmore continued.

"I will die for you." The hands slid down, allowing the circle to contract until their bald heads were all touching. The words were now a low hiss, the arms contracting hard across the torsos to right and left.

"Live for me. Live for me. Live for me."

Sealed in, communications checks completed, data arrays on her face shield, Ayliss followed Dellmore toward the ramp leading into the shuttle. All over the launch bay, double ranks of Banshees were lumbering onto the war chariots that would take them to the surface. Two shuttles over, a bizarre file of shrunken suits entering a standard-sized shuttle caught her eye. Mottled in gray and black, the recon rigs worn by the Spartacan Scouts attached to Breverton's company were terrifying in their minimalism. Life support, communications, gel rations, water, and a modest selection of hand tools, all built into a suit that had little armor. The scouts would be the first ones into the crater, and might need to worm their way through tight spaces.

"And you thought you had a tough job." Blocker's jovial words entered her helmet, and she turned to see him wearing a headset, combat goggles, and fatigues.

"Bear." Ayliss reached out with an armored glove that could easily crush the man's bones, gently running the outer fabric down his cheek. Realizing he couldn't see her face, she activated the interior cameras so that the image appeared in the goggles. "Wait for me, Bear."

"Wait? In three hours I'll be down there with you."

"How?"

"You asked me to make sure nobody got left behind, right?"

"You piloting one of the shuttles?"

"Better than that. You know those extravehicular bubbles the repair folks ride?"

"Yeah, but they use those in space."

"They're designed to work in atmosphere as well."

"That's not the point. They got no armor at all."

"Well then I better stay away from the shooting." Blocker gave her a crazy grin. "Listen. Those bubbles have two strong pincer arms, and they can fly really fast with a load. When Command gives the signal to run for the evacuation points, you just *know* some squads are gonna be too far away to make it in time. Me and my people will be swooping and scooping, and dropping 'em at the shuttles. Everybody comes back from this one."

"I wish you'd told me this sooner, Bear."

"Hey." The word was stern. "I did two full tours out here before you ever got across the CHOP Line. I earned my invitation to this party."

"I'm sorry. I forgot."

"Silly rookie." The grin was back. "Look at it this way. Now you can concentrate on your job. No matter where they send you, you *will* get out of there before we torch this place."

"Me *and* my squad. My entire squad."

"Count on it. Every wrench-turner and wire-router volunteered to fly the bubbles." Blocker's face came close. "I promised I would never leave you again, Little Bear."

"I love you, Dom."

"I love you, Ayliss. Now go kick ass."

In a small compartment many decks away from the busy launch bay, Christian Ewing came awake when a low buzzing rose from the console. Dozing in his seat while waiting for the latest data from Omega, he rubbed tired eyes before tapping buttons on the panel. Imagery of the planet surface rolled across the screens, while different views showed heat and soil readouts from the most recent wave of reconnaissance robots.

Initiating a filtering protocol of his own making, Ewing concentrated on the information deemed unimportant by the anonymous analysts and countless computers evaluating the data stream. As the steadily descending surveillance patrols failed to attract attention, and the launch hour for the Banshees approached, the focus had shifted almost entirely to the craters and their environs.

Ignoring the giant apertures in the ground, Ewing directed his efforts toward the ruins buried not far from them. The moth-creatures' arcane ritual had intrigued and disturbed him, and he'd found it impossible to stop thinking about their aerial dance. Various theories had been offered by intelligence officers eager to dismiss the mysterious flights that had so closely followed the dimensions of the underground structures. Ewing had found their surmises absurd.

Yawning, he applied a new layer of filtering. The latest reconnaissance flights had estimated the dimensions of the ruins beneath the soil, and he straightened up in alarm when the results appeared. The dead city closest to the crater assigned to Ayliss's squad was believed to be concentric circles of stone foundations radiating from an empty center. The new scans showed that to be wrong, and Ewing squinted at what was unquestionably a spiral shape. The ruins formed a single, curved line that looped around its origin and continued outward for miles.

"Doesn't make sense," Ewing muttered, refining the view while telling himself that this was alien architecture not bound by human engineering. "What was this? One long line of connected buildings? And why would they do that?"

His facile mind quickly developed and rejected a collection of explanations every bit as useless as the musings of the intelligence staff. Shaking off those inadequate ideas, Ewing called up the dimensions of the rocks themselves. The resulting data set his head tilting to one side in pensive confusion, until he shifted the view to a different city and saw the same result.

The foundation stones were rectangular slabs hundreds of yards long and wide. The overall sizes varied, but every one of them was fifty yards in depth. The readout said they were all cut from the same kind of indigenous rock, and the material glowed with energy soaked up from solar radiation. The filter swept over the images, revealing a second, muted store of energy directly beneath each of the slabs. It pulsed as if alive, stirring up a sickening sensation in his stomach. Checking his findings against three more of the cities, his fingers shaking as they flew across the keyboard, Ewing finally sat back in shock.

"How did we miss this?" he said to the air, before typing out the commands to download the results and then running out the hatch.

With a single command, the region of space surrounding Omega changed dramatically. Force warships burst into existence in a choreographed pattern that quickly surrounded the gray sphere from every direction. The distant security cordon didn't move at all, but its systems immediately linked in with the scanners and recon 'bots of the invasion ships. Advance warning was the key to preventing the escape of any alien vessel, and once that mechanism was fully established, the assault commenced.

With all pretense of stealth abandoned, a thick cloud of surveillance craft burned through the atmosphere and took up patrol routes. Thousands more of the recon robots plummeted through the clouds, taking over the sectors originally covered by their more secretive predecessors. With this low-level screen in place, the personnel shuttles launched in a seemingly random dance that saw them separate into twos and threes and then into ones in order to confuse any concealed devices that might track them from inside the craters.

The frenetic flights resolved into something that made sense once they were closer to the surface. Aping the cordon out in space, a far-flung perimeter made up of widely scattered Banshee squads took up positions surrounding each crater. Gunships, both drone and manned, raced back and forth above them to cover the wide gaps in territory. The suited warriors quickly deployed the ground sensors, established observation posts, and reported their general impressions in this, their first visit to the enemy home world.

As soon as the security rings were in place, a different cloud of flying robots descended. Focused on the five craters to be first examined, they performed a complex, surface-level ballet that saw some of them circling the apertures while others flew directly across. The data went straight to the fleet, showing nothing unexpected. Three of the five craters provided no indications of any unnatural activity at all; their rims were covered in vegetation, and their walls were riven with cracks and fissures that could have been centuries old. The remaining two, one of which had seen the launch of the Sim transport, showed stretches of denuded rock where the vines and plants had been blown down by the violence of the blastoff.

"Deep surveillance entering craters. Full alert." A mechanical voice warned the Banshees on the ground that the flying robots were about to dive below the surface. Although they'd heard the command hundreds of times in rehearsal, it still elicited sarcasm.

"Full alert. Did you hear that?" Dellmore called to the others. She and Ayliss were covering their portion of the perimeter from atop a small knob of large rocks and sparse trees. "Not half-assed alert. *Full* alert."

"Glad they cleared that up," Bullhead commented from a mile away. "I wasn't planning to give a hundred percent for at least another hour. But now I'm good. Alert, you might say."

"Hey Tin," Zuteck called. "You think the folks in orbit are on full alert? Or maybe getting another cup of coffee?"

"They can have all the coffee they want, as long as they're watching the ground we can't," the squad leader answered lightly. "I bet they're all sitting in the galley, though, writing medal citations for each other."

Broken up into pairs spotted along their portion of the extended perimeter, the squad members laughed. The overhead feed in their helmets was extremely good, combining the footage from the flying 'bots, surveillance drones, gunships, and the vessels in orbit. Their sectors had been chosen with care, allowing them to observe great stretches of largely open ground. From what they were seeing through their scopes and with the aid of the eyes above them, no threat was yet evident.

Minutes slowly passed, minutes where they all knew the surveillance robots were descending inside the gigantic shafts. Despite their forced insouciance, the desire to know what the craters contained was almost maddening.

"Tin, how come they aren't showing us the feed as they get it?" Lightfoot asked. "It's not like we could run off, if it was bad."

"You know the answer. If the bigwigs let us see it at the same time they do, we might get the dangerous idea that we don't need them."

"Wait." Ayliss spoke without meaning to, excited to see a small rectangle of new imagery in a corner of her display. "I think they're sending it now."

The view was far below the surface, the robots using night vision to record their findings. Enlarging the image, Ayliss felt a momentary stab of vertigo.

The surveillance 'bots were flying back and forth inside one of the undisturbed shafts, the transmissions from their cameras blending to provide a single view. The combined vista gave her the impression of being slowly lowered down the center of the crater, and Ayliss marveled at the sights. Hundreds of yards to either side the rock walls were cracked and crenellated, with intermittent clumps of vegetation that grew less frequent as the robots moved away from the sunlight.

Lowering her chin allowed Ayliss to look down the vertical tunnel, its walls green in the night vision and the bottom nothing but a dark circle an unknowable distance below. All she could determine so far was that nothing seemed out of the ordinary.

Another rectangle appeared on her display, this one blinking, so she switched to it. The robots were much deeper in this shaft, which she quickly identified as the site of the launch. The dark walls were bare, and appeared to be crosshatched with countless scratches.

"What do you think caused that?" Zuteck asked. "The launch?"

"I'm guessing it was more of those caterpillar things," Tin mused. "Look at the gouges. Some are small, some must be yards wide."

"Intel did suggest the worms come in all sizes." Legacy offered.

"You getting all that from a bunch of cracks?"

Dellmore scoffed. "The thrust to push that transport into space had to be enormous. They're lucky they didn't collapse those walls."

"Those aren't cracks." Tin spoke, and then paused when a line of precisely rounded holes appeared in the wall. "They had to build that entire ship—or at least assemble it—inside the crater. Something like a gantry had to hold it up, and they'd have to attach it to the rock."

"That's human thinking," Ayliss warned. "Remember what Varick said about that. The only thing that had to obey our way of doing things was the ship itself. Who knows how they made it, or launched it?"

"Careful, Rig," Cusbarina joked. "You start talking like that, you'll end up like Varick. Trapped in the staff world. They wouldn't even let her come with us."

The conversation ended when the footage reached the bottom of the shaft. The scattered Banshees studied the green-lit imagery, utterly baffled.

"There's nothing there."

"Look at the way the ground tilts. Shouldn't it be flat?"

"Can't tell if there are burn marks or not. That whole floor should have been scorched."

"Where's the launch pad? Where are the supports? Why aren't there great big holes in the rock for the fuel lines?"

"Wait." Legacy spoke. "They're focusing in."

The horde of flying robots had detected an anomaly in the inky blackness at the bottom of the chute. The view shifted around, revealing an extremely large fissure that formed an arch in the wall.

"Tunnel entrance," Lightfoot suggested, and then corrected herself when a similarly blocked aperture appeared on the other side. "Entrances. They didn't finish camouflaging them, but I bet that's what they are. They launched that ship, and then cleaned out the crater completely."

"**E**mpty?" Reena stared at the footage across an entire wall of screens. "How can it be empty? They launched a faster-than-light ship, loaded with sleeping Sims, from that crater just a few days ago."

"Intelligence believes this is confirmation that the caterpillar creature was one of many underground workers the shapeshifters control," Merkit answered. "It was big enough to perform a task like blocking off the tunnels leading out of the crater."

"Buy why would they do that? Did they realize they were being watched?"

"That's unlikely. If they spotted our surveillance— which was quite distant at the time—they would have stopped the launch. If they detected our recon after the blastoff, why waste time sanitizing the site? I would have expected them to initiate whatever contingency plans they've got in place, in case we ever found them."

"What if this is their contingency plan?"

"Hunker down and hope for the best, when they know we can blow this planet to bits?"

"I suppose not." Reena sagged in her chair, feeling the tension in her muscles. "So what caused them to empty out that crater and block it off?"

"To me, it sounds like a procedure they've been performing for decades. Think about it. Nothing on Omega's surface suggests anything is there. They know we've got the technology to send reconnaissance all over this planet, and every planet in this system, if we detected anything suspicious. So why leave something for the 'bots to find? They do a launch, and then they strip the place down. Nothing to see, nothing to report."

"They know we're here now, and that we're more than a few probes working the system. So why haven't they tried to run off?"

"I think the question is bigger than that. Why didn't the shapeshifters abandon this place, and even this part of the galaxy, when they first encountered humanity? Just using the DNA and the technology they captured from those earlier ships, they built an entire race of mutated humans to challenge us when we returned. They even gave them the tools to make more ships and weapons on their own."

Merkit paused for a breath. "So why didn't they use all that tech to make a fleet that could take them out of our way? Why didn't they go live somewhere else?"

"I'm assuming you have an answer for this."

"A guess, at best." Merkit's face went slack in thought. "I think they stayed here, and threw the Sims at us, because they *couldn't* leave. I have no idea what nailed them to this spot, but that's my conclusion. Why else would they go to so much trouble to fend us off, if they could have just left?"

"Hostility? Territoriality?"

"If that were the case, I would have expected to be under heavy attack as soon as we revealed our-selves here. With their intelligence and ingenuity, they should be hitting us with weapons we haven't yet dreamed of. And yet they're doing nothing."

"So what does it mean?"

"I'm offering another guess. I think this place is so crucial to their existence, or so sacred to them, that they wouldn't risk it in a battle. They can't abandon it, and they can't see it destroyed."

"They're *going* to see it destroyed, if we don't get some answers on the ground."

"We can shift to five more craters. See what they hold."

"No. Leave the Banshees in place. Send the de-molition 'bots into that crater and blow those tunnel openings clear. Have the Spartacans ready to go in right after that. That's why we brought them along."

"Yes, ma'am." Merkit rose, and started moving toward one of the consoles.

"General, let's stop screwing around here. Send recon 'bots into every one of the craters."

"Yes, ma'am." Merkit leaned in and began giving instructions to a communications technician.

"Madame Chairwoman?" Ulbridge's voice rose up from the arm of Reena's chair.

"What is it?"

"I'm talking to a very agitated commo man who's been showing me some interesting data from the planet surface. Specifically, the city ruins."

"Why is he talking to you? Doesn't he have a chain of command?"

"He says his chain of command is Dom Blocker, ma'am. It's Ewing, the man who killed Vroma Rittle."

"He met Ayliss on Quad Seven. Some kind of savant. So what's he telling you about the ruins?"

"He believes they're not ruins, ma'am. He believes they're incubators. Incubators for the next generation of shapeshifters."

CHAPTER 17

Jander Mortas awoke to darkness and pain. His mouth was gummed up with coagulating blood, and his entire body was soaking wet. His feet were numb, and his legs were stuck between what felt like two rocks. His head was throbbing with a steady beat, and at that moment he was racked with a coughing fit that seemed to come from his very core. Somewhere in the middle of that he realized his helmet was gone.

A distant surf was pounding an irregularly shaped shore, but the thunder came to him as a muffled murmur. His mind refused to engage its gears, but the blackness was intolerable and he felt his hands reaching for his eyes. The familiar lenses of his goggles met the tips of his fingers, and he remembered the devices shorting out when his dart hit the roof of the Ministry. Shock and fear surged through him, and he tore at the goggles. The strap holding the frames against his cheeks parted, and he blinked in the sunlight entering through the open observation window several feet away.

He was covered with transparent jellyfish that turned out to be exploded bags of water, and his legs were jammed between the two breaching charges. Mortas marveled that the explosives hadn't gone off, but then the sound of gunfire and explosions entered the tube. He couldn't determine how close they were, and looked at the opening to see a sky-blue sheet flapping against it. Puzzled, he reached up gingerly and caught hold of the harness that was still attached to the wall. His chest argued with him as he pulled himself toward the window, and then he was coughing again, uncontrollably, until a wet wad of blood and mucus finally caught in his throat and he spat it out.

The latch was in front of his eyes now, and he tugged at it with little hope. The hatch was dented badly, and it refused to budge. Now pulling with his arms and pushing with his legs, watching the mysterious blue fabric slapping the dart through the window and desperately wanting to be outside with it. Looking down at his torso armor with its pouches full of magazines and grenades, and recognizing he wouldn't fit through the opening.

Explosions getting closer, and then a loud burst of gunfire. Fear and frustration taking over as he raised his right leg and began kicking at the hatch release.

Squirming up a little more, now able to look through the window, seeing that the dart was on its side next to the gray walls of the Ministry. The blue sheet dropped away, revealing the six stories above decorated with a series of enormous blue drapes that hung from the roof almost to the ground. Torn in many places, tangled in a web of stout cords, a confusing jumble until his brain finally started working again.

"Parachutes. The chutes activated when I hit," he mumbled at the miraculous event. "Didn't know they were even there."

Kicking the latch once more, relief washing over his sodden form when it swung away with a screech and the damaged hatch popped open an inch. Looking for his Scorpion, and then seeing it at the nose, its butt fractured and its barrel bent. He placed his hand on the door, pondering whether to open it slightly or to get out in a hurry, when a shower of stones rattled across it and something heavy hit the dart near its tail. An angry clang punched into his ears, and he shoved the curved hatch open just to stop it.

Shielding his face when another shower of rocks fell into the dart, looking up at the roof where the railing was gone and the pointed noses of two darts jutted out into space. Seeing them both shift, pushed by something large and unseen, and then struggling to free himself and get away. His left foot tangled on a strap, fighting him, trapping him there, and then it came loose and he was rolling over the side. Emerging into air that smelled like smoke, hearing the booms of explosions many blocks away, and rifle fire much closer. Feeling a thump on his leg, and looking over to see that one of the breaching charges had come with him, its straps wrapped around his ankle. Scooping up the bomb, crouching, looking left and right to see where to go.

The survey of his surroundings froze Mortas in place. The street between the Ministry and a nearby building was strewn with dead bodies, most of them civilians. Two of Asterlit's green suiters were lying there as well, seeming to have been hacked to death. The other corpses were almost as bloody, having been hit by numerous bullets. The one closest to him was a woman in rags, slumped over an outdated rifle and wearing two bandannas in an effort to hide her face. Despite the disguise, it was obvious that her skin was orange.

Two of the other civilians bore the same coloring, and several more showed dark tracks on their faces that could only be birds. The Flock. The puzzle pieces came together, the answer to the question of what had happened to the Orange. They'd infiltrated the city, somehow avoiding detection, and the Orphans' attack had brought them out of hiding.

Mortas had no time to ponder this because his eyes found a second dart, on its side across the street in a pile of broken masonry. Its hatch was shut, and he slung the breaching charge across his shoulders before scrambling over to it. Crawling over the rock pile, seeing that the dart's nose was crushed and knowing it had followed his over the side. Unable to get the hatch open, tumbling fragments of carved stone out of the way, and finding that the observation window on this one was open to the air just like his own.

Trimmer's goggles were smashed, and drying blood marked his nostrils, mouth, and ears. His weapon was nowhere to be seen, but his helmet was still on and so Mortas unfastened the strap and took it. Looking in at the dead man, he whispered, "Sorry."

A figure stepped clear of the building not five feet away, oblivious to his presence. Green fatigues covered by a vest loaded with chonk rounds, the grenade launcher in his hands and his eyes on the roof of the Ministry. Mortas now heard the gunshots and the blasts up there, and realized that his people were still fighting for access to the stairs. The man in green wore a soft black cap, and his lips parted as he prepared to fire.

Rushing forward, swinging Trimmer's helmet, Mortas hit the side of the man's head so hard that he simply dropped. Ducking down to grab the chonk, and then feeling a hand roughly grabbing his armor and pulling him upright. Turning in fright and anger, only to stop in amazement at the joyous face of a madman. Inch-long birds flew from one cheek across wild eyes to the opposite temple, one smudged because they'd been drawn with ink instead of tattooed.

A workman's coverall and a rust-colored machete completed the uniform, and then the Flock member was yelling in his ear.

"Come on, Orphan! Kill with us! *Whole lotta good killing!*" He drew an ecstatic breath, but a machine gun thundered from a window in the Ministry and he disintegrated. Blood and matter slapped into Mortas, but he was already running across the street, the enemy gun sending sparks flying near his boots until he was up against the wall and then ducking around the corner. Crouching, laying the chonk down so he could don Trimmer's helmet, seeing a semicircular window at sidewalk level next to his boots. Strong bars blocked the aperture, but it was the perfect size.

Yanking out the safeties on the breaching charge, he twisted the arming timer and stuffed the bomb into the stone arch. A single bullet came from the other side of a small park across the street, and he caught a glimpse of more bodies out there before scrambling back around the corner. The machine gun chattered again, though not at him, and Jander saw the barrel protruding two stories over his head. A drone gunship appeared in the distance, fire streaming in a molten line at targets he couldn't see before he threw himself facedown on the sidewalk.

Trimmer's helmet connected with the communications in his armor, and desperate voices filled his ears while he waited for the breaching charge to detonate.

"We're trapped on the roof! Stop sending darts!"

"This is Hatton! We are encountering heavy resistance on the Joy Canal Road! Looking for a new route!"

"Do not fire up the Flock or the Orange! They're killing the CIP!"

"This is Wolf! We've captured a guard tower on the southeast corner of the wall! Swing around to the south!"

The bomb detonated, and the dampers in Trimmer's helmet clamped down on Jander's ears. Smoke and rock dust plumed up, and he grabbed a grenade from his armor while low-crawling through the cloud. Reaching the window, which was now a man-sized gash in the wall and sidewalk, he was about to arm the grenade when the shooter in the park sent a ricochet past his feet. Grabbing the grenade launcher, Mortas dived straight through the hole into the smoke.

He landed on the fragments of some office furniture, and then a bullet followed him through the breach and he skittered back against the wall. The chonk came up in a reflex, covering the open door, just before Jander realized he had no idea if it contained any bullets. Its grenades were still out on the street, so he popped the magazine and saw that it was indeed loaded. Slapping it back home, he peered through the lingering smoke.

A weapons rack stood open on the far wall, alongside several sets of shackles hanging on hooks. The rest of the room was wrecked, but the sight was enough to kindle a dull hope. By pure luck he might have landed in the cell block where Watt and the others were being held. Keeping out of the sniper's sight line, he moved to the door and swung the chonk around.

A long corridor lined with doorways stood empty before him. Littered with pieces of green uniforms, CIP identification badges, and a range of common items, it gave silent testimony that Asterlit's followers on this level of the Ministry had fled. Hugging the wall, checking each office as he passed, Jander quickly reached the holding cells in the building's center. Somewhere high above him, a giant stomped intermittently, sending a shiver through the entire structure. Outside, a gunship tore up the street with a stream of heavy slugs, but he heard none of it.

The cells were bare rooms with vertical bars where the corridor wall should have been, and there were only five of them. Two had been occupied when the attack commenced, one by a trio of Flock members wearing gray prison uniforms and the other by men in fatigues. Mortas stood at the bars, the grenade launcher becoming heavy in his hands, gravity pulling his jaw down, staring at the murdered prisoners.

Colonel Watt lay at the bottom of a pile of his staff officers, who had tried to shield him with their bodies when the massacre commenced. Captain Pappas lay across him, bloody rips in the back of his fatigue shirt. His vision blurred and the room seemed to spin, so he grabbed the bars and squeezed tight until a weak voice spoke.

"Jan."

Startled, he searched the pile until a single pair of open eyes blinked at him. Motionless, a large bald man with blood running from his mouth fought to raise his head.

"Major Thorn?"

"The colonel knew the brigade would come. When he heard the explosions, he was so happy."

"I wish we got here sooner."

"It was an ambush, Jan. We were never going to take over security here. Command sold us out." Thorn made a choking sound, more blood running.

"Take it easy, sir. I'll find the keys."

"Don't bother. I'm done. Can't move. They arrested us the moment we got here. Took us into the throne room, called us all sorts of names, said the Orphans were finished." Thorn gave a hollow laugh. "Colonel Watt punched Asterlit right in the nose, knocked him on his ass. You tell the boys that."

"You'll tell 'em yourself."

"Nah." Thorn's eyes dulled, his final mission completed. "They murdered us right here. They were all gonna run away, but they gunned us down first. You killed him, right? Asterlit?"

The building shook again, reminding him of the

fight raging on the roof and outside, but Jander decided a lie was in order because it wouldn't be a lie for long. "Oh yeah. He's dead all right."

The first two floors of the Ministry were likewise deserted, and he wasted no time checking them as he went up the stairs. The explosions and gunshots were inside the building by then, but he couldn't hear anyone on the radio. The battle outside seemed to be getting closer, and when he took a moment to look out a shattered window he saw ugly plumes of smoke rising to the west.

On the third floor he heard a radio transmission from one of the offices, terse words against a background of battle, and felt pulled toward the information they contained. It was CIP traffic, and they were panicking.

"Shoot at anything on the streets! We are bringing in the drones. Anyone outside a building will be taken under fire."

"I can't raise the air control HQ! And can someone please tell me what those flying torpedoes are?"

"How did they get into the SOA?"

The hallway showed the same signs of hurried flight, and he had to step over fallen handhelds and a single discarded boot before reaching the office where the radio was playing. When he pointed the chonk around the doorframe, he was greeted by the sight of three CIP officers preparing their getaway. Stripped down to their underwear, they were donning one-piece uniforms that probably belonged to the janitorial staff. Their green outfits were draped across two chairs, and an assortment of weapons sat on the desktop. They froze in place, eyes on him and then on the desk, and Jander waited for them to reach before he shot them all.

Mortas was almost back on the stairs when the fight on the top floors ended. Hoarse shouts and pounding bootsteps echoed inside the stairwell, and he pressed back against the wall while shadows flew past the door's small window. The chonk still contained the grenade that its previous owner had meant for the roof, and he waited until the green fatigues passed before yanking the door open. He was sighting between the railing's thin spokes when an avalanche of hand grenades came bouncing down the steps from above, and he had just enough time to throw himself back inside the hallway before they went off.

The dampers in his helmet kept the successive blasts from deafening him, but they kicked the door off its hinges and filled that part of the corridor with a concussion wave that left him stunned. He was rolling onto his back when the barrel of a Scorpion rifle appeared in front of his eyes. Remembering a similar view on the planet Roanum a lifetime before, he looked past the dark hole to see bloodstained cheeks under a set of goggles and a helmet. The rifle came down slowly, teeth showing under the blood.

"Lieutenant?" Easterbrook asked in a rough voice. Clearing her throat, she spat against the wall and then looked back at him, the smile widening. "You're alive! They said you went over the side!"

"I did." Starting to rise, seeing more armored forms in the stairwell. "Did we get Asterlit?"

"Throne room." A smoke-darkened hand pointed at the ceiling.

"He alive?"

"Maybe."

"No."

Mortas stepped over three dead green suiters when he reached the top floor. Two FITCO troops were covering the stairwell, and they congratulated him on his survival. His headset wasn't working at all, but Jander didn't bother asking for an update on the rest of the fight even though it was clearly in progress outside.

The throne room's double doors had been blown off their hinges, and the aroma of explosives was all around. Jander thought of his only other visit, and then remembered the scene of carnage in the basement prison cells. His hand was drifting toward the handle of Cranther's knife when he saw Asterlit's dead body sprawled in the far corner near his throne. He'd been stitched with several rounds at close range.

"We have to clear the roof. Push the darts over the side." Leoni stood just inside the doors, soot covering his armor. "Call Strickland. Tell him to send two loads of medical supplies pronto. And then find any medics on the Mound, stuff them into darts, and send them too."

"Sergeant." Mortas greeted him with a head bob at Asterlit. "He didn't run off?"

"Good to see you, sir." Leoni grabbed his armor and gave him a quick, affectionate shake. "Heard you did the big drop."

"I did. The parachutes deployed and got hung up on the roof. Only reason I'm here."

"Coulda sworn we removed all of those . . . doesn't matter." He pointed his Scorpion at Asterlit. "Yeah, the governor here didn't seem to understand we were mad at him. He was standing next to that big chair when we got the doors open. He looked right at me, and said something about having done nothing to deserve this."

"Guy was nuts." Mortas turned away, dismissing the image. "I found Colonel Watt and the others. The guards killed them before they ran off. They're in a set of cells in the basement."

"Fuck."

"I know." Mortas heard something crash onto the roof overhead. "What's the status? We winning?"

"Sort of. Turns out the Orange and the Flock had infiltrated the city. They came out of hiding when we attacked. We got a couple of messages from them; seems their pals on the Mound told 'em the Orphan Brigade was coming to town. It's chaos."

"I saw a few of them outside. Seems they took the heat off the rest of the attack."

"Lucky for us. A light infantry brigade with no fire support and a half-assed plan does *not* take down a city."

"You didn't mention that earlier."

"Didn't think we'd get this far." Another thump on the roof. "Listen, we've got a tough decision to make. Ordinarily I'd say we have to get out of this place pronto, but my new pals over there told us something interesting."

Jander looked across the room, where two FITCO troops were guarding three green suiters. The CIP men were stretched out flat on their faces, and he'd thought they were dead.

"What did they say?"

"You know how Roger was redirecting our missile strikes? Asterlit heard about that and figured it wouldn't be long until one of those rockets got reprogrammed to hit the SOA. So everything inside the wall is protected by heavy jamming. The apparatus is right here, in the Ministry."

"So this might be the safest place to be?"

"Looks like it. The gunships are tearing up the

streets out there, so I'm not sure where we'd go anyway." Leoni's normally buoyant features turned grim. "Not that it'll make much difference in the long run. Force units are being sent here to finish us off."

"You say the jammers are all somewhere inside the building?"

"Yes." Leoni gave him a measuring look. "What you cookin' up there, sir?"

"Asterlit controlled all the communications, too. We need to find that, and make a broadcast."

"What? Tell the rest of the Force to surrender?"

"No. Tell the rest of humanity what's going on here."

CHAPTER 18

"Captain, what exactly are we supposed to find out there?" Corporal Cusabrina asked from the bench seats on the shuttle.

"That's why we brought the devices along." Seated with her back to the cockpit and wearing an armored suit like the rest of the Banshees aboard, Erica Varick pointed at a row of the tripod-mounted machines. "These things measure a wide range of subterranean indicators, from seismic activity to heat, and we're going to plant them inside that buried city."

"Even though they never worked in training?" Dellmore asked.

"They worked fine in training, and they're operating the way they were designed right now, all over the target site. We had no idea what we were going to find down there, so these things just basically gather everything."

"I'm still lost here, ma'am," Lightfoot called out. "We're going to measure heat and tremors from the ruins of a city so old that it's completely covered with dirt?"

"Actually, the analysts think it's not a city at all." Varick paused while the rest of the squad groaned. "Yes, they got it wrong. In fact, if it wasn't for a communications specialist named Ewing—I think some of you know him—we might have missed this completely. The stones we thought were foundations are all the same distance from the surface."

"Why is that significant, Captain?" Bullhead asked.

"The stones are all the same kind, and they absorb solar radiation. The readings also show that something beneath them is alive. Ewing thinks it's an incubator for baby shapeshifters."

"What if it's a nursery for those caterpillar things?" Zuteck asked. "What if we disturb them?"

"So far, with troops running all around those craters, we haven't disturbed a thing. I doubt a squad in the middle of nowhere is going to cause much of a fuss." More groans, but good-natured this time. "Okay, I know I shouldn't have said that. Here we go—touching down in one minute."

The shuttles kicked up a cloud of powder when they lifted off, and Tin directed the squad into a wide perimeter even though there was no cover. Zuteck and Bullhead stayed with Varick, setting up their sensor, while the other three pairs headed out carrying the other devices. Jogging along with Dell, Ayliss checked the imagery and saw that nothing was going on anywhere nearby. Widening the scope, she smiled at the sight of the support area going up miles away. Temporary shelters where Banshees could be removed from their suits, ammunition stacks for resupply, and fuel bladders for the aircraft dotted the ground. Shuttles were already landing and shutting off, alongside a double row of the flying bubbles that Blocker had brought down.

"Rig, I'm not doubting your nutty pal with the knife, but I'm not seeing anything in the overheads that say there's a nursery under us." Dell said.

"Ewing sees things the rest of us miss." She giggled when they reached their designated position and started putting the machine into place. "He does hear things that aren't there, though, so maybe he's just wrong."

"Let's hope so. Hey, you catching the latest feed?"

"Yep. Just coming in." Ayliss tongued the new screen a size larger, so that she could view it while still scanning the empty ground to her front. The demolition robots had opened the two tunnels in the launch crater, after determining the blockages were largely cosmetic. Three shuttles had hovered long enough at the bottom of the chimney for the Spartacans to climb out in their special suits, and the footage combined the views from their helmets as well as the tiny drones that hovered nearby.

"A little surprised we're seeing all this." Lightfoot commented from the far side of the perimeter.

"And why's that?" asked Cusabrina. "You do know we're *all* going down inside those things eventually, right?"

"I was hoping they weren't lying when they said that was just a contingency."

"Keep hoping. What's the most important part of a fighting suit, as far as Command is concerned?"

"The commo."

"That's right. Once the scouts are deep enough in the tunnels, their transmissions are gonna fade. A nice long chain of Banshee squads, leading back to the surface, will make sure the honchos in orbit don't miss a thing."

"*That's* why they put us down here?"

"Sorry. Thought you knew."

"Well, there's a little more to it than that," Varick said, before remembering her tenuous status with the squad. "But probably not much."

"I'm starting to like Ewing's wild-goose chase more and more. Hey Captain, can we just stay out here? You know, until they call us back to the ship? Skip that whole tunnel thing?"

"Watch your sectors." Tin warned. "Captain, you getting any readings yet?"

"No. It's still going through its setup."

Ayliss returned to the footage of the Spartacans in the crater. The dark bottom was rough with fingers and fissures, and the lead scouts were taking their time getting across it. The view shifted to just inside the first tunnel entrance, where the broken rocks from the demolition littered the ground. Unlike the crater's bottom, the rock inside the passage was flat and level. The flying 'bots focused on those surfaces, showing thousands of circular rub marks. Remembering the giant caterpillar, Ayliss tried to think of what kind of appendage it or its cousins might have used to perform that work.

The feed took her back to the scouts, who were edging closer to the tunnel mouth. One was nestled against a short rock spire that stood up like a cracked tooth, peering inside, while the others likewise hid themselves. The reconnaissance robots were gliding down the horizontal passage, where the walls had taken on a fuzzy, almost stucco-like texture. The imagery shifted closer to this anomaly, switching from night vision to infrared.

"What is that?" Dell asked quietly.

"Readout says it's alive. Kind of like a moss."

"Moss? In this atmosphere?"

"A kind of moss that could grow in this atmosphere. Look at it all. It's everywhere."

"Could be a food source, ma'am." General Merkit relayed the opinion of analysts located elsewhere on the ship. "The robots are detecting a difference in age and thickness in large, geometrically similar patches. As if strips had been harvested and replaced."

"I suppose they have to eat something."

"Ma'am?" one of the technicians called, punching the keyboard to his front. "Important feed from Crater Forty-Seven coming in. There was a camouflage net inside the hole, and the 'bots have flown in underneath it. On display."

The largest screen switched from the inside of the moss tunnel to a disorienting tableau shot from above on a completely different crater. The center of the circular image looked like an open food can crawling with maggots, while multicolored, ribbed tubing ran inward from the wall at three points. Reena rose and stood next to Merkit, puzzled.

"This is an overhead view, ma'am." The technician explained as the description came through his headset. "They believe the center is a spacecraft under construction, and that the supports between it and the crater wall are more of the caterpillar creatures."

The picture fell into logical place, and Reena gasped in recognition. The food can was actually the truncated hull of the ship still being assembled, and the maggots were smaller versions of the caterpillar.

Hundreds of them, perhaps thousands, ranging in size from gigantic to mere slivers, working in concert. The supports were just that, the larger caterpillars extending from the walls of the crater to the fuselage of the vessel. In the gaps running down the chimney, gangs of the creatures could be seen inching pieces of machinery up the walls. Looking more closely, Reena marveled to see the myriad appendages performing complex tasks as they emerged from the tube-like bodies or disappeared inside them. Claws fastened down on bolts and screws, while others wielded welding devices and red-hot electrical irons.

"Look at that." Merkit pointed. "Their bodies adjust to the task. Do you think they've been mutated by the aliens, the same way as the Sims?"

"Doesn't matter." Reena turned to the technician. "Are we recording all of this? Every bit, with complete redundancy?"

"As ordered, ma'am."

"General, contact the command element and tell them to have those Spartacans get moving. We need footage of actual Sims being created, or stored in vats, or however these things are doing it."

"With everything we've seen and recorded so far, you're not going to have any difficulty convincing the rest of the alliance that we found the origin of the Sims, ma'am."

"I've never been worried about convincing *them* of anything." Reena's eye never left the screen, where the creatures kept on with their labors despite the intrusion of the recon 'bots. "Before we blow this place to bits, I'm going to need absolute proof that these things were making the Sims. After we've destroyed this place, we still have to make the Sims understand that the game is over."

"Looks like somebody guessed right," Varick commented as the footage of the partially assembled ship came into their helmets. "That caterpillar was one of their workers."

"Look at how many of them there are," Tin observed. "All different sizes, too."

"Could be billions of them, maybe trillions under there." Zuteck spoke. "Heck, under *here*, for all we know."

"I have a question." Bullhead interrupted. "The demolitions blew down the obstacles in the launch crater, and made a lot of noise doing it. The recon 'bots are deep inside those tunnels now, with the Spartacans behind them. Why haven't the aliens sent a few big caterpillars to block the robots and crush the scouts?"

"Maybe the same reason the workers on that ship haven't reacted to the robots filming them. Think they might be blind? Deaf? Both?"

"Discipline." Tin replied. "The aliens turned that first caterpillar around when it was running away from them. Its only escape was to kill itself. I bet the aliens have some kind of mind control over these things. What do you think, Captain? I mean, you met one of them."

"You may be onto something. The shapeshifter I met spoke inside my head without opening its mouth. And when we jettisoned the thing, it laughed the whole way down."

"Did you feel like it was able to make you do things?"

"No. It knew we were going to kill it, so if it could have stopped us, it would have. Maybe they can control the caterpillars that way, though."

"Uh-oh," Dellmore interrupted. "Showtime."

The footage from the flying 'bots in the Spartacan tunnel showed layers of moss covering the walls, but the dark expanse to their front now started to shimmer. The heat signatures of thousands of floating, bobbing points filled the void like a storm of fireflies, and then they filled the view. The cameras on the miniature reconnaissance craft blurred as the moths covered them, and then the image shifted. Farther back down the tunnel, obviously a composite of the feed from 'bots that hadn't been surrounded yet. Up the passage, the swirling dots of light seemed to coalesce in the air in tiny bundles, like floating rolls of dough congealing into balls, and then a large spark erupted from inside each mass.

"Did you see that?" Lightfoot asked. "They merged together and crushed the robots!"

More sparks followed, while the oncoming torrent seethed toward the next cameras. The process repeated itself, a blizzard of dots blotting out the view until the image shifted, then tiny eruptions and more moths. The tunnel was filling with them, and now the Banshees could see the lead scout. Flat on the stone floor, up against the wall, motionless.

The storm rolled down the passage toward him, but then the boiling lights swirled in a tight circle that generated a long, thin tendril. More robots were coming up, sharpening the picture, showing what appeared to be a whip-like cord reaching out from the cloud toward the supine body. Other cords appeared, wrapping around the first one as the horde of moths billowed closer.

"Muscle." Ayliss whispered. "Doesn't that look like a muscle fiber?"

The elongating bundle of twitching cords fused together, and then dived with alarming speed. Snake-like, it coiled around the Spartacan from head to toe. Now the width of a man's thigh, it detached from the cloud while the Spartacan's one free arm punched at it with no effect. The hideous picture of the constricting sinews and the struggling man ended a moment later, when the coil gave off a muffled boom and a spasm of light exploded from inside it.

"They crushed him!" Legacy stammered. "They formed a big tube of muscle, and they crushed him."

Explosions burst inside the oncoming moths, grenades thrown by the other Spartacans, and then the view showed the scouts rushing back down the tunnel.

"No effect. The grenades didn't hurt them at all."

"Get outta there, guys. Get outta there!"

The flickering storm lashed out, boiling down the passage while more tendrils started to form. A lone scout detached from the wall just in front of them, running into the cloud, cords whipping and grabbing him, but not before he detonated an incendiary bomb of some kind. The outline of the tunnel appeared as a stark circle, its center consumed by light and fire, the camera view retreating. The tendrils were gone, and the air showed numerous flaming bits that darted about before dropping to the floor, but then the mass returned. It rolled forward as a roiling fog, catching and destroying the recon 'bots still in the passage.

The view shifted to the crater, an overhead shot as five remaining Spartacans rushed over the broken rocks in full flight. The tunnel entrance pulsated with the approaching doom, and a shuttle dropped almost to the floor with its rear ramp down. The dark figures fled in terror, clawing, tripping, legs pumping, then the first one was aboard and the next one and then the swarm surged right into the back of the shuttle.

Tree-sized vines materialized out of the cloud,

man-sized branches that speared the sides of the shuttle while the clutching cords wrapped around the fuselage. Mercifully, someone in orbit cut the feed before it exploded.

"**M**y God." Reena stared at the screen even as the crater's bottom started to fill with the moths. The flying robots ascended ahead of them, showing that the cloud was growing exponentially. "General Merkit, initiate the emergency evacuation protocol."

"Yes, ma'am." Merkit bent over one of the technicians, speaking quietly.

On the screen, a salvo of rockets slammed straight down into the crater. The view switched to higher-altitude reconnaissance, showing the massive aperture as an innocuous hole just before it belched light and flame and then smoke. A second salvo struck home, blowing the smoke out into a wispy fog that hugged the ground. Holding her breath, Reena strained to see through the obstruction.

Undiminished, the cloud of moths spewed forth from the opening and spread out like ants surging from their ruined home to do battle.

"Ma'am?" Merkit was next to her. "General Immersely."

The Banshee commander's face appeared on the screens. Seated in the center of a tactical operations center on a different warship, she was an immobile form surrounded by troops speaking urgently into headsets and typing rapidly on control panels.

"Madame Chairwoman, I'm going to need authorization to employ every weapon available." Immersely spoke slowly, in a voice of steely calm.

"You already have that authorization, General." Merkit answered.

"Not all of them. I'm going to need the therm-bombs to get my people out."

"Those were designed for the tunnels." Merkit shook his head. "No one's going to be able to emplace them now."

"I'm aware of that. I'm planning to use them as air bursts."

"They were designed for confined spaces. You use them in the air, the effect's going to be considerably diminished."

"I certainly hope so." Immersely's facial prosthetic twitched. "I'm going to be detonating these things right over my people."

The first shuttle flight to be brought down by the moths sent down a distress call heard all over the surface.

"Hey, is anybody else getting readings near me? Eye in the sky, you seeing this?" The pilot's broadcast quivered with near-panic.

"Mark your location." a robotic voice answered.

In helmets all across the plain, aerial imagery widened until the blinking cursor appeared. It was a flight of three shuttles, heading for one of the pickup zones to begin the evacuation.

"What are you seeing?" the pilot shouted. "I had no readings at all, and suddenly the alarms are all going off!"

Increasing the resolution showed nothing at first. Then flashing red dots appeared on the screen all around the shuttles, the alarm cursors quickly forming a wide cloud of heat signatures that enveloped the three craft.

"Engine failure! Engine failure!"

"Something's blocking my intakes!"

"They're moths! There's a million of 'em!"

All communications from the shuttles ceased. The Banshees watching on the ground knew the link hadn't been severed by Command, because they got to watch the three stricken craft fall all the way down.

"**M**ultiple swarms rising from craters. They're disappearing from the scopes—looks like they're scattering." The technician in front of Reena chanted the latest reports. "Another shuttle flight just went down. There were no warnings until they were on them."

"They know how our systems work, and they've figured out how to get past them." Merkit kept his voice low, as if trying to figure out a puzzle. "Look at the screen. They're intercepting the evacuation flights."

All across the target area, Banshee units were moving toward the pickup points. Bright flashes kept exploding inside the craters, missiles impacting steadily. Smoke drifted from most of the holes in elongated clouds. Drone gunships had dropped low enough to be seen from the ground, covering the troops as they moved.

"Madame Chairwoman, I think they're trying to trap our troops on the surface."

"What would that accomplish?" Reena asked, forcing herself to stay seated and to focus her thoughts. "They know more than our systems—they know how ruthless we can be. They know we'll blow this whole planet to bits, with our people still down there, if we have to."

"Everything we've seen says they were relying on not being found. For whatever reason, they're tied to this place. And now that we're here, perhaps they're going to take as many of us with them as possible."

"Ma'am?" General Immersely appeared on the screen. "The ground element is being cut off. Request permission to join them."

"Denied. You'd never get down there anyway. They're picking off the shuttles . . ." Reena's word trailed off.

"I have an answer for that. I'm going to bring the

ground element together, and then burn the surface and the air with the therm-bombs. Their suits should protect them. After that, I'm going to drop missiles all around them except for two shuttle lanes, one in and one out. You have to let me go down there."

"Give me a moment, General." Reena broke the connection and looked at Merkit. "They *do* know us, right? Jan and Varick said the thing reached into their minds."

Merkit frowned, until comprehension reached him. "That's how they're intercepting the flights. They knew the whole plan as soon as we put people on the ground."

"General, this is Chairwoman Mortas." Reena reopened the connection. "I'm going to need you to trust me."

"**S**tay here? Why?" Tin answered Captain Breverton's call.

"The company's been ordered to break up into squads and head out on different headings. Somehow the aliens figured out where our pickup points are, and you saw what happened to the shuttles. They haven't been going after individual craft that are flying random patterns, so Command figures the aliens won't gather for a single bird.

"Each squad is going to be picked up at an unspecified time and place, because we don't know how the aliens identified the pickup points. You weren't supposed to be where you are, so you'll be fine."

"When can we expect our ride?"

"I just told you—no one knows the timing. Don't do anything to attract attention, and be ready to move."

"Understood." Tin switched to the squad's internal communications. "But I sure don't like it."

"Hey, we're the only ones who don't have to hump out into the wasteland." Dellmore tried to sound optimistic.

"Right." Lightfoot chimed in. "We're already there."

The others all laughed, and even though their suits were soundproofed Ayliss couldn't help noticing that the merriment was a low whisper.

"Captain Varick?" Zuteck called.

"Go ahead."

"You are officially a jinx."

"Thanks. And here I thought I was just rusty."

"Hey," Cusabrina hissed. "We might not have to wait long. Look what's coming."

Ayliss widened the view in her helmet, observing the numerous short, dotted lines of Banshee suits spreading out across the flat. Gunships ran routes over all of them, and target markers dotted the imagery for missile strikes, but the first shuttles appeared to be coming in. Three ships came flying along alone, each from a different direction, clearly on intercept with three of the widely scattered squads.

"You'd think they'd throw in a little diversion, wouldn't you?" Legacy asked. "Maybe a little zigzag?"

"That's messed up." Varick agreed. "All that effort to fool the moths, and now they're coming straight in."

"Fuck!" Dellmore shouted. "Look what's popping up."

The dreaded convergence of the aliens started all over again, like a recurring nightmare. Red dots flashed ahead of the lone craft, their number increasing by the second until they formed a crimson cloud.

"Why aren't they diverting?" Ayliss asked, dumfounded. "They're going right into it."

The answer came in the form of a loud mechanical voice that overrode all other communications.

"All units! All units! Take cover! Take cover! Take cover!"

The Banshees flung themselves down, hugging the dirt, and Ayliss looked up at the last moment in the direction of the nearest shuttle. Miles away, an eye-burning dot of white light burst into life and then blossomed into an orange line in the bright sky. A boom like the birth of the universe followed, and the damping mechanisms in her suit did their best to keep it from rendering her deaf.

Pressing her entire body against the soil, Ayliss cringed inside her armor as the sunlight was replaced by a yellow glow that raced toward them. A second crash of thunder passed over, followed by a blast of heated wind that lifted her into the air and threw her back several feet. The imagery showed an ovular fireball expanding where the nearest shuttle had been, and understanding came with it. The shuttle had clung to its suicidal course because it was unmanned. Remotely piloted, it had been intended to draw the deadly swarm because it was carrying one of the thermal bombs.

Another shockwave, this one from the opposite direction, as if the enormous explosion had burned up the very atmosphere around it and now a hurricane of other gasses was rushing in to fill the vacuum. Dirt swirled up and would have blanked out the sun if the orb could be seen through the fireball that stretched across the firmament. Lying there, feeling the heat slowly dissipating across her armor, Ayliss shut her eyes because she didn't want to see what had happened to the Banshee squad closest to the blast.

"Rig? Rig?" Dellmore calling.

"I'm here." Ayliss didn't open her eyes. "Everybody okay?"

The different voices called out, proof that they were all alive. Varick answered last, and Zuteck responded.

"Hey, Captain?"

"Yeah."

"You are officially our good luck charm."

"What about the squads?" Reena demanded. "Are they alive?"

"Yes, ma'am." The screens were slowly returning to normal, as if the trio of enormous fireballs had given retina burns to every camera covering the battlefield. "The last one just called in. Said they were a little singed, but all right."

"What's surveillance saying? Did we burn those things up or not?"

"The three concentrations are gone." Merkit pressed a finger against his earpiece, relaying the messages. He gave Reena a hopeful look. "I think it worked."

"Get the second shuttles in right away."

"Already inbound," Merkit answered. "Amazing. We couldn't have done this near unarmored troops. The blast, the concussion, the heat, the vacuum . . . would have killed them all."

"Are the next shuttles ready?"

"As soon as we've picked up these three squads, we'll do it again with three more. With any luck, the aliens will stop coming after us."

"Shuttles inbound, ma'am." The warning made Merkit go silent, and they watched as the markers for the individual craft appeared in three different parts of the screen. "Squads ready to board."

The cursors blinked in flight, each time moving closer to the pickup points like water bugs kicking across the surface of a lake. Reena's mind was racing with the different variations of her plan, cooked up by Immersely's staff in case the aliens reacted faster than expected. More unmanned flights, some with bombs and some without. A kaleidoscopic dance that would keep the detonations from knocking down the other ships.

The shuttles were almost to the pickup points, where the Banshees were marking their locations. Evacuating in this fashion would take many hours, unless the aliens retreated back inside their caverns. Reena's thought shifted to the bigger question of what their opponents had hoped to accomplish with their devastating foray aboveground. Even if they'd killed every human on the surface, it wouldn't save them in the long run.

"Shit!" Merkit caught himself too late.

The dots were back, forming quickly around the descending shuttles and the waiting Banshees.

"Why can't we detect them?" Reena shouted impotently, knowing the moths only appeared on the scanners when they gathered in large numbers. She grabbed the console in front of her as the red cloud grew, her fingers whitening. Forcing herself to let go, and refusing to push the horror and disappointment away. "Put it on speaker. Let me hear it."

"Ma'am, there's no reason—"

"Let me hear it!"

A burst of static belched across the room, immediately followed by frantic calls.

"Perimeter! Tight perimeter!"

"Grenades only at this range! Don't use up your flame fuel!"

"It's gonna land on us!"

The shuttle's cursor disappeared in the crimson mist, just a few hundred yards short of touchdown. A series of booms rattled the speakers, and then the cloud was surrounding the Banshees.

"Give it to 'em, sisters! Burn 'em down!"

"There's too many of them!"

"They've got Temple! *They're crushing her!*"

A rattle of gunfire, and then another explosion, and then silence.

The low hum of activity that was always in the background of the operations room was now missing. Technicians sat in various postures, some staring at the screens, others bent over in thought, while the remainder tapped out communications or whispered into headsets. Reena stood stock still, her lips parted slightly, and Merkit paced back and forth in a slow trudge near the back wall.

Someone had muted the audio, but it was all there on the monitors. The presentation automatically focused in on enemy contact, the view dropping to show the markers where individual Banshee squads were being surrounded and killed. Missiles rained down in a useless ring around some of them, a reflex call for protection that had always worked in the past.

Incendiary rockets, not anywhere near as powerful as the therm-bombs, burned the ground and the low vegetation and even a few of the moths before the swarm closed in.

General Merkit stopped pacing, pointing at one of the monitors. "What's going on there? What are those machines?"

On the screen, transparent globes fitted with engines and outsized pincer arms were carrying individual Banshees through the air. A tech enlarged the image while another answered.

"Those are extravehicular maintenance craft, brought down to the surface by the units supporting the Banshees, sir. No one seems to have known they were there. They're scooping up the squads that are closest to the swarms and flying them out of danger."

"How many of those things are available?"

"Impossible to say. No one's directing them, and so the different support outfits are all mixed together. It's pretty confused."

"Find out how many of them are down there."

"General." Reena spoke with resignation.

Merkit flinched, knowing what was to come. "I'm here, ma'am."

"No matter their numbers, those machines are only prolonging the inevitable. There's no need to continue this. Order the fleet to move to minimum safe distance."

"There has to be something we haven't thought of."

"Hear that?" She raised her left hand, palm up with the fingers spread, swinging it slowly from the elbow. "Not a word. If anybody's got the solution, they're keeping it to themselves."

"How about . . ." Merkit's mind raced. "We cut the feed to the squads. That way they won't know if a shuttle is approaching or not. The aliens can't read their minds for information they don't have. We can still see where each squad is located, so we send a remote-piloted shuttle to each of them. They see it, they run on, it takes off."

"Blind them? How are we going to explain that to them?"

"That's the thing—we don't tell them. We can't."

"Ma'am?" one of the techs called out.

"What is it?"

"The aliens just broke off one of their attacks." The man pointed at the screen, now focused on the missile-torn plain around one Banshee squad's position. "A squad assigned to Crater Thirty-Nine is reporting that the swarm flew away all at once."

"Let me speak to them."

"This is Sergeant Littlefield." a tired voice answered. "Who's this?"

"This is Chairwoman Mortas. How did you drive the aliens away?"

"We didn't." The words came through as exhaustion mixed with awe. "They had us. They fuckin' *had* us. And then they just . . . left."

CHAPTER 19

"**T**he tanks are blasting holes in the wall!" Lieutenant Wolf reported from somewhere on the SOA's perimeter. "We're gonna have to fall back."

Mortas listened to that report, and many others like it, from a vault buried under the Ministry. The prisoners had shown them the secret subterranean passage, but even so it had taken the nefarious talents of Leoni's drivers to gain access to Asterlit's bunker.

"Gunships using high explosive rounds!" Major Hatton called out from several blocks away. "They're chewing up the buildings around us. Displacing to the north."

Other reports carried similar tales of a losing battle. The Orange and the Flock were out in force, killing the green suiters in large numbers, but the units converging on the city were all hardened HDF. Protected by rocket fire and armored vehicles, they were grinding their way forward and squeezing the Orphans into a pocket that was getting smaller and smaller.

In addition to the medics that had arrived in a recent salvo of darts, Strickland had found a pair of communications specialists who volunteered to help Jander work the sophisticated equipment in Asterlit's vault. The gear had been left running when the normal operators had fled, but the new radiomen weren't sure they'd managed to transmit any messages off-world yet.

"Sergeant Strickland, you can stop sending people." Jander called back to the Mound. "The Force is closing in on us. Load up another salvo of darts with ammo, and then send everybody away."

"I'll do that, but I'm coming in on the last one" Strickland answered. "If I'm gonna get executed, I want to be with my own."

A muted blast thrummed against the bunker's heavy walls, suggesting that the rocket-jamming gear was beginning to fail. Sergeant Leoni was up on the roof, firing anti-aircraft missiles at any gunships that tried to get close while FITCO drivers emptied the latest darts and shoved them over the side.

"I hear you. Make it quick. And tell anyone there who isn't an Orphan to say they had nothing to do with us."

"Aw, shit." Strickland's words rang with disappointment. "Won't be seeing you, sir. Inbound rockets."

"No!" Mortas shouted, as if to drive them away with his will. "Get down! You can make it!"

"Oh, that's doubtful." Strickland answered just as a succession of earthquake-sized explosions pounded over the speakers. The transmission ended.

"They killed them." Easterbrook whispered at his elbow, a blood-soaked field dressing wrapped around her head. Much of the bunker was taken up with other wounded and the medics, but no one had been able to convince her to sit quietly. "They're gonna kill us all, aren't they, sir?"

"It's all right," he murmured, squeezing her shoulder while cold reality crystallized in his guts. One of Cranther's comments came to mind, and he gave a lame grin. "It's a lot cleaner when Command kills you on purpose, than when they do it by accident."

"We've got confirmation!" one of the communications men shouted, bouncing in his chair. "Sir, we've been broadcasting your message off-world for almost an hour!"

"Who's telling you they heard it?"

"Your first choice—the Holy Whisper radio net. The Whisper is rebroadcasting even as we speak."

Mortas blew out a long exhale, and then gave Easterbrook a hopeful glance. "We might not be dead yet."

The speakers came alive with the address he'd recorded an hour earlier.

"This is Lieutenant Jander Mortas of the Orphan

Brigade. I am broadcasting from the Celestian Security Ministry in Fortuna Aeternum. Orphan units have attacked the Seat of Authority because Governor Damon Asterlit murdered our commanding officer, Colonel Jonas Watt, along with his entire staff."

The others had gone silent, even the worst wounded gritting their teeth to listen.

"We have captured the Ministry and much of the Seat of Authority, and we have killed Governor Asterlit. We are under heavy attack by Human Defense Force units, and I ask you to rebroadcast my words to anyone who will listen."

The room shook with another detonation, dust drifting down around them.

"Governor Asterlit had committed numerous crimes before murdering Colonel Watt. He had secretly reopened several mines in areas that the rebels never captured, and transferred Celestian citizen refugees to those mines. Right now, this very moment, they are being forced to work in exchange for their food rations.

"If you believe that the rebellion ended the slavery on Celestia, you have been misled. Video evidence of the new camps at the mines has been smuggled off-world by Orphan officers, and I ask whoever now has that footage to release it immediately. Your friend Erlon Pappas died so you could have that evidence.

"The Orphan Brigade has removed Asterlit's government, and I am begging you to direct the HDF units attacking us to cease fire. Please rebroadcast this message, and if possible, send it to Chairwoman Reena Mortas."

Jander looked at the nearest specialist. "Who confirmed receipt?"

"Someone claiming to know you, sir."

He punched a button, and a young male voice came through the speakers. "This is Dru Clayton, from the Holy Whisper station on Roanum. I know Jander Mortas personally, and he is a man of honor and a man of peace. I am rebroadcasting his message, and urge every one of my brothers and sisters to do the same."

"You think that will do it, sir?" Easterbrook asked, one hand clutching his armor while the other pressed against her head.

"Not sure. Maybe nobody's gonna listen to a bunch of pacifists."

One of the commo men turned in his seat. "I can't think of a better group to call for a cease-fire."

"**W**here'd you get the boomers?" Mortas asked Sergeant Leoni once he emerged on the roof. The jamming was still working, and several FITCO troops were firing the rocket launchers at the building across the street. Sited on lower ground, it was a good three stories shorter than the Ministry.

"You wouldn't believe the arms room they had

here." Leoni was crouched by an unbroken part of the stone railing. No darts remained on the expanse, which was now covered in spent missile tubes and chonk casings. "Boomers, chonks, anti-aircraft, and tons of ammo. Looks like they figured they might have to use this place for a last-ditch defense."

"They were always terrified of the people they abused," Jan commented. Outside the distant wall surrounding the SOA, billowing clouds of smoke and soaring flames said that much of the city was rapidly disappearing in fire. "Fortuna Aeternum. Eternal Fortune. Look at it now."

"For what it's worth, I liked your message, sir."

"We got an answer from the Whisper, and they're rebroadcasting it. We're sending it out to as many stations as we can. Not sure it's gonna be in time."

"The tanks have knocked down the wall to the north." Leoni pointed. Gunships roared back and forth in front of what must have been a large armored assault creeping down the narrow streets. "The Orange and the Flock are holding them up, but that's not going to last."

A tree-sized rocket sailed down out of the atmosphere toward them, and Mortas shouted a warning just as Leoni grabbed his arm to keep him from going flat. The missile veered off course long before it would have impacted, wobbling in flight before erupting in the mud flats outside the city. Leoni laughed.

"The jamming takes a little getting used to. The

drivers don't even notice them anymore." Mortas looked at the far edge, where the troops were still firing boomers. "Some of the CIP got in there, started lobbing chonk rounds at us. About the only thing that can reach us that doesn't have a guidance system."

"They're gonna find a way to get past the jamming. And even if they don't, those tanks will knock this whole place down when they get here." Mortas made a decision. "Come on. Everybody down to the bunker."

"With all due respect, sir, I'm not interested in being cornered. They're going to execute us all anyway, so I think I'll stay put."

The stark finality of Leoni's statement hit him like a blow. The words took the high likelihood that they wouldn't get out alive and turned it into a certainty.

"What about them?" Mortas pointed at the soldiers on the bare edge, where the darts had completely destroyed the railing.

"Same opinion. Everybody who wants to be downstairs is there already." Leoni peered over the railing, at the front of the Ministry. "Look at all those big wide stairs. I was thinking how much I'd like to just sit out there. Eat a little lunch, watch people walk by."

"You may yet." Jander tried to control the rising doubt. "Who knows what that message might do? Come down to the bunker; we're just playing for time now."

"It's been a pleasure working with you, sir." Leoni extended a bloodstained hand.

He took it, staring into the older man's eyes. "Don't do this. Come with me."

"We'll hold 'em off as long as we can, sir. But when they come banging at that door, make sure they don't take you alive."

CHAPTER 20

"**W**hy are they breaking off the attacks?" Reena asked, watching the monitors showing several embattled Banshee squads that were now in the clear. "Is this a trick?"

"Doubtful," Merkit replied, his eyes flicking over the various screens. "What would they hope to get? A few more shuttles?"

"Ma'am," a technician called, rising from her seat and pointing. "Look at Crater Forty-Seven."

Reena stepped up to the monitors. The crater that held the partially assembled spacecraft was completely changed. The busy worms and caterpillars were almost all gone, and the truncated fuselage was no longer in the center of the shaft. It was pressed up against one side, and all three of the mammoths that had been holding it upright had coiled together. She watched in fascination as the circular hull bent, shivered, and then crumpled under the weight and the pressure of the beasts.

"They're destroying it." Merkit spoke in awe. "And where did all the others go?"

"Show me the ground around that crater." Reena ordered, and the view changed after a few keystrokes. Leaving small clouds of dust, the other workers from the shaft were rushing across the open much like the worm that had killed itself. "Where are they going?"

"Their azimuth will take them to the nearest ruins, ma'am," the technician responded. "Incubators, I mean."

"What about the other craters?" Fingers flew across the consoles, tightening in on different holes but showing no surface activity near them.

"Forget the holes," Merkit ordered. "Show us the incubators."

At first the empty plain over the buried stones appeared inactive, and the different monitors flashed and flickered as each image changed. Suddenly, a voice called over the speakers.

"Look at the ruins near Crater Nine!" The image appeared on the largest screen a moment later, and the entire room went silent.

Numerous sinkholes seemed to be appearing on the dead gray ground. First they resembled black pinpricks that grew into large dots, and then they collapsed inward. Reena's face was squinching up in puzzlement when one of the cave-ins burst upward in a shower of dirt, broken rock, and fragments of what looked like a golden honeycomb. The explosion resembled a tornado for a moment, but as the broken materials flew away the tubular body of an enormous worm came into resolution. Towering higher and higher, it slowly came to a stop in the air before turning and heaving its entire length down onto the surface.

The ground fractured and collapsed all around the strike, a giant fissure running away from the worm as it extended hundreds of arms and started burrowing in a frenzy. Other holes likewise erupted, revealing even larger caterpillars. They smashed the dirt with their elongated bodies, and then dug right back among the buried stones. Rock flew everywhere, and in one instant Reena was sure she saw the gaping maw of one of the beasts chewing up the honeycomb.

"What is that golden material? Is it food?"

"No, ma'am." A different technician stared at lines of data rolling across a console screen. "It almost exactly matches the scans for the moth-things. They must have been asleep inside them."

"What do you know?" Reena turned to Merkit, astonished. "Ewing was right. They are incubators."

"And the workers are destroying them." Merkit snapped his fingers. "When the aliens came out to fight us, it must have broken whatever hold they had on their slaves. They're wrecking everything in sight."

As if to confirm that, the screens showed similar carnage at other locations. The unremarkable terrain hiding the stones was exploding with geysers of rock, honeycomb, and caterpillars, and then the heat signatures of the swarm flew into view at one of them. A giant red cloud, it converged on the worms destroying the incubators.

"It's not working." Merkit shouted. "Look at them! They're ignoring the moths. They just keep on smashing and chomping away."

"General." Reena grasped his sleeve. "Order the evacuation. Get all of our people out."

"**W**ill you look at that?" Lightfoot crowed from the far side of the perimeter. "Those worm things are tearing up the town!"

"They don't seem to like the ruins any more than we do," Legacy offered. "Captain Varick, maybe we should get out of here before one of those wrecking crew pays us a visit?"

"Hang on." Tin ordered. "The shuttles are coming in. The moths have their hands full with the caterpillars, so it's a full-on evacuation. Get ready to move."

"Can we leave these hunks of junk behind?" Dellmore asked, and Ayliss looked over at the silent monitor they'd been guarding. A moment later its dull dome lit up with a deep blue light, and a blast of electronic beeping and twittering came through her helmet.

"Hey, anybody else getting that?" Cusabrina called. "My hunk of junk just turned on."

On the *Aurora*, Reena was trying not to clap her hands as the screens showed shuttle after shuttle touching down and flying out with squads of Banshees and Spartacans. The carnage at the various buried sites had escalated, to the point that the shapeshifter swarms were physically assaulting the worms. Coalescing into a mindboggling array of spear-like weapons, the aliens were fighting a doomed battle while their workers chewed up the honeycombs.

Around the craters, more and more creatures were emerging. All of them were tubular in form, but their sizes ranged from tiny to enormous.

"Look at that," Merkit said. "They're uncountable. Those tunnels must go for thousands of miles."

"Sir?" One of the technicians waved him over. "The ground monitors have finally synced up with the aerobots. Here's the imagery so far."

The screens shifted to an overhead view of the plain surrounding the selected crater. One moment it was a scene of tumult, with the worms climbing the shaft and then racing away, and then the surface became almost transparent. At an unspecified depth, a network of tunnels appeared as if right on the surface. Twisting and turning, they connected enormous caverns that hummed with electricity and light.

"Focus in on that one there," Reena ordered, pointing at a rectangular vault filled with what appeared to be Transit Tubes. The screen filled with the image, and Reena snarled, "There it is! Look at it, General! Rows and rows of 'em! *Sims!*"

Tin's squad had come together again, forming a wide circle around the monitor that Varick was minding. The imagery in their face shields was a kaleidoscope of shuttles and rampant destruction, the flights picking up the separated Banshee squads while the shapeshifter swarms fought their erstwhile workers.

"This is crazy." Varick muttered, examining an illuminated screen on the side of the device. "These things are supposed to image the ground, but this one's uploading data at an incredible rate."

"What are you saying?" Tin asked. "That the ruins are some kind of supercomputer?"

"No—these places clearly hold millions of the moths in some kind of stasis. Ewing thought they were incubators, but how would that account for all this information?"

A wisp of smoke rose from the glowing blue dome, and Varick took a step back. Sparks popped from the lead stuck in the dirt, and then the entire device began to rock and hiss. With a sudden bang, the dome burst free and flew several yards in the air while flames briefly flickered inside the machine's overloaded circuits.

"Too much data?" Bullhead joked. "I remember studying for a test one time—"

"Uh-oh," Cusabrina grunted. "Look what's coming from the north."

Ayliss adjusted the display, and then wished she hadn't. A wave of red dots was rolling toward the ruins, and no shuttle flights were anywhere nearby.

"Evac! Evac!" Tin shouted. "We are about to get swarmed! Anyone close by, divert to this location and pick us up!"

"Why are they coming here?" Zuteck asked as the squad reoriented itself to face the oncoming threat. "No worms, no shuttles . . . what did *we* do?"

"The monitors," Varick answered, unclipping her Fasces and stepping into line. "We've got the only ones probing the incubators, or whatever these things are."

"Oh, you are definitely back to being a jinx, Captain."

"Fire control, we have a concentrated cloud of aliens about to hit us." Tin spoke calmly while Cusabrina motioned the squad down. "Request incendiaries."

"We see 'em. On the way. Hang tough."

"Heads down." Cusabrina just got the words out

when the missiles landed. Once again Ayliss felt the shockwave lift her, heated air in a world that had turned to nothing but fire, and then she was dropped on her stomach. More blasts erupted in the flames that engulfed them, slapping her back and forth. The suit protected her as it always had, creating a surreal environment where Ayliss should have been burned to a cinder but instead watched the inferno from its very center until it simply blew out.

"Up! Up! There's more!" she heard Tin shouting, and then saw the mass of black flecks charging toward them. Without thinking, Ayliss raised the Fasces and squeezed the trigger. Fire roiled from the barrel in a hungry jet, blowing through the swarm, lighting hundreds of them and dropping their ashes to the ground as she swept the flame back and forth. The rest of the squad was nearby, other horizontal tornadoes of fire drilling into the cloud, but it wasn't any good, there were too many of them, her cameras were suddenly blotted out by a million fluttering wings, and then she was knocked over.

Firing from a sitting position, running out of fuel in that barrel, tonguing the next one up and shooting the jet into the swarm. Buffeted by what felt like high winds, and then a flesh-colored tree branch struck her so hard in the side of the helmet that she fell over, stunned. The swarm shifted off of her, and lying there Ayliss saw it all happen, unable to move, unable to act. Fibers emerging from the moth cloud, twisting, coiling, growing, and then one of them was holding a Fasces and driving the barrel straight into Cusabrina's shoulder joint and blasting high explosive rounds straight into her armor.

"Therm-bombs! Drop 'em right on us!" Varick shouted from somewhere. "I been roasted before—it's *nothing*!"

The tendrils wrapped around Zuteck, lengthening, expanding, pinning her arms and her rifle against her torso while she screamed for someone to shoot them off her. Dell stepping up, ricochets bouncing off of Zuteck's armor as the constricting cords broke and regrew and then Zuteck's suit exploded right in the middle of them.

"Dell!" Ayliss wheezed. "Run, Dell! Run!"

Dellmore turned to face her, the interior cameras activating, and her partner was regarding Ayliss with a beatific smile. Dellmore tossed the empty rifle away and pulled a grenade from her armor just as the surging muscles caught her.

"Rockets inbound! Rockets inbound! Take cover! Take cover! Take cover!" The words rebounded inside Ayliss's ears, and she fought her way up onto an elbow just as the bands tightened around Dell and the grenade went off, the confined space of the tendrils blowing them off of her like rotten vines and tearing her suit in half.

"Dell," Ayliss whispered, her armored hand reaching for the two pieces of the suit. The swarm recognized she was still alive and dived, the terrible sinewy bands forming, and she was still too dazed to reach a grenade and her suit was making horrible grinding sounds and then the rockets landed. The constrictors evaporated right in the middle of the explosions and the fire, and then the ground gave way underneath her and she fell into darkness.

Reena stood in front of the screens, too conflicted to move. The evacuation was proceeding at a rapid pace, and the unit markers of entire Banshee companies were quickly disappearing from Omega's surface. Under the dirt, the mapping of the aliens' world continued to serve up breathtaking revelations. The ground monitors, though linked in with more powerful systems flying over their heads and in orbit around the planet, were already indicating that the tunnels and caverns extended inside the planet far beyond their range.

But it didn't matter. Before her eyes was a steadily resolving subterranean complex of astounding proportions. Moss-covered tunnels alternated with laboratories where sophisticated machines still hummed and spun and shook with the generation of humanoid life. Enormous subterranean factories forged and shaped and twisted the tools, weapons, and ship parts that would be brought together in the craters that had been launching the Sims into their endless war for decades.

"Ma'am?" Merkit appeared next to her. "Ma'am?"

"Yes, General."

"We've received an urgent communication from the Holy Whisper Elders. There has been a significant development on Celestia."

"Whatever it is, it can't even come close to what we're doing here." Reena dragged her eyes from the screens. "What is it, and why did it come from the Whisper?"

"It involves your stepson."

CHAPTER 21

"This is General Morris Zillinger." A stern voice came over the speakers in Asterlit's bunker. "I am the commanding officer of the Tratian armored division that is about to knock the entire Ministry down around your ears."

"Fuckin' Tratians," one of the commo men spoke in a weary voice. "Gotta make everything an announcement."

"I offer you no clemency, and promise I will do my best to see any survivors executed for mutiny."

"Guy knows how to sell it, doesn't he?" a wounded FITCO driver muttered from the wall behind Jander. The vault was now filled with bandaged troops, and rockets were steadily chewing through the upper floors.

"If you come out with your hands up, I will accept

your surrender and see you are safely transported to whatever authority will oversee your courts-martial."

"That's it, Lieutenant." The nearest radioman took off his headset and pushed away from the console. "They've blocked our transmissions. Now we can only hear."

"I will give you three minutes to come outside. After that, no surrenders will be honored."

Mortas looked around the room. A heavy explosion slapped the reinforced ceiling, and small chunks of plaster rained down. Grim faces returned his gaze, some immobile while others were checking their weapons. Remembering Sergeant Leoni's decision not to let himself be cornered.

"I won't lie to you. They're going to kill us all, whether we surrender or not." He made his words loud enough to be heard over the bombardment. "Never forget we did the right thing here. We rid this world of an evil government, and we told the entire galaxy about the suffering and injustice that goes on here to this day. If Command can't see that, then I have no interest in letting them call me names as they walk me to the gallows."

He took his Scorpion rifle from a nearby table and made sure it was loaded. The motion sent many of the wounded struggling to their feet.

"I'm going out shooting. It has been an honor to lead you."

"Then lead us out, sir." Easterbrook pushed herself up, fresh blood on her lips. "We'll make them wish they never fucked with us."

Jander took her arm across his shoulders. All over the room, FITCO troops and support personnel from the Mound paired up to assist the wounded. Jander started toward the enormous door, even then sliding open on silent hinges. With the bunker unsealed, the roar of the explosions surged in like the howls of ravening beasts.

Easterbrook coughed once, then again, and then her entire body was wracked with a fit that sent dark blood streaming from her nostrils. Mortas gently lowered her to the floor, sitting her up against the wall while she raised glazing eyes.

"Aw shit," she whispered. "Look at me. Couldn't make the last twenty yards."

Her chin sagged to her armor, and Mortas released her. Standing, he looked back at the others. "Let's go."

He was several steps out into the ruined corridor when the speakers bellowed behind him.

"Attention! Attention! Attention all Human Defense Force units! This is General Euton Marbrook, commander of all HDF personnel on Celestia! By order of Chairwoman Reena Mortas, I command all Force units to cease fire immediately! I say again, cease fire!"

Pinned under the rocks, Ayliss Mortas rested in an inexplicable state of contentment. A dark space opened up far above, showing that the sun was setting on Omega. She should have been concerned, knowing that sooner or later the fleet would blow the entire planet to bits, but nothing could override the flow of thought that was spilling through her.

Her brain practically buzzed with the sensation, and she numbly decided that this was how data banks must feel. Facts and concepts and innovations rolled across her mind, and even recognizing that they were in no way human failed to disturb her in the least. Ayliss tried to focus on a single thread as it went by with the current, something about a civilization that had once traveled across the expanse of space with enormous solar sails as their only locomotion, but the information refused to sit still. It was like sitting in the middle of a crowded room, surrounded by brilliant conversation, but without the ability to hear more than a few phrases clearly.

A vibration thrummed through the rock, sending a jolt of muted pain from her left arm. Turning her head inside her helmet, she saw that the limb was caught beneath what must have been a titanic amount of rock. Two of the slabs came together in an unbroken seam, and her arm was between them. Her diagnostic readout said the appendage had been crushed all the way up to an inch past her elbow, but the pressure was so great that the suit hadn't lost its integrity.

Another shudder, this one larger than the first

one, started her wondering about an earthquake, but then the knowledge stream returned. It was different now, broken and panicked, and Ayliss swore she heard voices.

Devouring us. Our servants turned against us. Helpless.

Not the servants. The humans. Found us.

Too old. Too tired. Too late.

They're going to exterminate us right here in our home.

She tried to make sense of the words, and then didn't need to. The flow now mated with her own knowledge, prompting Ayliss to remember the caterpillars savaging the other ruins across the plain. The swarms had broken off their attacks on the Banshees to combat their own workers and protect what slept under the stones. Ewing had believed the ruins were incubators for young aliens, and he'd been close with that estimate—just in the wrong direction.

Not incubators. Hibernators. The final stage of an individual moth-thing's life cycle, when it could no longer shapeshift or fly or even move. They would simply lie there together, communing with each other, living repositories of everything their race had learned over the eons. The younger shapeshifters flew over the hibernators at set intervals, the telepathic link grown weak with age, in order to share their latest discoveries and call up pertinent data.

All to be lost, now that humanity had found the planet that the aliens could not abandon because their ancestors could not be moved. The irony of her own predicament, trapped with them as Armageddon loomed, reminding her of a calf on a distant planet that died just because it got separated from the others. What had Breverton said about her squad?

You weren't supposed to be where you are. If that were true, the chances of anyone finding her before the planet was blown to smithereens were practically nonexistent.

The current flowed in again, the aliens remembering how they'd come to create the Sims in the first place. The tale unfolded in her mind as if she'd actually lived it.

The shocking arrival of the human factory ship so long ago, attracted by what the home world contained, all the raw materials needed to create new equipment for the deep-space explorers. Observing the invaders as they dug into the planet's rich veins, then searching the interlopers' minds to learn with terror that there were more of them, that plumbing the depths of space was their calling. That they would despoil the home world before realizing that an ancient civilization lived within it.

A superior civilization. A race that had infiltrated, subjugated, and destroyed many species whose intelligence far outstripped that of the humans.

Studying the trespassers and then taking on their forms, boarding the ship and replacing the crew until they could seize the vessel intact. Learning its secrets, how its innards were capable of creating other ships like it, and that its laboratories could generate human life.

Deciding then and there to oppose the invaders using their own machines, creating and arming a species much like the humans, just more brutal and more focused. A designer enemy that couldn't regenerate itself, that fought its cousins for habitable planets far from the uninhabitable home world. The Sims.

The Sims, who had been intended to destroy mankind and then die out—except they'd failed. Leading to the desperate decision to infiltrate the humans yet again, this time to gain the secret of the Step. The war, and the invaders' sophisticated technology, had come too close to the home world and the ancient generations asleep inside it. They'd considered the gamble an unavoidable risk, as the only way to preserve the race.

Tears rolled down Ayliss's cheeks as she experienced their fear and anger, and finally their resignation, now that all was lost.

"Rig." The voice was low, scratchy, but Ayliss knew she should have recognized it. She looked to her right, and gasped.

Likewise pinned under the dark rocks, Legacy had activated her helmet cameras so that Ayliss could see her. Only her upper torso was visible in the small space, but Ayliss didn't see much of that.

Her horrified eyes recoiled at the graying skin and the puckering lips of an old woman who was as young as she was.

"Lisa? What's wrong?"

"Suit breach," she wheezed, eyes slitting in pain. "It's one of my legs. Can't get to it. Can't seal it."

Ayliss reached out with her right arm, trying to find a handhold to pull herself closer, knowing it was pointless.

"Don't struggle." Legacy made a deep choking sound. "You'll end up like me."

"You're going to be fine." Ayliss lied, and then tried to broadcast. "Any Banshee unit, anyone at all, do you read me?"

"They're all gone, Rig. I already tried."

"They can't be! They knew we were here. They were going to pick us up."

"They think we're dead. And they're right." More choking. "Oh, this *sucks*. My mother died from a suit breach."

"You're not going to die. Look at me. Help is on the way. I know it is."

"Hey Rig, was I hallucinating, or did you feel it too?"

"Like voices were inside your head? Brilliant voices? Millions of them?"

"Yeah." Legacy turned off her cameras, returning the image to the canted angles of her helmet. "What did we destroy here, Ayliss?"

"I'm not sure."

She got no response.

The voices entered her mind again. The rocks imprisoning Ayliss rumbled constantly now, punctuated by deep belches that suggested a major seismic event was occurring nearby. She wasn't forced to wonder what they were, though.

Where are the young ones? Why aren't they defending us?

The humans killed them. Or enough of them to free the workers.

How awful. To be erased by such a low intelligence.

Let us not die with that notion. Let us remember what we achieved.

Ayliss's mind floated along with the alien group consciousness. She struggled to concentrate on her own dire situation, but it was too hard to fight off the other signals. Her brain sang with revelations and wisdom and unfathomable images, remembered vistas in far-flung regions of space that no longer existed, hundreds upon hundreds of civilizations that had lived and died before humanity had ever come into existence. It was a comforting distraction, even as she sensed the carnage only a few miles away, the worms chewing through the stones and the honeycombs and their feeble inhabitants. Ayliss shut her eyes and watched a star explode, so long ago that the light had already come and gone.

Light. The darkened sky had mated with the edges

of the crevice, forming a single shroud of black, but there was an undeniable flicker there. It passed over the hole again, and the voices went silent as she shouted.

"Here! Here! I saw your beam! Come back!"

The light returned instantly, and then shone straight down into the small cavern. A Banshee helmet appeared, and Ayliss heard the voice of a woman she'd thought was dead.

"Dom! Over here!" Tin called, but the effort sent her into uncontrollable coughing. Armored gloves reached through the aperture, slowly peeling back a sliver of rock to widen the fissure. "Hang in there, Rig. We're here."

"I thought you were all dead." With Cusabrina and Zuteck and Dell.

"No. Just a little overcooked."

"Who—" She couldn't bring herself to finish the question, and instead looked over at Legacy's lifeless suit. More hands were clearing away debris, and other lights were entering the space.

"Varick's with us. Bullhead and Lightfoot, too. Haven't found Legacy."

"She's gone. Down here with me. Suit breach."

"Okay, back off." She heard Blocker's voice, and the hands disappeared. "Ayliss, can you send me the feed from your cameras?"

She gave the command with a dry tongue, and a moment later a long, tapering metal claw entered the crevice. Using her view, Blocker's machine gently shifted one enormous, cracked slab out of the way. The light beams streamed in, and she was able to see the big man working the controls inside the protective bubble. Even in her weakened state, suspicion rose up.

"How did you find me?"

"I had Orton put a special tracker in your suit." A boulder ascended, clutched between the machine's giant pincers, and another bubble's fingers took it away.

"I told you—my entire squad. Not just me."

"I figured you'd *be* with your squad. But the firestorm blew them half a mile away." The bubble pressed against the hole, and she could see sweat running off his face. "I told you on Quad Seven. I will never leave you again."

"Sarge, we shouldn't move any more of these." She heard Jerticker speaking from somewhere behind Blocker. "Her left arm's been crushed. We take off that pressure, who knows what shape the armor is in."

Fear entered her stomach as Ayliss looked at the smooth wall where her arm ended. Blocker exhaled, his cheeks rounding, and then tapped his headset. "Chief, you seeing all this?"

"Yep." Ayliss recognized the gruff tone of Chief Scalpo, the Banshee troop's hardened physician's assistant. "You're almost outta time. Crimp the suit just below the armpit, and then cut the rest loose."

"Oh Lord." Blocker whispered.

"Back out, Sarge." Jerticker offered. "Let me do it."

"No." Blocker extended one set of pincers until they held Ayliss's upper arm. "She's my little girl. I'll get her out."

"Hold on." Varick came crawling past the bubble, her gray suit unrecognizable. Its paint had blistered straight off, and the armor was charred. She slid over Ayliss, pointing. "Put the pincers right here. That's the nearest crush point."

"Crush point?" Ayliss tried to keep her words calm. "What's that?"

"What a newbie. Didn't they teach you anything in Basic?" Varick stayed close, even as a second set of pincers moved into place near the rocks. "The crush point is like a tourniquet. You crimp a suit right there, it seals it off."

"Varick, you're gonna have to move." Blocker warned. The captain rested a gloved hand on Ayliss's chest armor, and then wriggled away. Ayliss could see the big man again, and the cold certainty on his features scared her even more.

"So that's what you looked like. All those years in the war."

"Shut your eyes, Little Bear. We'll have you out in a second."

Ayliss tongued the cameras inside the helmet so Blocker could see her forced smile.

"It's okay, Bear. I trust you."

"Sarge, we gotta hustle." Jerticker called. "Those worms are almost on us."

The alien current flooded back into her mind, but this time it was a hurricane of screams and anguish. Ayliss gasped, feeling the honeycombs tearing and rocking as giant jaws and merciless claws tore into the ancient shapeshifters. Someone squeezed her upper arm hard, and then harder, and then she started screaming too.

"So what about that crazy announcement?" Lieutenant Wolf sat on the cracked stone steps of the Ministry, next to Jander. His left boot was missing, and his bandaged foot was propped on a piece of fallen masonry. They were surrounded by weary soldiers, the less seriously wounded who were waiting for eventual pickup, and Mortas had stopped to talk. "Somebody said the war is over."

"I heard that broadcast with my own ears. There's a super-powerful communications center inside." Mortas looked out over the cratered square in front of the building. Troops from the HDF units that had been assaulting the SOA only hours before were now guarding it and sorting through the dead. Broken stone from the Ministry's missing top floors was scattered all around, and he thought of how they resembled ancient Roman ruins because he didn't want to think about Leoni and the others from the roof. "It was definitely my stepmother."

"Really?" Prevost asked, two steps down and wrapping a bandage around Greeber's upper left arm. "The war's actually finished?"

"Kind of. She said Command found a planet where the Sims were being made, and that the Banshees attacked the place. In the end they had to nuke it, but right now in the war zone our people are pulling back to give the Sammies some room."

"What good's that going to do? Can't talk to them."

"She explained that. This gang of linguists caught a major break a while back. They finally worked through enough of the bird-speak to build a simple translator. They're broadcasting all over the war zone, asking for a cease-fire."

"A major break?" Prevost tied the bandage and then looked up at Mortas. "That was you, wasn't it? That secret mission you were on. You *did* talk to them."

"Yeah, we did. Through one of the shapeshifters."

Wolf snorted. "Your old girlfriend from Glory Main?"

Jander instantly thought of Varick, and then realized Wolf was referencing the oft-told story of his having had sexual congress with the original alien. He snorted as well.

"Hardly. I killed this one myself."

"And we always wondered why you aren't married." Prevost laughed.

"Lieutenant Mortas," a Tratian soldier in full combat gear called from the bottom of the stairs. "Can I speak with you?"

Jander put a hand on Wolf's armor, and stood with pain. Now that the battle was over, every muscle seemed to hurt. He carefully weaved his way through the rock fragments and resting Orphans. When he reached the bottom, the Tratian soldier came to attention.

"Cut that out. War's over. Haven't you heard?"

"No, sir." The man appeared confused. "Is that true?"

"My stepmother *never* makes a public statement that she can't back up."

"Sir?"

"Never mind. What is it?"

"We've got a small party from the Orange, requesting to see you."

"What, are they all deaf? We've had the PSYOP drones broadcasting for hours—if they stay away from us, nobody gets hurt."

"There's this kid, seems to be their leader. Says he knows you."

"Oh no." The words were almost inaudible. He hadn't been able to give a thought to Leeger during the chaotic fighting. "They carrying a body?"

"Yes, sir." The confused look had returned. "How did you know?"

"Take me to them."

His feet hurt as he walked across the small broken rocks that seemed to be everywhere. Smoke rose over much of the rest of the city, and drone firefighters with bulging bellies could be seen dumping retardant in several places. As they went down the block, he watched a flight of medevac shuttles lift off from somewhere near the river.

He knew they were getting close when the looming hulk of a Tratian tank came into view. A temporary barricade of rolled anti-personnel wire blocked off the street twenty yards in front of the tank, and a cluster of Tratian soldiers stood watching seven orange-colored civilians sitting next to a stretcher. Jander tried not to look at its motionless occupant.

The boy called Sunlight stood up from the group, wearing oversized fatigues blackened with soot. One side of his orange hair appeared to have been flattened, until Mortas got close enough to see it had been singed away. The other rebels, four men and two women in ragged clothing, made no effort to stand. Like the troops he'd left on the steps of the Ministry, they looked too tired to do much of anything.

"It's all right. Let him through." One of the Tratians punched a signal into a handheld, cutting the electricity in the wire, and then pulled one segment back. The orange-hued child walked through, lips pursed. He walked up to Jander, tears cleaning away the dirt on his cheeks.

"It's our father," he whispered. "He's dead."

CHAPTER 22

"I thought we were done." Olech spoke to Mirror as they walked across a sunny plain covered with waist-high grass. "You told me why your people avoided mine after studying us in the Step. I figured that was it."

"No matter how much it hurt, that was the answer you sought when you climbed into that capsule." Mirror wore a dark, high-collared suit with the red ribbon of the Unwavering, and when Olech looked down he saw the same image. "You'll be taking that message back with you."

"Back?" Hope leapt inside him. "I'm going home?"

"Of course. You risked everything coming here, even death, so why wouldn't you go home?"

"What's happened while I was gone? Jan looked so different, so . . . used up. What about the others?"

"Time has indeed passed in your realm. The war with the Sims is over. With our help, Reena found the planet where they were being manufactured and annihilated their authors. She believes that you somehow sent her that location. In a way you did; consider it an acknowledgment of your genuine willingness to sacrifice yourself in that cause."

Before he could ask about individual family members, Olech smelled an odor that sent his blood surging. The sun still shone overhead, but the tall grass was no longer an endless sea. Burned away in patches hundreds of yards wide, it sent up tiny curls of smoke in numerous spots.

"No." Olech hissed, seeing a long, tall hill rising from the blackened grass. Much of the rise was mud, and it slowly populated with mashed and mutilated bodies that disappeared in the undergrowth. He couldn't see the top, but he knew it by heart.

"This is an important experience for you, Olech. For both of us."

"No!" he yelled. "I already went through it. So it is *not* both of us."

"You directed the defense of that hill for two days and two nights, even though you were only fifteen and a private. Older men, even some NCOs, managed to join you without offering to take charge. You cobbled together a force that at one point numbered two hundred soldiers."

"That was only at the end. We never had more than a hundred until the Sims ran off. Couple of times, we were down to fifty." Olech turned away from the hill. "But that's not where we are right now, is it?"

"You recognize the terrain."

"I almost died right over there." At the base of the hill, the shell of a burned-out truck stood out from the ashen ground and the remaining grass. Bodies were strewn around it, many of them missing limbs. "This jerk of a captain finally showed up and took charge after we won. He never acknowledged what I did, but he knew. That's why he sent me down the backside here, with a message for battalion. He didn't want me around."

Memories flooded back, making him cringe. The explosion, the ground opening up, the mindboggling pain, the certainty that he was going to die, right there, alone. "Please, Mirror. Not this one."

A breeze greeted him from the spot where Mirror was standing, and when he looked up his twin was gone. Breath coming in short gasps, terror welling up, realizing that there hadn't been any fear before it happened because he hadn't known it was coming. Now, armed with that knowledge, Olech saw that it was far worse. Shutting his eyes, waiting for the sensation of becoming his younger self, the footsore boy who hadn't eaten in days, who'd defended the hill where his platoon-mates had died. Who'd then stomped off down the hill, furious at the stupidity of the people who had such enormous control over his life.

Remembering that very anger on the night he'd agreed to help Horace replace the government. Recognizing for the first time in many years that his true reason for helping with the Purge had been his hatred of the overblown fools in Command who'd cost him so much.

Olech's eyes opened in bewilderment, finding that he was standing in the same spot, but still focused on the awful truth about why he'd become the principle architect of the Purge. Lips parting while he wet them with his tongue, looking around for Mirror, wondering if for once he'd earned a reprieve.

Hearing a noise, Olech looked up the hill and saw a tall, thin boy in tattered olive drab clomping down the trail. Mud in his hair and on his face and on his clothes. One boot looked dipped in the stuff, completely brown while the other was black. Another recollection lost over the decades. How could he have forgotten the artillery barrage that tore off one boot heel and left him flat-wheeling from position to position, encouraging the men and directing their fire? How later, when things were quiet, he'd taken a brown-colored boot off of a dead boy who'd almost been his size.

The noise he couldn't identify turned out to be words, angry mutterings as the teenaged soldier reached the bottom of the hill.

"Fuckin' asshole. Captain. Kiss my ass, *Captain*. Lost a hundred guys up there, Sims attacked over and over and over and over and I held 'em off. Me. Private Mortas." Eyes not seeing the ground, or the cracked engine part jammed in the dirt. "I shoulda stayed lost. I was safer on my own. I should just walk off."

The memory returning, the one that had been literally blasted out of his mind, of tripping over the metal and sprawling into the grass where the mine had lain all that time, hundreds of soldiers had marched or run right past it, but he'd landed almost on top of it.

Finally understanding what Mirror had meant, about this being an important experience.

"Mirror! *No!*"

The entire world exploded, throwing dirt and grass and junk from the battle into the air. Olech was running, mouth wide but eyes narrow, afraid to see what it had looked like because the one blessing of being hit like that is you don't see what you look like.

The boy was on his side, curled up in a ball, arms wrapped around his stomach, not moving, too hurt to move, too scared to move. Olech threw himself down in front of him, but not before seeing the torn fatigues and the bloody meat. Grabbing Mirror's face with his hands, only to see his own eyes wide in horror, the mouth open in a soundless scream.

"*Hurts!*" Mirror shrieked. "Ohmy*God*ithurts!"

Pulling him in, fearful of making it worse but

knowing that wasn't possible. The eyes were an inch from his own.

"I'm dying, Olech." Real terror on his features. "I'm gonna die right here."

"No, no you're not." Arms around his head, hugging him fiercely. "I know it hurts, it hurts like hell, but you don't die. I didn't die. I lay there for hours, and it never got better, and I kept bleeding but I couldn't let go of my guts, but they did find me. They will find you."

"Gonna die."

"No. You went home. Because of this. You're going home."

Olech's eyes burned with the overhead light, and his mouth was so dry that he couldn't wet it with saliva. His hands came up, reaching, and pressed against the transparent cover of the Transit Tube. No Mirror, no blood, no grass, no war, no one. His head jerked painfully as he looked left and then right, seeing he was back in the capsule that had launched him on the mission to meet whoever or whatever had given mankind the Step.

Mirror.

It wasn't an illusion, or a memory. His body was real, and he'd been returned to it. He found a bottle of water set into the compartment's wall, and drank so quickly that half of it ended up on the cushions. The cushions of a luxury Transit Tube befitting the Chairman of the Emergency Senate. Olech hit the release, and scrambled out of the container.

The capsule wasn't moving, but all its systems were online and the air was warm. Grabbing another water bottle, he tottered on weak legs to the nearest porthole. Seeing he was right where his mission had started, very close to the blue planet where he'd been born. The place he had so longed to return to, the whole time he'd been with the entity that said time didn't exist. The entity that said its race would shun mankind, not because of its capacity for bloodshed, but because humans could convince themselves that the violence and the theft and the cruelty and the gossip and the indifference all had a good reason.

The arm with the water bottle hung down by his side, and he rested his forehead against the window.

"Mirror? Can you hear me? Can you give us another chance?"

" . . . our heroic troops suffered enormous losses in the final battle."

Ayliss was sure she knew who was speaking, but the volume kept cutting in and out as she rode the painkillers. She'd briefly regained consciousness inside a machine shop of some kind, with power drills and hammers sounding all around while a thousand hands dragged her from inside a crushed can and a hundred voices told each other to be careful. Fire had leapt up her left arm, and she'd passed out again.

"The planet code-named Omega was the source of the Sim enemy. Their creators were the shape-shifting aliens encountered earlier in the war." Ayliss grinned with her eyes shut, giddy to finally identify the speaker. Reena was giving a speech. "Because Omega is now gone, and the aliens making the Sims have been wiped out, I have ordered our troops in the war zone to fall back into a defensive posture."

A needle was probing for the vein in Ayliss's right arm, and a harsh light turned her eyelids red. Hands lifted her onto a narrow table, and suddenly she couldn't stay awake.

"Is she going to be all right?" Reena again, this time right next to her but also far away. Ayliss fought the crushing weariness, but couldn't manage to open her eyes.

"She's a fighter." Dom. Dom on the other side. "She's going to be fine."

"I've got the best re-gen surgeon in the Force lined up. Her new arm's going to be exactly like the old one."

"Takes a long time to grow a new one."

"The Sims accepted the cease-fire. We've got time."

Deciding that the insane conversation was a hallucination, Ayliss stopped listening.

"**L**ook who's finally awake." Blocker leaned over her, grinning warmly. "Thought you'd sleep through the next war."

Her vision was blurry and her mouth was dry, but Ayliss reached up with her right arm, trying to hug him. Her left arm was caught in the blankets, and she struggled to free it until Blocker's hand came down on her shoulder.

"Hold on. Your arm's gonna be inside that thing for months." She turned to look, seeing a huge white machine with blinking lights that was practically in bed with her.

"My arm," she croaked. "You cut off my arm."

Blocker held out a covered bottle with a drinking tube, and she sucked down the water while he spoke.

"Only way to get you out. It was crushed anyway."

Memories slowly returning. Cusabrina and Dellmore and Zuteck, killed by the moths. Legacy trapped with her, hearing the voices but dying from the planet's poisonous atmosphere. Tin and Varick helping to rescue her.

"Is it over?"

"Omega's nothing but an asteroid cluster now. They almost blasted the place while you and I were still down there."

"No, I mean the war."

"We've got a cease-fire, and a prototype of a translation device that sometimes lets us communicate with the Sims. We've pulled back from every contested planet in the war zone, with the promise to leave them all."

"The Guests won't like that. Watch out for Zone Quest."

"Don't give them another thought. Your stepmother is one thorough individual. She's got this flunkie named Kumar, used to work with Horace Corlipso, and then switched to the Guests. He's testified that ZQ conspired with Damon Asterlit to keep the mines on Celestia open, using Celestian citizens as slave labor. The entire ZQ board's under arrest, and Reena's in the process of dismantling the whole organization."

"Celestia? Are they still fighting there? How is Jan?"

"Well . . . that's a long story. But the fighting is over, and Jan's alive." Blocker nodded, remembering something. "And so's your father. His capsule reappeared, right where it vanished, with him inside."

"How can that be?"

"They're blaming it on some kind of Step hiccup. The mission clock in his capsule showed only an hour had passed, from the moment he disappeared to the instant he was picked up. On the Bounce they're saying he time-traveled."

"Saying."

"Yeah." He whispered in her ear, "He's a little messed up. Thinks he communed with the entities that gave us the Step. None of that's the official story; publicly they're saying he's convalescing somewhere. Luckily there's so much big news that he's been pretty much lost in the echoes."

"There's more? How long have I been out?"

"Three weeks. They always induce a coma after starting a regeneration." He let that sink in. "Like I said, Reena's one thorough lady. She recognized the rebels as the new government on Celestia. Then she made a big speech admitting she knew what was going on there pre-rebellion, and didn't do anything about it."

"Why would she admit something like that?"

"So she could resign, and take the entire Emergency Senate with her. She's staying on until the elections. The first elections since Larkin died."

"You watch. The same dirty crowd will end up in charge."

"Oh really?" Blocker straightened up, smirking.

"What?"

"The Mortas name still generates a lot of loyalty. Especially for the young woman who grew up on the Bounce, worked in the Veterans Auxiliary, fought off the Sims as the governor of a colony of discharged vets, and then lost an arm winning the war."

"What the hell are you talking about?"

"You've been nominated for Interplanetary President, and the numbers are looking very, very good."

"You're joking, right? That's a joke."

"It is not."

She looked at the machine again, tears starting to flow. "Because of this? Because I lost an arm on Omega? How many of my sisters died there? Breena got shot with her own Fasces. The moths ripped it out of her hands and killed her with it! Dell . . . they wrapped around her suit, and she had no choice but to blow herself up! And what about the rest of the squad? What about Bullhead and Lightfoot? Why haven't you told me if they're alive?"

"Ayliss!"

"What?"

"Varick, Tin, Bullhead, and Lightfoot all made it out with us. We lost a lot of people, but more survived than didn't." He laid a hand on her forehead, brushing back an errant blond hair with his thumb. "And your reaction makes me very hopeful that you *will* be selected to take charge—instead of that same dirty crowd."

"I can't take office, anyway. I'm a fugitive. And so are you."

"Not with ZQ getting broken up. Now that they're out of the way, Reena's had a chance to massage what happened on Larkin. The new story is Rittle was trying to murder *you*."

"But that's the truth. He tried to murder us all, on Quad Seven."

"Yes, he did. But somebody convinced Margot Isles to amend her statement about the fight in that passageway, saying Rittle came after us and got killed in the scuffle. We're all in the clear. You, me, Tin, and Ewing. In fact, I've been discharged from the Force."

"Discharged? Why?"

"Reena thinks you might need someone to head up your security detail."

"You cut off my arm."

Blocker gently slid his hand behind her, pressing his cheek against hers. "The whole time I was doing that, I was wishing there was a way for us to trade places. I would have gladly done that for you. I would die for you, Little Bear."

"Live for me, Big Bear."

CHAPTER 23

The sun was reaching for the horizon when the slim figure in black came up the hill. Using the new trees for cover, she alternated between short dashes and long crawls. Her dark hair was cut short, but her almond skin bore no camouflage. She was peering over a large rock near the summit when a child spoke to her.

"You are really noisy."

Tin smiled evenly, her muscles sagging to the ground as she turned. A boy with orange skin and a bush of hair the same color was squatting a yard away.

"I told them I wanted to do this at night."

"Wouldn't have mattered. Lucky for you you're not armed."

"You have to be Sunlight."

"I don't have to be anything."

"I'm Tin. I work security for Jander's sister."

"Heard they made her the new boss."

"She's the Interplanetary President." Tin rolled over, resting her head on her palm. "And she's all right."

"She won't stay that way. They won't let her." Sunlight stood, motioning her uphill. "But with somebody noisy as you guarding her, maybe she won't be around long."

Tin also stood, brushing dirt off the suit. "Maybe you could teach me how you sneaked up like that."

"See out there?" Tin scanned the rest of the base and the surrounding plain. Though still guarded by Force troops, the Mound had been transformed. The support units were all gone, and their bunkers had been turned into dwellings. People of all ages, some orange and some speckled with bird tattoos, were working on garden plots all over the slope.

"I'm not much of a farmer."

"Neither were they. The Whisper gave us the fertilizer caps they made from the Sims' mud munitions, and now they're teaching us how to use them." Sunlight pointed out at the open plain, where families of feral hogs moved around in the distance. "But I meant outside the wire. You want to learn how to move, go out there."

"With all those ugly things? No thanks."

"Yeah." Sunlight started up the hill. "They did get outta hand. But we're working on that too."

Blocker and the rest of the security team secured the top of the hill just before the sun set. An armored mover came up the road soon after that, and Erica Varick stepped out in the uniform of a Banshee major. She walked up the remaining incline, but was intercepted by Dru and Felicity, members of the Holy Whisper from Roanum. They hugged and laughed, but Varick kept her eyes on Jander, standing with his back to a sprawling hilltop garden.

"She's quite a soldier, Jan." Beside him, Blocker spoke without moving his lips. "And a fine-looking woman, too."

Dressed in tan fatigues with no adornment except some dirt, Jander only nodded. "If you like burn scars."

"She says you do."

"What else does she say?"

"No more than that." Blocker walked off toward the tree line, where a woman in black fatigues was crawling across the ground next to Sunlight.

Varick came up the rise alone, a challenging tilt to her chin. "It's good to see you, Jan."

"Major."

She shook her head. "Okay, I'll play along. *Lieutenant*."

"I know why you're here."

"I doubt that."

"I'm done with the Force."

"I once told you that when I was finished with the war I was going to find a tall mountain and never come back down." Erica put her hands on her hips and looked at the lush vegetation behind him. "No matter how you decorate it, this little mound of yours isn't going to cut it."

"A lot happened here. A lot of good people died here. The last ones were killed by Command."

"And now we've got a new president, a real Senate, and a chance to make sure things like that don't happen again. This is no time to quit."

"Not happen again? The lies have already started up. They never even stopped. They said the Force deposed Asterlit on Reena's order."

"What would you have wanted instead? Your entire brigade court-martialed for mutiny? More good people killed by Command?" She stepped closer, the vertical cheek scar shining. "The Orphans marched at the very front of the victory parade, and then they got disbanded. The ones who wanted to stay in uniform got reassigned, and the rest were discharged with full benefits. Except you. You became a farmer."

"I'm good at it." Jander looked over his shoulder at the low wall and the greenery that overflowed it. "You should have seen what this place looked like when I got here."

"I heard. The whole galaxy heard about the Red House. You did the right thing there. And you did the right thing again when you killed Asterlit. But there's a lot left to be done. Come with me, Jan."

"The Banshees don't take guys."

"It's not a Banshee assignment. We've got a tenuous cease-fire with the Sims that could blow up at any time. We've got a translation device that is *far* from perfect, and we can only communicate long-distance. We promised to give Sam every Hab in the war zone, but he sure as hell doesn't trust us to leave him alone. Especially in the future, now that he knows there won't be any more deliveries of young Sims."

"How did you prove that to them?"

"The aliens were launching new Sim transports every few weeks, one at a time, with the entire complement asleep. A pre-set course took them far away, to a spot where hundreds of those ships were just sitting there in space, waiting to be awakened."

"We didn't get that story on the Bounce."

"Too many people would have wanted us to just blast them. But we told Sam where they were, and let him go through our cordon with one ship. That's what sealed it. They didn't trust the footage from Omega, but seeing all those new ships, all those bodies in sleep tubes, and realizing we could have killed them all . . . that did it."

"So what do you need me for?"

"The Sims are going to grow old and die out. Even with robotic defenses—and you can bet they're working on those right now—they'll reach a point where they couldn't hold us off no matter what weapons they develop. Somebody's got to hammer out a system that protects them until they're all dead. You were invited by name."

"You mean our new president is ordering me."

"No, dumbass." Varick's lips curled affectionately. "Remember that gray-haired Sammy on Roanum, the one with the face scar? He's a *very* big honcho with them. He refused to talk to ambassadors, scientists, linguists, even Reena herself. That clunky translation machine worked really well just one time—when he said he only trusted the two soldiers he met on Roanum. You and me."

"You and me?"

"It's always been you and me."

Dru's voice broke the silence from down the hill. "If you don't kiss her right now, Jan, I'm going to."

Jander glared over Varick's shoulder. "I don't think Felicity would like him kissing you."

"Well you know how to prevent that." Their lips brushed lightly, doubtfully, and then Varick rested her forehead against his. "You better hurry with this. Your sister's waiting in the mover."

Ayliss sat in the back, in a spacious compartment that included a large rectangular box that covered her left arm. Light reflected off a nest of whitened scars on her right cheek, reminding Jander that he hadn't seen his sister since shipping out almost two years before. So much had happened, so much had been lost, so many had died. He settled into the cushions facing her, and spoke.

"Murderer."

Ayliss's lips pressed together, but she nodded. "Mutineer."

"President Mortas."

"Captain Mortas."

"So I've been told. Since we're all getting promoted, what's happened to the old guard? The Chairman and the Chairwoman?"

"Father actually contacted the entities that gave us the Step. They want nothing to do with humanity, and he isn't accepting that. He and Reena are with the Step Worshipers, on their research ship. They could both use a break, so the family reunion's going to have to wait."

Jander slid forward until he was on the edge of the seat, his hands clasped and his forearms on his knees. He looked deep into the blue eyes, searching.

"Did you get the poison out, Ayliss? Did you get your fill of it?"

She tilted her head in a motion he recognized. Despite her efforts, a tear rolled across the bridge of her nose.

"It was a poison. But I wasn't the one who drained it. All the people who died around me did that. Too many people died around me."

"I know. Same here."

Jander knelt and carefully embraced her, feeling his sister's one good arm pulling him in. The two of them cried for a long time.

On the Step Worshiper vessel *Delphi*, the duty day had largely ended. Members of the crew were of course going about their endless watches, but the rest of the ship's complement had for the most part sought out their bunks.

Mira Teel, their leader, sat up in her quarters wrapped in a comforter and drinking tea. Despite Olech's disheartening news, she'd dreamed vividly during the day's transit. Perhaps the race represented by the creature named Mirror did indeed intend to keep humanity at a distance, but she was certain that they were still listening. And that was enough.

Curled up together in a single bunk not far from Mira's quarters, Olech and Reena were enfolded in the deepest slumber either of them had experienced in decades.

In a small compartment lined with consoles and monitors, Christian Ewing leaned back in his chair with his eyes serenely closed. A pair of headphones covered his ears, and one of his hands swung back and forth, describing a short, flowing arc without end.

ACKNOWLEDGMENTS

My deepest thanks go to my editor, Nick Amphlett, for providing key insights that greatly magnified this story's big moments. As the final book in the Sim War series, *Live Echoes* had to answer important questions without explaining every little detail, and Nick's editing made that happen. I'd like to extend special thanks to my publicist, Camille Collins, for her imagination and her efforts in finding new ways to let more people know about the Sim War novels.

Several of my West Point classmates have given invaluable feedback on this series right from the start. Many thanks to Michael McGurk, Meg Roosma, Duane O'Laughlin, and Ginni Guiton for their time and talents. Their impressions and improvements greatly contributed to bringing this story to life.

ABOUT THE AUTHOR

HENRY V. O'NEIL is the pen name used by award-winning mystery novelist Vincent H. O'Neil for his science-fiction work. A graduate of West Point, he served in the U.S. Army Infantry with the Tenth Mountain Division at Fort Drum, New York, and the First Battalion (Airborne) of the 508th Infantry in Panama. He has also worked as a risk manager, a marketing copywriter, and an apprentice librarian.

In 2005, he won the St. Martin's Press Malice Domestic Award with his debut mystery novel, *Murder in Exile*. That was followed by three more books in the Exile series: *Reduced Circumstances*, *Exile Trust*, and *Contest of Wills*. He has also written the theater-themed mystery novel *Death Troupe* and two books in a horror series entitled *Interlands* and *Denizens*. His website is www.vincenthoneil.com.